MOLLY'S ROCKER

Susan M. Hoskins

Nancy E. Doherty, Editor

ISBN 978-1-950647-80-4

Names: Hoskins, Susan M., author.
Title: Molly's rocker / Susan M. Hoskins.
Description: Second edition. | Broomfield, CO: OF Love Creations,
2021.
Identifiers: ISBN: 978-1-950647-80-4
Subjects: LCSH Kentucky--History--19th century--Fiction. | Kentucky-
-History--20th century--Fiction. | Tobacco farmers--Fiction. | Family-
-Fiction. | Rural women--Kentucky--Fiction. | Farm life--Kentucky-
-Fiction. | BISAC YOUNG ADULT FICTION / Historical / United
States / 19th Century | YOUNG ADULT FICTION / Historical / United
States / 20th Century
Classification: LCC PS3608.O7795 M65 2021 | DDC 813.6--dc23

Published by OF Love Creations
Broomfield, Colorado

Publishing assistance by BookCrafters, Parker, Colorado.
www.bookcrafters.net

Author's Note

*"We thought there'd come a day when folks got over
their hatred of coloreds and the white people who loved them.
But they never did."*

As you will read in the pages to follow, I wrote *Molly's Rocker* after I discovered my husband's grandmother's old rocking chair in the attic. It was the only thing saved from a fire that destroyed her home. My husband, Larry, knew very little about the details of his grandmother's life, other than she had lived in Upton, Kentucky, with her husband, Elijah, and their six children, including Larry's mother, Tula Mary.

Yet, as I sat in her rocker for the first time, I began to imagine in great detail what it was like to be Molly, a tall, plainspoken, courageous woman, who confronted danger, loss, inequality and bigotry throughout her life. What I learned in the process of writing her story affected me deeply, and it's why I believe this novel is particularly relevant today.

It was a late November day in 2015 when I realized why Molly's story is so timely. Sadly, while many things in our society have changed since the late 1800s and early 1900s, hatred for those of different skin colors and beliefs still exists.

My daughter, her husband and their two young sons were

preparing to move from El Paso, Texas, to Denver, Colorado. I was there to assist with the move and help care for the boys. I was completing the first draft of *Molly's Rocker* that morning while the children were in preschool. My daughter was at work and asked me to watch for the mail carrier. She had lost her key to the mailbox and needed to retrieve her mail. She warned me to be wary of engaging in conversation with the deranged woman who lived across the street.

As I was watching for the mail carrier, I wrote perhaps the most meaningful statement by Molly in the novel. It read: "We thought there'd come a day when folks got over their hatred of coloreds and the white people who loved them. But they never did."

Just then, I glimpsed the mail truck coming up the street. I hurried outside, only to encounter the dreaded neighbor. She asked who I was and where I was from. I told her I was from Kansas City. She then went on a tirade about the University of Missouri's football team and their protests about racial bigotry. She quoted a well-known conservative radio personality who had stated that all of those agitators should be flown out of the country wherever they wanted to go, but never to return to the United States because they did not love our country. I excused myself to talk to the mail carrier, who was listening to the same hate-filled rhetoric blaring from his radio on the mail truck. He, too, asked where I was from and went on a similar diatribe about freeloaders who worship their black Muslim president. It was then that I knew Molly's words were unfortunately both prophetic and enduring.

Since that fateful day in 2015, we have seen even greater episodes of vitriol, violence and the rise of white nationalism. It's been devastating to watch our country torn apart along racial and political lines. There is a deep divide between those who seek equality for all of us and those who cling to a past when white men ruled the country.

We have clearly not healed the wounds of hatred and discrimination that profoundly affected Molly and those she loved.

But her love, courage and gentle wisdom can provide guidance to us even today, especially with our children and grandchildren.

Molly Then – You Now!

Everyday life was quite different in rural America during the late 1800s, especially for children. There were no computers, video games, sports teams, televisions, automobiles, electricity or even indoor plumbing. Children, if they were fortunate enough to go to school, attended the first through the eighth grades in a one-room schoolhouse. The school year revolved around the planting and harvesting of farm crops. Children were expected to work alongside their parents tending the crops if you were a boy, or doing cooking and house chores if you were a girl. Molly did not like being relegated to doing house chores, which her mother called "a woman's duty." She much preferred working with her brothers in the tobacco fields.

Life was hard back then without the modern conveniences we now take for granted. Yet despite the fact that her education was limited, Molly confronted many of the same issues as a young girl that you face today.

We may think we have come a long way in dealing with discrimination, but the truth is that in the 2020s, children still experience the pain of not being accepted because of the color of their skin or their family's culture or religion. During the past few years we've seen an eruption of hatred and violence against people of color or those of the Jewish faith. And even though there are many more career possibilities for women in our society today, gender inequality remains in the work force and in professional sports.

It might surprise you to know that school bullying is not a new phenomenon, as you will read in the pages to follow when young Elijah Fry first attends school. And one of the most important lessons Miss June taught Molly was that it's OK to be different and to feel like you don't belong. Molly learned that there's great value in accepting yourself just the way you are by embracing your own uniqueness.

Because our life experiences seem so dramatically different from those of our grandparents or great grandparents, we think they couldn't possibly understand what we deal with on a daily basis. It rarely occurs to us to seek their guidance regarding our challenges. We erroneously believe that those living decades before us cannot appreciate the challenging problems we face now. That may be true for some, but it is not the case with Molly. Her simple wisdom is timeless. She has a great deal to teach us about living a rich and full life with simplicity.

Molly faced her challenges with courage and grit. She was true to her convictions and spoke plainly from her heart. Despite adversity, she always chose love over hate. I invite you in the chapters to follow, to listen to Molly as she speaks to you across time. May her story cause you to ask yourself how you would deal with the same issues she faced, including discrimination and oppression. What you may discover is that you and Molly are not that different. Molly, may, at heart, be like you now.

Molly's Schoolhouse

Molly's Schoolhouse is an innovative learning tool based on the timely themes of the touching historical novel, *Molly's Rocker*, a meaningful and enriching reading experience for upper-elementary and middle-school students. The authentic exploration into this powerful story provides the basis for rich, multigenerational dialogues on a wide variety of topics vital to our lives today.

Molly's Rocker follows the fortunes of an ordinary farm girl living through extraordinary times, from the wide-open America of the 1870s, through the Great Depression to a modern-day nation on the brink of World War II. As she sits in the rocker she loves, Molly tells her remarkable tales in her distinctive voice, capturing the drama inherent in a humble farm family's struggle to survive during times filled with strife. In vivid detail, she chronicles her challenging childhood; her long, fulfilling marriage to a kind but troubled man; and, finally, her unconventional bond with a man of color. Throughout her life, Molly confronts danger and loss, together with inequality and bigotry, but she is a woman of grit and heart who resolves to live as she sees fit, braving the consequences.

The intent of *Molly's Schoolhouse* is to assist students in deeply reflecting upon the timeless wisdom that Molly's story conveys.

Meaningful reading passages, discussion questions and exercises explore themes that are as culturally relevant today as they were long ago. This enriching experience is intended for a wide variety of educational environments, including progressive, charter, private and public schools, homeschool and learning-pod settings; and after-school study groups.

By presenting engaging opportunities to deepen discernment, *Molly's Schoolhouse* provides students with the opportunities to genuinely think about and discuss how vital historical lessons can inform our world today. Students are also invited to explore and develop their own creative writing and artistic talents, as Susan M. Hoskins unveils her own processes and experiences in unfolding Molly's story. Through discussion questions and exercises, students are encouraged to explore the brilliance of the written word.

Our young people are our future. *Molly's Schoolhouse* presents a profoundly powerful invitation to participate more meaningfully in an empathic, socially conscious world, a world that the students of today are capable of creating. The guidance offered by Molly's tender and touching story can help show the way.

Acknowledgements

Thank you, Larry Hoskins Roggenkamp, for introducing me to your wonderful grandmother through photos, memories and subsequent research. Thank you for allowing me to become Molly for a short period of time, in order to understand life from this remarkable woman's perspective.

Thank you, Patricia McLaughlin, Larry's beloved sister, who was the first person to read *Molly's Rocker* and to approve of the story I envisioned for your family. Your love and support mean the world to me.

Thank you to my dear editor, Nancy Doherty, for always speaking your truth and challenging me to become a better writer with every draft of the manuscript. Your vision, expertise and belief in the novel motivated me to see this project through to its ultimate conclusion.

Thank you, Deborah Hirsch, my queen of the comma, for throwing down the gauntlet during the final proof of the manuscript to ensure consistency, accuracy and authenticity of dialogue. It's no easy task to assume the voice of an uneducated heroine who lived so long ago.

Thank you, Susan Danz (the other Susan as I fondly call her), for your brilliant work designing the website for *Molly's Schoolhouse*, and for working so diligently to help me create the content for the innovative learning experience. Without you, I would not have envisioned the release of a second edition of *Molly's Rocker* for upper-elementary and middle-school children.

Thank you, James Neely and Victoria Moore, of Unzipped Design, for your beautiful cover design, featuring a photo of Molly and her rocker. I truly value both your talent and your friendship.

To the young readers who are now being introduced to Molly, I hope you come to love her as much as I do. Her simple wisdom can be a guiding light for all of us now.

To my readers over the years ... thank you for taking this amazing journey with me. You are the reason I go through this incredibly challenging process. Please keep thoughtfully reading books that intrigue you, and together let's keep the lines of communication open for our mutual growth and healing.

And, finally, for those of you in my baby boomer generation, please remember two things. We have a story to tell that will be lost soon unless we share it with those we love. We are the bridge from the past to the future. Let us help those we love see life from our unique perspective and experiences. Likewise, it is never too late to pursue your passions and dreams. My husband and I founded our business, OF Love Creations, to share our love of photography and books with others. All of us have talents to share and a purpose to fulfill at every stage of life.

Prologue

"Love Finds a Way"

"We need to leave NOW, Mr. Larry. The dump closes at four o'clock sharp!"

Mike set a dusty chair down on the driveway. The chair rocked back and forth slightly, its fate teetering in the balance.

"I got everything cleaned out of the attic," Mike said. "Most of it's going to the dump. But there's one old piece you need to see."

I joined Larry to have a look.

"The chair's wobbly. It's not in very good shape."

"Is it worth anything?" Larry asked.

"Not to me," Mike said. He turned the chair over and pointed to a wooden brace holding the seat together. "It's been patched and repaired too many times."

"My dad did that," Larry said. "The seat split in half. He reinforced it with a brace so Molly could still use it."

"Who was Molly?" I asked.

"My grandmother."

"You want to keep it or should I throw it on the truck?"

Larry looked at me and then at the chair.

"Go ahead and take it," he said, after some hesitation.

I don't know if it was the sound of his voice or the look in his eyes, but something about his response made me uneasy.

"Leave it, Mike," I said. "I'd like to have a better look at it before we decide."

"Suit yourself, ma'am."

Mike's truck was packed full of remnants from our former lives. Larry and I had recently married. Our children were grown, with families of their own. I'd sold my house and moved into his. We'd accumulated a lot of furniture over the years and now we had nowhere to put it all. The time had finally come to dispose of the stuff we couldn't use and our kids didn't want.

Mike was our local junk dealer. He went through the attic looking for treasures. He found a few items he thought he could sell. The rest of it was going to the dump.

I have an appreciation for beautiful antiques. This broken-down old rocker was no fine piece of furniture. Yet I found myself drawn to it for no apparent reason. I couldn't tell if it was made of pine, maple or something else. The wood on the seat looked different from that on the back. The arms were worn, and the stain had been rubbed away. There were two large spindles holding the back of the chair to the seat and seven small spindles in the middle of the back. Several of them felt loose. The seat was almost as worn as the arms.

Larry carried the rocker into the kitchen and set it by the window. The afternoon sunlight exposed every flaw. You couldn't miss the variations in the shades of wood or the prominent crack in the seat. Hardened globs of glue were everywhere. We stood together shaking our heads at the rickety old thing.

I eased down into the rocker, hoping it wouldn't break beneath me. It wasn't the least bit comfortable, but someone had spent a lot of time in it. I rocked back and forth and it creaked loudly.

"Just thought of something," Larry said. He went into the bedroom and soon returned carrying a large, cardboard box. He set it on the kitchen table and cut through the tape with a knife.

"What's that?" I asked, joining him at the table.

"Some things I thought you might like to see."

The first item he took out was an old photo album. One snapshot showed a smiling couple with their daughter and two sons. By the look of the mother's dress, I guessed it was taken in the early 1950s. There were several more photographs of children at different ages, and one of an old woman cradling a baby.

I recognized my husband immediately as the oldest of the kids. His smile had not changed, nor his snappy blue eyes. He looked pretty cool in his Radio Flyer wagon.

"That's my mother, Tula Mary, and my father, Chet," he said pointing to the couple on the couch.

He turned back to the photograph of the old woman rocking a baby. "That's Molly holding my baby sister. I was 8 when she came to live with us. Her house burned down, and she lost everything but this old rocker."

Larry looked fondly at her photo and then at the rocker. "Molly used to sit in this rocker around this time every day, talking about her life in Uptonville, Kentucky. I still remember the sound of the chair creaking as she rocked back and forth, telling me one story after another. I loved those times. I never got bored. Molly didn't get very far in school, so her grammar wasn't always the best, but she had a way of making her memories come alive. She would get so into her stories that she'd start talking to the characters like they were right in front of her, and then she'd talk back in their voices. Listening to her was like watching a movie of her life—except she never left the chair."

Next, he took an old writing book from the box. He showed me the yellowed handwritten pages. "And this is my grandfather's story of his life before he met Molly. He began writing it down when he was a boy so he wouldn't forget his early years with his mother. Molly gave it to my mother, Tula Mary, after he died. Molly remembered his story as a boy like it was her own."

Larry reached down to the bottom of the box and pulled out a weird-looking machine. "Oh, wow, look at this!"

"What is it?"

"This is one of the first tape recorders sold for home use. I'd forgotten all about it."

He then took out several boxed reels of tape, all carefully labeled.

"My dad got all this as a surprise for me after Molly came to live with us. He knew how much I loved hearing her stories. He wanted me to record them so I wouldn't forget her."

"What a great gift! Does the recorder still work?"

"I have no idea," he said. "I haven't seen this stuff since I was a kid. But let's give it a try."

We sat down at the kitchen table as the afternoon sun began to fade. Larry plugged in the vintage recorder, then carefully fit the first reel of tape onto the left spool and threaded a few inches of it into the empty reel on the right. When he turned on the power switch, the reels began slowly turning. The first sound we heard was the creaking of the rocker.

And so it happened that the extraordinary tale of *Molly's Rocker* almost died with her, hauled away by the junk dealer Mike. That it didn't, that I'm telling it to you now, might be called luck or a twist of fate. But I believe it was meant to be. Love always finds a way to share its story.

MOLLY

Chapter 1

"Born a Girl"

Living life is like growing a crop of tobacco. It takes hard work to make it through a season. Some years, the good Lord gives you just the right amount of sunshine and heat to grow a fine crop. After the harvest, you sell the tobacco for a decent sum of money and you feel good about your lot in life. But then there are the years when bad things happen, like a drought or a long hard freeze. That's when all you can do is grit your teeth, wipe away your tears and start all over again. My life was like that. There was a whole lot of good that happened to me mixed up with a heap of bad. I loved tender and I cried hard. But I wouldn't have traded my life for nothing.

I was born on October 10, 1879, on a tobacco farm near Uptonville, in Hardin County, Kentucky. I was named Mary Molly Van Meter. I was the youngest of seven children and the only girl. My pa was Dutch and my ma Irish. That made for an interesting mix of seeds. Pa wasn't mean, but he was strict. I don't remember him being much fun. Ma wasn't like him. She was kind and pleasant to be around, except when her Irish temper got ahold of her. You never wanted to get Ma mad 'cause she could flick a switch harder and faster than Pa.

Ma had thick dark-brown hair and green eyes. She had a fine

figure, and her dresses fit her good. I failed to get Ma's good looks and for that I was truly sorry.

Pa was tall and skinny with light-colored hair. His people came to America from Holland. They settled in Ohio. That's where my ma and pa met, but they left there when they got married. Pa's family was big, and he liked to tell stories about his kin. My favorite was the one about Polly Van Meter. She was my pa's great-grandmother. She was married to a fella by the name of John Evans, who was the commander of the fort where they lived.

Polly tended to people who lived near the fort when they got sick. She'd ride out on her horse with her dog beside her and a rifle strapped to her shoulder, in case she came across Injuns who wanted to take her scalp. Polly had a keen eye and steady hand with a rifle. One day, she and the other women were alone at the fort when them Injuns attacked. None of the other women were as good a shot as Polly, but they loaded rifles and done the best they could. Polly ran from one porthole to another, firing off her rifle 'til the Injuns ran away, carrying the ones she shot on their backs.

After the day she drove them Injuns away, they left her alone and let her go about her business without fear they'd take her scalp. She was a straight-shooting woman who wasn't afeared of nothing. I liked to think I favored her some. She made me proud to be a Van Meter.

Ma didn't talk much about her people other than she grew up with three sisters. I asked her why none of her kin, or Pa's, ever came to visit us.

She said, "Pa's people and mine don't get along 'cause they're Baptists and my kin are Catholic. They turned us out when we got married, so we left Ohio and made our way here."

I knew what it meant to be a Baptist 'cause that's what we was, and Ma came to church with us. I didn't know what a Catholic was.

"What's a Catholic, Ma?"

"It's too hard to explain, Molly."

"Are you still one?"

Ma said, "No, I promised your pa I wouldn't be Catholic no more."

"Why did you do that?"

Ma stroked my hair and looked at me tender. "I loved your pa, and that's what he asked me to do when we got married."

Her lips turned down when she said that. I wondered if she was sad about not being who she was before she married Pa. I wished I'd asked her about that, but we got busy fixing supper and I forgot.

Ma and Pa wanted to have lots of young'uns to make their family and help out on the farm. Times were hard, so you made as many babies as you could just in case some didn't survive. They named their first four sons after Pa's kin. Pa's name was Jacob. My first brothers were named Joost, Jansen, John and James.

Joost, the oldest, was the best-looking of the lot. He had yellow-colored hair, and girls acted silly around him when we went to church. Jansen was quiet and stayed to hisself most of the time. He was serious like Pa, and I never felt at ease around him. But he tended to the land good, and Pa favored him a lot.

I loved my brother John. He looked like Ma with brown hair and green eyes. He made up stories for us to play about going to far-off places and having big adventures. I liked it best when he lifted me up on top of his shoulders. He told me to look out as far as I could see.

"There's a whole other world out there, Molly, besides our farm."

I would squint my eyes and strain hard to see some other kind of world, but all I saw was our tobacco fields. I didn't tell John that 'cause I didn't want him to put me down. The wind never felt as good on my face as when I was up on his shoulders with his hands wrapped around my legs.

James wasn't like my other brothers. He didn't look like the rest of us. He had red hair, and you couldn't tell if his eyes were green or brown. But here's the one thing I knew about James. He loved John like he loved no other. Whatever John said, it was true for James. And that's just the way it was. They was brothers and best friends.

Ma told me that she thought her next baby after James would be a girl, but it was another boy instead. They got tired of names that began with the same letter, so they named this one Isaac and the last one Edward. Isaac was curious about everything. He wanted to know why frogs made a croaking sound and why ants carried things up hills in straight rows. He'd ask Pa questions like what made grass green and why did the tobacco plant sprout pink blossoms. Pa got tired of his questions and told him to get on about his chores. But I could tell that Pa was proud of Isaac for being smart.

Edward, my youngest brother, was the one I favored most. He wasn't strong like the other boys and he got sick easy. Even though he was a year older, he was always smaller than me. There was something about Edward that made me want to hold him and keep him safe. He cared about people and critters. He and Isaac was different in this regard. Isaac was all about holding a butterfly by a wing so he could study it good. Edward would tell him to be gentle so he didn't hurt it.

Ma waited a long time for a pretty little girl to love, but she got me instead. My hair wasn't thick like hers, but thin and dull-brown. I got Pa's sharp features and scrawny build. Folks said I was too tall for a girl, but I had nice eyes, like Pa. The way I felt was, if I wasn't gonna be pretty, I wished I'd been born a boy.

I asked Pa why they didn't have more young'uns after me. He said, "Your coming was too hard, Molly."

"What's that mean?"

"You was turned the wrong way," he said. "Your feet come out first instead of your head. We thought we was gonna lose Ma after you got pulled out."

I wasn't sure why it mattered whether your feet came out first or last, but I guessed I'd done something bad right from the start. "I'm sorry, Pa. I didn't mean to come out wrong."

Pa patted my head. "Ma got better in time, but she couldn't have no more babies after you." He got quiet for a moment, then he said, "We thank God for the ones we got."

He was my pa, and I respected his word. But I got a hole in my heart then that never went away 'cause I knew he and Ma wished their last baby turned out better than the one they done got.

Chapter 2

"Cold Eggs"

Our house wasn't nothing fancy. It was built out of weathered wood and had one door and two windows. We spent most of our time in the big room that had the fireplace and our table and chairs for eating. We liked to sit by the fire at night telling stories while Ma mended our clothes. Me and Ma got food ready to cook over the fire in a small room off to the side. It had a cupboard for canned goods and a place for Ma's pots and pans.

Back behind that room was a tub where we took turns once a week having a warm bath. We hauled in water from the well out back for cooking, drinking and bathing. Ma made soap strong enough to get the dirt out of our ears and britches, but you sure didn't want to get it in your eyes or have Ma scrub your mouth with it for saying a bad word.

Ma and Pa slept back off the main room. They kept me in a crate, in with them 'til I got too big. Then Pa built me a wood bed to sleep on, and Ma sewed up a curtain to pull around it.

My brothers slept up in the snuggery over the main room. It was called a snuggery 'cause it stayed warm from the heat rising up from the fireplace. Soon as it got dark, the boys would climb up the ladder, but I could hear them talking quiet way into the night. I felt lonely being downstairs by myself. I asked Ma if I could sleep up with the boys, but she said it wouldn't be fittin'. I didn't understand that at the time since she was a girl and Pa a boy and they slept together. But I came to understand later.

When Edward was sick, Ma let him sleep downstairs so we could tend to him good. She'd make him a bed of quilts right next to me. I'd wipe his face with a wet rag when he was hot to the touch. And when he couldn't sleep, I'd make up stories to tell him. Ma always made sure we said a special prayer for Edward when he got sick. I waited 'til she went to bed and then I'd say my own prayer.

"Jesus, make Edward better but take your time, please. I like it when he stays with me."

It was scary going to the outhouse alone at night. I could hear all sorts of critters making noise and was afeared one of them would get me. The boys kept a slop jar upstairs to use at night, but I didn't have one 'cause it was too hard for a girl to use. I learned early on how to hold my pee 'til morning. That lesson served me well up 'til the time I became an old lady.

From the time I was little, I had to get up at four in the morning to help Ma milk the cows and get eggs from the hens to fry up for breakfast. I learned how to make batter for biscuits and shape them proper for cooking. The older boys brung in water from the well and got the fire going good. When we set breakfast on the table, the sun was just starting to wake up. Ma made me wait with her to eat 'til the menfolk got through.

I reckon I was seven years old when I asked her how come she did that.

"That's just the way it's done, Molly," she said. "Pa and your brothers have to get to their chores. It's our job to make sure they have a proper meal."

"But that ain't right, Ma. We got chores to do just like them. Besides ..." Ma started going red in the face, so I shut my mouth.

"Go on," she said. "Besides what?"

"My eggs are cold by then. They don't taste as good."

"Get used to it, Molly. It's a woman's job to be a proper wife and mother. That means putting the needs of the menfolk ahead of our own."

"Who says, Ma?"

"God does. It's in the Bible."

That didn't set well with me. I thought God created everybody equal so nobody had to eat cold eggs.

It was hard work keeping our place clean with six boys and Pa tracking in dirt, especially when they was tending to the tobacco. When it come time to plant or harvest the crop, me and Ma worked in the fields, too.

It takes near on half a year to grow tobacco. After the last snow, Pa made a bed for the seedlings we got off the plants from the year before. He needed a day that was warm and not windy, and we planted them there to give them a proper start. Once they come up, we took them out of the bed and planted them in neat rows in the field.

We hoed the tobacco in June and July to keep the weeds out. In August, we topped the tobacco by cutting off the pink and white flowers that grew on them. When the leaves turned gold in September, they were ripe and had to be cut right away. Me and Ma helped to cut the plants. Then Pa and my brothers would spear them onto big wooden sticks to dry in the sun for a few days before hauling them to the barn in our wagon.

A man's tobacco barn is even more important to him than his house. The barn has to be precisely built with crisscrossing wooden beams that go clear to the roofline and then come down in rows to about eight foot off the ground. That's so the last plants have room to hang. Every beam in the barn is needed to hang the sticks of tobacco.

Hanging tobacco to cure is something to see. You got to hang the sticks of plants from the top beams of the barn and work your way down. To do that, the boys had to scramble up on the lowest beam and wait for Pa to hand them the first stick. Two of them would hold onto it while the others climbed up to the next beam. Once they was steady on their feet, they'd grab ahold of the stick, while the boys below climbed to the beam above them. The boys had to work close together to make sure nobody lost their balance and fell. They'd hand the stick of tobacco off, back and forth, 'til they got to the top of the barn and hung the first plants to cure. After that, they'd come back down and start all over again.

I had to beg Pa to let me climb up on the beams to hang tobacco. Ma didn't think it was fittin' for a girl to do a boy's job. Pa let me take a turn now and again, especially if Edward was sick and they was shorthanded. One evening, we was all tired from hanging tobacco in the barn. Me and Ma served up supper, and then we sat down to eat our own. I looked around the table. We had body water clinging to our hair and faces and dirt on our hands that washing up didn't clean. Pa had it, my brothers and me, too. We was alike and we was equal.

I said out loud, "I like working tobacco."

My brothers all looked at me and grinned. They didn't say nothing, but I had a feeling they knew what I meant. Supper tasted extra good that night, though I couldn't tell you what we had.

Chapter 3

"Pastor Brown"

Every Sunday, we went to church. Weather didn't matter a lick—it could be sunny, raining or snowing. Pa hitched the mules to the buckboard and loaded us up for the four-mile ride across the railroad tracks and a stream. Our white church had three rooms and fifty members. There was the place for worship and another room for Sunday school. We had a meeting hall where we had dinner when folks died or got married.

The preacher and his family stayed in a house called a parsonage next to the church. And behind the church was a cemetery where a body could get a proper Christian burial when the time came.

I didn't mind going to Sunday school 'cause the teacher read us stories about Jesus. But sometimes we had to go to worship service with Ma and Pa. My butt got sore sitting on the hard wood benches, especially in summer when it was hot and crowded.

Our preacher's name was Jonathan Brown. He had a loud voice that scared me bad. Pastor Brown was a big fella. He wore suspenders, but his belly hung over his pants, and his shirt popped open sometimes when he got agoing about Jesus and getting saved. There was nothing he liked better than thumping his Bible and yelling about sin. When he hollered real loud, he got short of breath, and we worried he would fall out then and there.

Sticking his finger right in my face, he'd shout, "You got to be saved, otherwise you're gonna burn in hell for eternity!" Scared the tar right out of me!

Pastor Brown was hard to look at 'cause he had hair growing out of his nose and ears. His wife, Penelope, was fat like the pastor and short. She never said much. She kept her eyes on the floor. I wondered if he scared the tar out of her, too.

Sometimes at night when I heard a loud noise, I wondered if it was the end of time and the world was crashing in around us. Those were the nights I kept my eyes open as long as I could and prayed real hard.

"Lord Jesus, save me!"

I'd wake up the next morning mighty grateful to be alive.

You could start school when you was six, but I had to wait 'til I was almost eight and Edward was nine. That's on account we didn't have a schoolteacher for a couple of years. Back then, they had strict rules for teachers. Men could take one evening a week for courting and two evenings if they attended church regular. But any teacher who drank liquor, went to pool halls or got shaved in a barbershop got fired.

My older brothers had Mr. Guthrie for a teacher, but he got caught in Elizabethtown doing things he shouldn't. Late one night, I heard Pa tell Ma that Mr. Guthrie was seen drinking whiskey at a tavern with a lady of the night.

"Who caught him?" Ma asked.

"A fella by the name of Harold Bradley. He said he went to the tavern to have dinner and saw Guthrie drinking whiskey and making a fool of himself with that woman. Bradley couldn't wait to get back to Uptonville and tell folks what he seen."

The next morning I asked Ma, "What's a lady of the night?"

Her mouth got crooked, and I could tell she was thinking hard before she spoke. "She's a sinner who needs to be saved, Molly."

"Oh no!" I cried. "She's gonna burn in hell! Pastor Brown said so!"

Ma looked pleased when I said that. That gave me an idea that I thought she would like even better.

"Let's bring her to church with us on Sunday so Pastor Brown can save her."

Ma started stirring them eggs real fast. She told me to go on about my business. Nothing more was said about that lady of the night. To this day, I laugh when I think about asking Ma if we could bring her to church.

For the rest of that year and on into the next, nobody went to school. Isaac wanted to know why they couldn't find a teacher to take the place of Mr. Guthrie.

Pa said, "I reckon a man doesn't want to live here in Uptonville when he could get a job somewhere else."

"Why is that?" I asked.

Joost said, "That's 'cause folks think we're backwards and don't know nothing."

"That's not true," said Ma. "It takes a special person to be a teacher. A man can come to a strange town and make it home. It's not the same way for a woman, especially if she's unmarried. Who'd look after her?"

Up to now, young'uns went to school in town where a man teacher could rent a room. That wasn't fittin' for a woman in those days. And a woman teacher couldn't be married back then, either. With no teacher wanting to live in Uptonville, the school stayed closed, 'til Pa got an idea that changed everything. He went straightaway to see Pastor Brown.

"Pastor Brown, I think we ought to build a new schoolhouse right next to the church. We could advertise for a good Christian woman to come teach our kids."

"But where would she live?" he asked. "We can't have a woman just living anywhere."

Pa smiled. He'd thought it all the way through. "Why, she could live right here with you and Mrs. Brown! Thataway she could tend to your young'uns when she wasn't teaching school."

"What about keeping the boys in line?" the preacher asked. "Don't we need a man to do that?" Pa grinned. "Ain't nobody gonna misbehave on church ground. That would be sinning in God's own house. A man would whip his boy crazy for doing that."

Pastor Brown thought it over and decided Pa had a fine idea. He sent out notices to Baptist churches as far away as Louisville, looking for the right person to come teach us. That's how he found Miss June. We started building the schoolhouse in the summer of 1887, right after the tobacco got growing good. Back then, country folks helped one another build their barns and houses, so they were glad to come together for the schoolhouse. Mr. Macon, one of the church deacons, was good at figuring out what a building should be like and then drawing a picture of it. He met with Pa and the other men after church one Sunday to decide what supplies they needed to get started. Pastor Brown's wife called the ladies together to plan meals to feed folks while they was working.

The day they began, every member of the church and all their young'uns showed up to help. Before we got started, Pastor Brown gathered folks together to offer up a prayer that God would show favor upon us and be pleased with our work. Then Mr. Macon met with the menfolk to show them the plan and divide them into teams with specific jobs. I got lucky and got a special job 'cause there were enough older girls to help the women with the food.

Pa said, "Molly, we need you to be a fetcher."

"What's that, Pa?"

"That means if a man needs a tool he don't have, you go find it, or fetch him a drink of water if he wants it."

"I think I'll like that job. If I get too busy, can I ask Edward to help me?"

He said that would be fine, so we ran our little legs off fetching supplies and water. We took our meals in the meeting hall, and all of us had a good time. By the end of the week, we had a building to be proud of. It wasn't nothing fancy, built of plain wooden timbers, from the roof to the walls and the floor. Even the benches that we sat on were made out of the same wood. Luckily, that wood was sanded good so we didn't get splinters in our butts.

Pa said I'd been a fine fetcher, but there was one more thing we had to fetch for the schoolhouse, and that was a wood stove to keep us warm. Me and him went to order the stove from Albert Fry, who owned the general store. I'd only been to town a time or two. I'd never gotten to go alone with Pa, and I felt real proud riding up front with him in the buckboard 'cause I was such a good fetcher.

Back then, the town wasn't very big, but I thought it was a grand place, with a bank, a hotel and a train depot besides the general store.

Mr. Fry had three stoves for sale. Folks had chipped in what they could, and we had just enough money to buy the one Pa thought would keep our little schoolhouse good and warm in the winter. He lifted me up on the counter so he could settle up with Mr. Fry. While I was sitting there, a man I'd never seen before come in the door. His skin was the color of chocolate, and his hair was real curly. Mr. Fry said, "Jacob, this here is Isaiah Jackson from over at Doc Middleton's place. He works for me in the afternoons and on Saturdays when he's not busy tending to Doc's tobacco."

Pa shook the man's hand.

"Who do we have here?" Isaiah said, looking at me.

Pa told him my name was Molly.

Isaiah reached out his hand to me, and I shook it politely like Ma taught me. He had a strong grip. I liked looking at his face 'cause it was different from any menfolk I knew. I guess he didn't mind me looking at him hard. Smiling pleasant, he said, "Nice to meet you, Molly."

Mr. Fry told Pa he and Isaiah would bring the stove to the schoolhouse the next morning. When we was leaving, I turned around one more time to look at that fella again. I waited 'til we were up in the buckboard before I asked Pa, "Why is that man's skin so brown? Did he stay out in the sun too long?"

"No, Molly, that's the color God made him."

"Why did God make him different like that?"

Pa looked at me gentle and said, "I reckon you'll have to ask God."

"Does he have kin around here?"

"I don't know, Molly. We don't have many colored folks in these parts."

"Where do they come from?"

Pa was patient while I asked my questions. As we started out of town, he told me how colored folks were brung here from Africa to grow tobacco crops for white men.

"How come we don't have coloreds to help us grow tobacco?"

"Used to be that coloreds were slaves," Pa said. "Slaves didn't have no say in who owned them. Our kin never had slaves. We didn't think it was right."

Pa told me about the Civil War and how, finally, President Lincoln said coloreds should be freed. I had a lot more questions about that, but soon enough our time together was over and we had to get about our chores. When I was getting down from the buckboard, Pa said, "You're a smart little thing, Molly. You take after your ma like that."

My insides felt warm when he said that 'cause, sure enough, I didn't take after Ma in no other way. I was glad I was smart. I couldn't wait to start school and get book learning so I could read and write.

Chapter 4

"Miss June"

The night before the first day of school, I was so excited, I couldn't sleep. I got up before sunup to get eggs from the chickens like always. Me and Ma cooked up two big pans of biscuits with jam. Plus, Ma had a surprise.

"I got some salt ham to go with your eggs and biscuits. You gotta have a full belly to learn proper."

We didn't keep hogs on our farm. Pa had to buy ham from another farmer, so we got to have salt ham only on special occasions. It sure tasted good with them fried eggs and biscuits. Ma packed up extra biscuits and jam in a pail to carry to school for dinner.

That year, my brother Joost was sixteen, so he couldn't go to school no more. It didn't matter a lick that he couldn't read or write good. Being fourteen, Jansen could go to school another year, but he didn't like being around people. He begged Pa not to make him go. He said it was a waste of time since he didn't care nothing about book learning. All he wanted to do was grow tobacco, and Pa did a fine job teaching him how to do that.

Ma wasn't keen on the idea, but in the end, they decided that Jansen was stubborn like Pa, and it would do no good to make him go to school. Besides, Pa needed him on the farm. That left John, James, Isaac, Edward and me.

Ma lined us up and checked our hands, ears and teeth to make sure we was clean.

"Now listen to me good," she said, eyeing us hard. "Don't go shaming me and Pa. Mind your manners. Hear me?"

"Yes, ma'am," we all said together.

Growing up, Pa didn't go to school but a year or two, but he was smart enough to run the farm and grow tobacco. Ma got more book learning than Pa. She told my brothers to learn as much as they could, since they'd have to make their own way if they didn't stay on the farm to help Pa.

"What about me, Ma? Am I gonna have to make my own way?"

"I ain't too sure about you, Molly," she said at first. A few minutes later, she told me I'd find a good man to marry and have babies.

That morning, Ma worked up a sweat trying to fix my hair. She brushed it 'til I thought it would fall out, but there wasn't nothing she could do but braid it. I remember she just shook her head and put the brush away. "You go on now, Molly. I done the best I could."

I must have been frowning, 'cause then she said, "You look pretty in the blue dress I made you."

I didn't believe her. She was just being kind.

Pa hitched up the mules to the buckboard and hauled us to school that first day. He wanted to make sure we got there on time and in good order. After that, we had to walk to school and back.

Miss June was a spinster lady. I don't know how old she was, but Ma said she was past her prime for getting married. I reckoned that meant she was at least twenty years old. She was tall and skinny like me. She had big teeth and smiled a lot. That year, Miss June had twenty-one young'uns to teach. Me and Edward was in the first grade. School went clear up through the eighth grade, with all of us learning in the same room. That first morning, Miss June was waiting for us outside. She greeted everyone, then lined us up by age with the boys on one side and the girls on the other.

Then she rang the school bell for the first time so we could go inside.

By then, Miss June had been living with the Browns for near on a month. We'd seen her several times at church, and she knew each of us by name. She had us little kids take our places first in the front of the schoolhouse, up close to her. Miss June had a place ready for each of us to sit, with the girls on one side and the boys on the other.

The middle-grade kids sat behind us. The oldest boys and girls were in the back of the room near the wood stove. That was handy so the boys could keep the fire going all day and fetch drinking water from the well. We all drank out of the same cup in the bucket. Miss June's desk was built up on a platform so she could look out over the whole room.

We began our day by reciting the Lord's Prayer. Miss June then read us a Bible story. After that, she went to the blackboard and wrote down a word. She called it a character word, and we'd get a new one every day. One of the big kids had to read the word and tell us what it meant. Then we spelt it out loud. She told us we had to practice living the word all day at school. That first day, the word was *polite* 'cause she wanted all of us to be nice and get along.

Each of us kids got a tablet with our name on it and a pencil to write with. Miss June had whittled down the nubs of them pencils so they'd be just the right size. We was real proud of our tablets and pencils. Miss June told us to keep them under our seats when we wasn't using them and never take them home. In them days, nobody took schoolwork home 'cause we had chores to do.

Before she got started with lessons, Miss June told us to pay close attention while she explained the rules. She expected us to follow them every day.

"Rule One: Silence is golden. I don't want any of you talking unless I call on you to answer a question, and there is to be no whispering among yourselves."

She waited before going on to make sure we understood.

"Rule Two: Raise your hand if you want to answer a question. If I call on you, stand up and speak up so the other children can hear you."

Again, she waited and looked at us before she went on.

"Rule Three: Raise your hand if you want to go to the outhouse. I only want one boy or one girl going at a time. And be quick about it, or I'll send someone out to look for you. Understood?"

"Yes, ma'am," we said.

"Rule Four: Sit quietly in your seats when not standing to answer a question, and don't *fidget*."

I raised my hand like she said. "Miss June, what's it mean to fidget?"

She smiled and said, "It means to wiggle around in your seat like this." And then she done showed us by moving her hiney from side to side in her chair. We all laughed.

"Rule Five: Boys have to take their hats off in school."

"Rule Six: Everyone has to work together to keep the schoolhouse neat and clean. Boys will keep the fire going and bring in drinking water from the well. Girls will take turns sweeping the floor at the end of the day."

"Rule Seven: Older children will help the younger ones with their lessons."

Miss June had one final thing to say on the subject. She looked us each square in the eye. "Breaking the rules means bad trouble. Understood?"

"Yes, ma'am," we said. We knew what happened if we did something bad at home. We didn't want nothing like that happening at school.

In the morning, we had fifteen minutes to go out and play. Dinner was at noon and took an hour 'cause we got to go outside once we'd finished eating our biscuits and jam. We got one more recess in the middle of the afternoon. School ended at four o'clock.

This is how our lessons went that day and most days thereafter. Miss June started with us little kids. We used McGuffey primers to learn to read. The first one had pictures with words, like a picture of a cow and then the letters c-o-w. That's how we learnt to sound out letters. After that, she taught us how to add and subtract numbers.

The other kids had work to do while we was doing our lessons. After she finished with us, Miss June asked the big kids, like John, to recite their lessons out loud. They did reading and arithmetic. Miss June was smart 'cause she saved the middle kids for last. Thataway, they could hear what us little kids was doing and be reminded of what they already learnt. Then they'd hear what the big kids was learning and get a head start on what they'd get to study next. It made them real smart and like learning new things. I think that's what made Isaac want to be a teacher.

The bigger kids helped us little kids, and we all got along. We learnt how to be *polite*.

When four o'clock came, I didn't want to go home. I come to learn that Miss June didn't like it neither when school was over and she had to go back to Pastor Brown's house. She didn't favor his two boys much. They were named Matthew and Luke from the Bible, but I don't think Jesus would have liked them a lick. They behaved hateful to Miss June when their pa wasn't around. The preacher's wife wouldn't do nothing to those boys when they was bad. She skittered about like she was afraid of her own shadow.

Miss June made me feel smart. "You learn quickly, Molly. Why, you could become a teacher one day if you work hard. Although I must say, we have a lot of work to do on your grammar."

Grammar meant the way I put words together like *was* and *were, them* and *those*, and *come* and *came*. I always got them— those—words mixed up and still do to this day.

Chapter 5

"Triangles, Circles and Squares"

At recess, Miss June liked to join us little kids. We played tag and hide-and-seek. She'd hitch up her skirts and run just as fast as we did. One day at recess, I asked her if we could play Polly, like I did at home with my brothers. I told her all about how Polly killed them Injuns when they attacked the fort. She squatted down in the dirt so she could look me straight in the eye. "That game wouldn't be proper to play at school, Molly."

"Why not?"

"There is always more to any story than what we think we know. Folks believe that the Indians are savages who kill people for no good reason. But the truth is that the Indians were here first, and we took their land away from them."

I had to sit with that awhile 'cause I'd never heard things explained to me like that before.

Miss June said, "We won't play a game that involves killing people. But Polly sounds like she was quite a woman in her day. She had *gumption*, and I admire that."

I wasn't sure what Miss June meant by that, but I grinned anyway 'cause gumption sounded like a good thing.

Sometimes I felt like I just didn't belong, especially when Miss June didn't come outside at recess. If Miss June got a game going, boys and girls played together. But when she wasn't around, they stayed to themselves. I wasn't like the other girls 'cause I was used to playing with my brothers. I didn't much care for girl talk. I didn't care a lick about how good-looking a boy was or if his pa had a big farm. I wanted to play ball with the boys, but they didn't want nothing to do with me 'cause I was a girl. So I had nowhere regular to belong.

One day, Miss June come outside and found me sitting on the step by myself, hugging my knees with my head down.

"What's wrong, Molly?"

"Nothing."

"Come on now. I know better than that. Let's go inside and have a talk."

She sat down beside me on a bench. She had a way of making me feel like I could tell her things. So I told her how I felt about not fittin' in. She got up and went to her desk. When she come back, she had a wood puzzle in her hand.

"Tell me what I have, Molly."

I said, "This here is the puzzle you done showed us when you was teaching us about the shapes of things."

"That's right," she said. "What shapes am I holding in my hand?"

"You got five circles, four squares and three triangles."

"Good girl, Molly. You paid attention during that lesson. Now I want you to take one of the triangles and put it in the round hole."

I wasn't sure I heard her right.

She said, "Go on. Do like I asked."

Well, no matter how hard I tried, that little piece wouldn't fit in the round hole. "Won't work, Miss June. You got to put the square piece in the square, the round piece in the circle, and the triangle where it fits. Can't mix them up."

"That's right, Molly. That's how it is with you and me. We sometimes feel like we're triangles trying to fit in round holes."

"You feel like me?"

"Yes, I do, Molly. Lots of times I feel like I'm different than other folks."

"Does it make you sad?"

"Not anymore 'cause I figured something out."

"What's that?"

"It's OK to be different. That's what makes you special. See what we got here? We have more squares and circles than triangles. When I'm around you, I feel like we're cut from the same shape and fit together good."

Miss June took a triangle and put it in the right place on the puzzle.

"Look for other children that make you feel the same way."

After our talk, I went back outside and looked around the playground. Edward was different, too. He was a triangle 'cause he couldn't play hard like them other boys. He got short of breath. I wasn't too sure who else might be cut from the same shape as me, but I made up my mind to find out.

Miss June dressed up pretty for school like she was going to church. My brothers, John and James, had a crush on her. They was always asking what they could do to help her besides fetching wood and water. Most of the kids treated Miss June with respect, but for the Cole brothers, who didn't respect nobody. One day after lunch, they put a cow paddy on her chair. Miss June didn't see it. She just sat right down in the mess.

Oh my! We thought them boys would get a lickin' for sure, but Miss June didn't make a fuss. She got up and cleaned the mess off her skirt, but it still smelt bad. What she did do was spend a lot of time that afternoon around Roy and Charlie Cole, so they would have to smell her stink.

The Coles lived in a run-down old shack about a mile down the road from the schoolhouse. Pa said they was no good and to stay away from them. Roy and Charlie were about the same ages as John and James. There was something about them two boys that made my skin crawl. I stayed as far away from them as I could, and my brothers did, too.

The Coles had a little girl about Isaac's age named Sarah and a boy just a tad bigger than me called Jesse. Sarah was shy, and her hair smelt bad. Miss June took her outside when the weather was warm and tried to wash her up some. Jesse didn't talk plain, so he stayed to hisself most of the time. None of them Coles ever had clean clothes to wear to school.

One morning at recess, I caught Jesse taking biscuits from our dinner pail. He was chewing on one with crumbs falling out of his mouth and had another one in his hand. I started yelling at him to put our food back. He didn't do nothing but stare at me. I kicked him hard in the shin.

Miss June heard the ruckus. "What is going on here?"

"Jesse stole biscuits from our pail!"

"Is that true, Jesse?"

Jesse hung his head and nodded.

"Put the biscuits back where you found them and go outside. I'll have a word with you in a few minutes. But first, I want to talk to Molly."

"What do you have to say for yourself?" she asked.

"I didn't do nothing wrong," I said. "It was Jesse who was stealing."

I was so mad, I spit on the floor.

"That's enough, young lady," Miss June said, raising her voice. "Sit down and get ahold of yourself."

I sat down like she asked, but my heart was racing and my cheeks felt hot.

"What do you know about Jesse and Sarah?"

"I know that they ain't got no manners and they stink."

Miss June took in a deep breath. "There's a whole lot more you don't know, Molly. Jesse and Sarah's pa gets mean when he drinks, and beats them and their ma, too. I'm sure he beat Roy and Charlie when they were little, and that's why they're not right in the head."

I knew Pa didn't cotton to ol' man Cole, but I didn't know why.

"Molly, here's what I want you to think about. It's a sin to steal.

That's a fact. But those children don't get enough to eat at home. Have you ever gone to bed hungry?"

"No, ma'am."

"I hope you never do because your belly starts hurting so bad, you can't sleep. That's probably why Jesse and Sarah are tired all the time and don't learn well."

My stomach started hurting just thinking about that. There were times I wanted more supper, and there wasn't none. But that was just 'cause Ma's cooking tasted good and not 'cause I was still hungry.

Miss June said, "I don't have the heart to punish Jesse for being hungry. But he didn't steal food from me. He stole it from you. What do you think we should do?"

I couldn't answer her right away. I was feeling ashamed for kicking Jesse, especially after hearing that he got beat regular by his pa.

"Don't do nothing to him, Miss June. I'm sorry I acted like I did."

I didn't say nothing to my brothers when we had our dinner that day, but Edward always knew when something was bothering me. On the way home, he asked me what was wrong.

I told him about Jesse and my talk with Miss June. Edward cared about people, and he couldn't stand the thought of those kids being hungry. When we got home, he told Ma about them.

"We got to help them, Ma," he said. "I can give them part of my dinner."

"You'll do no such thing, Edward. I'll take care of it."

From then on, Ma bundled up extra food to send with us for them. She didn't say nothing to Pa about it 'cause he wouldn't take kindly to helping that family.

On that next morning, when I handed Jesse the bundle as we were putting up our pails, I said, "Our ma made us too much dinner. We'd be obliged if you and Sarah would help us eat it. Pastor Brown said it's a sin to waste food."

His eyes got big when I said that. I think it was the first time I ever saw him turn his lip up from a frown to a smile. I said the same thing the next day and the day after that.

After a while, I just handed him the bundle of food and didn't say nothing more about it. Jesse smiled big at me after that, and his sister, too. Me and Edward started helping them with their lessons. I asked Miss June if I could sit beside Sarah so I could make sure she was learning good, and Edward did the same thing with Jesse. We got to where we liked them good and played with them at recess. One afternoon, Miss June said that I'd been living the character word of the day. The word was *kindness*.

Here's what I figured out. It didn't matter that Sarah's hair smelt bad or that Jesse didn't talk plain. We was cut from the same shape and fit together good. Edward, Sarah, Jesse and me were triangles, and there was no way we fit in anybody else's hole. It was lonely sometimes 'cause there were only four of us at school like that, but it felt good when we got together. A triangle is a triangle. Ain't no way it's ever gonna be a circle or a square. I come to find out that I'd always live my life as that triangle. Not everybody liked me 'cause I was plain-spoken and liked to work in the tobacco field instead of the house. But I got along just fine with folks who were different like me.

Chapter 6

"Little Women"

Friday was the best day of the week 'cause we got to do special things. We had spelling bees that I liked a lot. We'd choose up teams and go up against each other. Sometimes it was the girls against the boys, and sometimes Miss June mixed us up. I always did good with them spelling bees 'cause I liked sounding out words. Give me most any word, and I could figure out how to spell it. Well, except for big words that made no sense, like gumption.

Isaac liked the arithmetic bees best. That boy had a way with numbers. Me and Edward … well, not so much. But it was still fun getting to play them games.

On Friday afternoons, my favorite thing to do was to listen to Miss June read stories out of big fancy books she got from Louisville. She was mighty fair about choosing a book that the girls would like and then one for the boys. One of the books she was most proud of getting was the one about Tom Sawyer and Huckleberry Finn 'cause it only got printed a few of years before. John and James liked this book the best. They'd talk all the way home about the adventures them boys had and how they wanted to go to Missouri and see what they seen.

James especially liked anything to do with rivers and boats.

"Molly, one day I'm gonna live on the Mississippi River, just like Tom Sawyer did," he said. "I'll have me a fine steamboat and go up and down the river all day."

"Can I go with you?"

"Well, of course you can. You're my little sister, after all."

"Promise you'll take me with you?"

"I promise," he said, and I believed him.

The book I liked most was *Little Women*, which was about four girls growing up during the Civil War. Miss June said the book took place in Massachusetts. I wanted Miss June to think I was smart. I raised my hand and stood up to ask my question.

"Where is Mass … a … toot …sits?"

Miss June said, "It's in New England, which is a long way from Kentucky, Molly. It's on the east coast of America by the ocean."

I kept thinking about that book while we was walking home that day. When we got to our farm, I asked John to put me up on his shoulders so I could look out beyond our fields to see New England. He smiled and lifted me up.

"Can you see it, Molly?"

"Yes, I can."

"What's it like?"

"Well, I'm not too sure yet what it's like, but it comes right after the old England that got all wore out. That's why it's called new."

John didn't say nothing when I said that. He just squeezed my legs good before he set me down.

Them girls in *Little Women* was named Meg, Josephine, Beth and Amy. I liked Josephine the best 'cause she was what you call a tomboy. That means she wasn't very ladylike. They called her Jo, and she had big hands and feet like me. I told Miss June that Jo was a triangle and I think we would have made good friends.

One Friday afternoon when Miss June was reading *Little Women*, I got scared bad. Edward had been feeling poorly all week and couldn't go to school. Ma said he was hot with fever and not hisself. His throat was hurting him bad, and he didn't want nothing to eat.

Miss June got to the part in the book where little Beth got bad sick from the scarlet fever, and they didn't know if she was gonna make it. I felt my dinner come right up in my throat when I heard that. I stood up and raised my hand.

"What is it, Molly?"

I had trouble getting my words out.

"How do you know if someone has the scarlet fever?"

"My understanding is that they get a sore throat and high fever."

"Oh no! I think Edward might have the fever."

"Does he have a rash?"

"What's that?"

Miss June pointed to her neck. "Red spots on his neck or belly."

"I don't know, Miss June! I got to go find out!"

I ran out of that schoolhouse just as fast as I could. Miss June sent John after me, but I was running so hard, he couldn't catch me. I fell down and scratched up my knee and tore my dress, but I didn't care a lick. I had to get to Edward. When I ran into the house, I found Ma was sitting with him.

I could hardly get my breath from running so hard. "Ma ... does Edward ... have red spots?"

I didn't wait for her to answer. I got down beside him and looked at his neck, then I lifted up his nightshirt to see his tummy.

"Molly, what's gotten into you?"

"I was scared he had the scarlet fever like Beth in the book. But he's OK, Ma. He don't got red spots."

Edward wanted to know what all the fuss was about. Then he asked Ma for some soup 'cause his throat felt better and he could swallow. I hugged him silly when he said that.

When John come in the door, he told Ma I was in a heap of trouble for running out of the schoolhouse. I was afeared she'd tell Pa and I'd get a whipping for sure, but she didn't.

She kissed me on the head and said, "You are a good girl, Molly, for loving Edward that much. I'll have to see if I can mend your dress."

Later on, when Isaac and James got home, I got a surprise, but it wasn't a good one. They weren't alone. Miss June come with them in Pastor Brown's buckboard. I said a fast prayer to Jesus when I saw her 'cause I knew I was in trouble. After she said hello to Edward, she asked Ma if she could have a word with me outside.

My leg started twitching as I waited for her to come out of the house. I was scared. Miss June come out and sat down on the step beside me.

"What do you have to say for yourself, Molly?"

"I'm sorry ..." I started to say but then I stopped. I knew it was a sin to tell a lie and I wasn't sorry for what I done.

"Miss June, you can whip me if you want, but I ain't sorry for what I done."

"Leaving school without permission was wrong," she said.

"But I had to make sure Edward didn't have the fever."

"What you did was wrong even if you had a good reason. You made a poor decision because you didn't think things through."

Miss June gave me a good talking to about what I could have done instead of running out of the schoolhouse. The next day, I had to stand up at the front of the room and tell the other children I was sorry that I made a poor decision. Miss June wrote that word up on the board for the character word of day. *Decision.* Then she asked me to tell the other children what I might have done to make a better one.

"I could have asked you if me and my brothers could leave school early to check on Edward."

"That's right, Molly. I would have said yes because you would have had your brothers along to make sure you were safe. From now on, let's all work together to make good decisions when problems come up."

Chapter 7

"Slammed Door"

It was a hot July day in 1888 when a stranger come up to the house to introduce hisself. Pa and my brothers were way out in the field, so they didn't see him. Me and Ma was fixing up noon dinner. The man got off his horse and knocked on the door.

"Morning, ma'am."

"Morning," Ma answered back, stepping out on the porch.

"My name is Sean O'Reilly," he said, taking off his hat. "I come to make your acquaintance. My wife, Bridget, and me live just down the road. We bought the Dickens place."

"Come in, Sean. I'm Maureen Van Meter, and this is my girl, Molly."

Sean was a big fella with specks of red in his hair and in his beard.

"You look hot," Ma said. "Sit down and I'll fetch you a drink of water."

"I'd be obliged, ma'am. Thank you."

I was staring at the stranger crooked 'cause his way of talking sounded different than ours. Ma thumped me on the head and whispered to mind my manners.

"I met some folks at the general store the other day. They told me about you and your family. They said you was Irish."

"I'm Irish, but not my husband."

"Well, that's why I come to meet you. Our kin is Irish, too."

Ma smiled. "I thought I heard a bit of the brogue in your voice. I've lost most of mine."

"My wife's having our first baby in a few months."

"That's wonderful, Sean. I'm sure she's pleased as can be."

"She's not herself these days."

"Is there something wrong with the baby?"

"No, ma'am. Don't think so. She cries a lot 'cause she's missing her kin. We come here from Elizabethtown to farm. It's hard on her not having folks like us around."

"You mean 'cause you're Irish?"

"Irish Catholic, ma'am."

Ma got a look in her eyes that I ain't never seen before, like she had a sharp pain she couldn't do nothing about.

"Would you care to stay for dinner, Sean? The menfolk will be coming in soon."

"No, ma'am, but I thank you."

Ma said, "I would be pleased if you and Bridget would have supper with us on Saturday. Come at five o'clock."

Sean took Ma's hand and pumped it good. "My Bridget would like that, ma'am. Thank you."

Ma stood in the door and watched him put on his hat, climb up on his horse and ride away.

"You feeling OK, Ma?"

"Yes, Molly. Why do you ask?"

"I never seen you look like this before."

Ma told me to go on and serve up the plates for dinner and not say nothing to Pa about the man's visit.

"Why?" I asked, but then she gave me a look. I shut my mouth and got busy with dinner.

After everyone got fed, Ma told me to wash up the plates and the boys to go on back to work 'cause she needed a word with Pa.

I made pretend that I was doing what she told me, but I kept real quiet so I could hear their talk.

Ma said, "That fella who bought the Dickens place paid us a visit this morning."

"Decent fella?" Pa asked.

"Seems to be," Ma answered. "His wife's having a baby. I've invited them to take supper with us Saturday evening."

"If you think it's fittin'," Pa said. "What's their name?"

"O'Reilly. Sean and Bridget O'Reilly."

"They Irish?" Pa asked, raising his voice some.

"Yes," Ma answered. "Catholic, too."

"Now, Maureen, you know how I feel about that!"

Ma told him to hush 'cause I was in the other room. But I could hear her plenty good.

"You listen here, Jacob Van Meter. I've done what you asked since the day we married. But now, I'm asking you to treat them good and mind your manners. You hear?"

Oh lordy! I'd only heard Ma raise her voice like that when she was about to fling a switch. I strained to hear Pa's answer. All I heard was the door slam behind him.

Chapter 8

"Who I Really Am"

That Saturday morning, Ma started making supper right after the menfolk finished their breakfast. We grew most everything we ate on our farm. We kept plenty of chickens and at least two milk cows. Every year, we planted a big garden so we could eat fresh all summer, and then canned what was left for the winter. The only things Ma bought in town was coffee and flour, our shoes, and cloth to sew for our clothes.

This was the time of the summer when our berries grew wild. Ma told Edward and me to take our pails and fill them with the berries that were black, not red, 'cause those was the ones ready to eat, and to wash them up good before we brung them in the house.

Then she sent us back out to the garden to pick green beans, carrots and potatoes. We sat on the porch and snapped the ends off them green beans 'til our thumbs and first fingers got sore. After that, I cleaned the skins of the potatoes and the carrots with a knife, being careful not to nick them. When it was time, Ma cooked all them vegetables in a kettle over the fire. Back in them days, you had to use special heavy pots with handles that hung on a metal pole in the fireplace to cook your food.

I made bottoms for pies out of flour, lard, eggs and milk on the table we kept in the little side room. After I stirred everything up good, I rolled the dough out flat and thin, just like Ma taught me. Edward got the fire burning just right, so it wasn't too hot or not hot enough. Ma cooked up the bottoms first in iron skillets, and then added the blackberries for filling. Oh my, were those pies good! We didn't have them very often, so I reckoned the O'Reillys were special people.

The worst part of the day was killing two hens to fry up for supper. Ma got her bucket and big knife, and then sent me to fetch the poor critters. When I went into the coop, the hens started making a fuss. They must've known what was coming. I grabbed the first one by the legs and took it out to Ma. We walked away from the coop so we wouldn't frighten the other hens more. She got that critter by the neck and flung it round and round 'til we heard its neck snap. It flopped around some, but when it got still, Ma laid it on the ground. Then she sent me back to the coop to get another one. When I brung it to her, she said, "Molly, it's high time you learnt how to wring a chicken's neck proper. Let me take the legs while you get ahold of its neck. Grab on tight with your right hand."

I did what she told me but I didn't like it a bit. That poor chicken squawked and fought me good, but I held on tight. Ma put her hand on top of mine for a minute to steady me. Then she said, "All right now, keep a tight hand and turn a circle as fast as you can. Don't let go for nothing!"

Its wings was flapping everywhere, and I thought I'd lose my grip for sure. I was hollering so loud, I didn't hear its neck snap, but Ma knew when it was dead. She told me I done good and to lay it on the ground. She cut off the hens' heads and then turned them upside down so their blood would run off into the bucket. That part made me feel like I wasn't sturdy on my feet.

Once all the blood was out, we took them over to the porch and sat down to pluck out each one of their feathers. Then Ma had me fetch water from the well so she could clean them good. After that, she took the chickens inside and cut them into pieces, coated them with flour, and fried them up in her iron pan over the fire. It was a lot of work, but Ma's fried chicken was worth it. Still, I hated having to wring that chicken's neck and watch the blood come out.

It got plum hot in our house with all the cooking, even with the windows and door open. From time to time, we had to go outside just to catch a breath. Ma made Pa and my brothers wash up good at the well when they come in from the field. The house started to cool down just as the O'Reillys come up in their buckboard. Me, Ma and Edward went out to greet them. Pa and the rest of the boys stayed inside.

Sean helped his missus down, and Ma walked out to welcome her. There was something about Bridget O'Reilly that reminded me of Ma, even though they didn't look alike. She had blue eyes, and her hair was made of curls, not straight pieces. Her face had freckles on it, and her belly was big with a baby. She had a gentle touch when she shook my hand.

As they walked in the house, I whispered in Edward's ear. "I like her even if she is a Catholic." I wanted to remember to ask Miss June what that meant.

Ma made introductions. Then we served up supper, and everyone crowded around the table. Ma told me to sit down beside her, and all of us ate supper together. That made me happy 'cause I got to eat my food before it got cold.

After we'd tasted some of Ma's fine cooking, we started talking.

Bridget asked Ma, "Where did your kin sail from?"

"They came from Cork," Ma said, "around 1800."

"Oh my, we haven't been here near as long. Our people sailed in 1848 after we lost everything in the famine."

Always the curious one, Isaac asked, "What's a famine?"

Sean said, "It's when people die 'cause there's not enough to eat."

"Why wasn't there enough to eat? Didn't you have farms like us?"

"Hush," Ma said, "mind your manners."

"It's quite all right, ma'am. I like a boy who asks good questions.

Our kin had small plots of land, and they grew potatoes. We were poor folks and potatoes was all we had to eat."

Edward's eyes got big. He looked down at his plate of chicken, potatoes, carrots and beans, and then he looked up at Sean. "That's all?"

"That's right, son."

"What happened?"

"The blight hit Ireland hard and killed all the potato crops for a decade. People were starving 'cause they had no food to eat. A lot of them died. The lucky ones, like our kin, made their way to America."

John said, "Miss June's been teaching us about immigrants and how they came to New York on boats. How did you end up here?"

"Looking for a better life," Sean said. "Some of our kin sailed over long before we did. They found their way to Kentucky and settled in Elizabethtown."

James said, "I'm gonna own a fine boat someday."

"Well, I'm sure it'll be a better boat than what they sailed across the ocean in."

"What made you want to move to Uptonville?" Joost asked.

"We've been looking for land to farm for a long time at a price we could afford. The Dickens place suited us, and with the baby coming, we thought the time was right to settle here."

Ma looked at Bridget and smiled.

"When you having the baby?" I asked.

"Early in the fall," she answered, rubbing her belly. "Sean thinks we're having a boy, but I know it's a girl."

"How do you know that?"

Bridget had a sweet look on her face when she answered me. "I just do."

Pa, who hadn't said nothing up to now, asked, "What crops you gonna plant?"

"I'd like to learn to grow tobacco," Sean said. "I was hoping maybe you'd show me your barn."

Pa grunted and went back to eating his supper.

When he got done, Sean sat back in his chair and said, "Ma'am, that was a fine supper, and I thank you."

Pa said, "I'll take you to see the barn."

"I'd be obliged."

Never one to talk much to strangers, Jansen hadn't said a word during supper. But as Sean stood to go with Pa, he said, "The tobacco crop's growing good. You want to see it?"

"I would," Sean said.

Ma told Pa and my brothers to take their time showing Sean around the farm. She told Edward and me to go play outside.

"What about washing up the dishes, Ma?"

"That can wait," she said. That's when I knew there was something really special about the O'Reillys.

Ma fixed them up a drink of water and went out on the porch to visit. Edward and me was playing a game in the dirt off to the side of the porch where they couldn't see us, but I got a look at them from time to time. I acted like I wasn't listening to their talk, but I was. I didn't hear all of it, but what I did hear made me wonder about things.

Bridget told Ma about her kin and how much she missed them, especially her older sister, who lived in Elizabethtown. Ma told Bridget about her sisters and how she hadn't seen them in the seventeen years she'd been married to Pa.

"Do they live far away?"

"Not that far," Ma answered. She got quiet for a minute, then said, "My pa said I wasn't his daughter no more when I married Jacob."

"Mind if I ask you why?"

"He isn't a Catholic. His kin felt the same way about me 'cause I'm not one of them. We came here to start a new life."

"Your husband doesn't take to us being Irish Catholic, does he?"

"He made me promise not to be a Catholic no more when we got married. I go to his Baptist church now with our young'uns."

They sat quiet for a spell, and then Ma said, "I miss being who I really am."

Bridget leaned over and took Ma's hand. When I heard Ma sobbing, I told Edward to get up so we could go play somewhere else. I didn't understand what she'd just said and I didn't want to hear her cry.

Chapter 9

"Getting Saved"

When fall come that year, I couldn't wait for school to start. That turned out to be the year Edward found his calling and four boys got in a mess of trouble.

The Sunday before school began was a big church day for the Van Meter family 'cause me and Edward was getting baptized. My other brothers had already been dunked in the river, and now it was our turn. We took an extra good bath on Saturday night, and Ma dressed us up in white that morning. We didn't go to Sunday school like normal. We had to come to preaching and sit up front.

Pastor Brown worked up a sweat talking about how our sins got washed clean by baptism. He made me and Edward stand up before the congregation and say real loud that we wanted to be saved. Then he marched us down to the river that we crossed coming to school. I was glad it was a warm sunny day so the water wouldn't be too cold.

The preacher waded into the river first. We'd had plentiful rain that summer, so the water come up above my knees. Pastor Brown stood between me and Edward. He looked like a giant standing over us with one hand on me and the other on Edward. His fingers felt like a vice gripping my head so I couldn't go nowhere. Even though I'd seen my brothers get dunked, I was still scared about what was gonna happen.

I could see Ma standing beside Pa at the edge of the river. I wanted to shout out for her to come get me, but I knew I'd get in big trouble for that. I was hoping Edward wasn't feeling as scared as me.

Pastor Brown began. "Romans 6:3-4 says: 'Know ye not, that so many of us as were baptized into Jesus Christ were baptized into his death?"

Now that got me shaking. I wasn't ready to be baptized into death. I was only nine years old.

"Therefore, we are buried with him by baptism into death: that like as Christ was raised up from the dead by the glory of the Father, even so we also should walk in the newness of life."

I felt the preacher's fingers gripping my head even tighter. Then he said, "Molly and Edward, do you want to be baptized into Jesus?"

"Yes!" we shouted out.

"I baptize you in the name of the Father, Son and Holy Ghost!" Then he shoved our heads down into the water. I hadn't closed my mouth all the way, and water got in. When he let us up, I was coughing hard and spitting out water.

We was shivering when we got out of that river, and I couldn't wait to dry off and get home to have supper. Edward kept talking about how good it felt to be saved for Jesus. I smiled like I agreed, but I was just glad it was over with.

Come October, I got to see a baby born. Ma and Bridget became good friends that summer. Ma went over to the O'Reilly place every couple of weeks and helped Bridget get ready for the birth by fixing up a little bed in their room and sewing clothes for the baby. Bridget asked Ma to come for the baby's birth. Ma said she'd be pleased to help deliver the baby. She started making preparations just as soon as she saw the baby drop down in Bridget's belly. She told me that was how you could tell the time was short 'til it comes.

We was finishing our noon dinner one Saturday when Sean come riding up the path to our house in a fury. He knocked on the door and shouted out for Ma to come right away. The baby was coming.

Ma tried to calm him down. "I'm sure we've got plenty of time, Sean. It's Bridget's first baby, and that can take awhile."

"No, ma'am," he said, trying to catch his breath. "Her water spilled out last night, and she's been having pains since before first light. They're getting closer together now and harder."

"I'll get my things," Ma said. "Isaac, go hitch up the mules to the buckboard. Molly, you want to come with me? It's time you learned about birthing babies."

"Yes, ma'am," I said. "I'll get my things." I didn't have no things to get, but Ma had said that, so I guessed it was important.

"Ma, can I go, too?" Edward asked. "I can be useful," he said. "I'll look after Sean and keep the fire going."

"All right," Ma said. "Let's go."

Ma kissed Pa on the cheek and told my brothers to look after theirselves 'til she got back.

Ma could drive a buckboard just as good as Pa, and we got to the O'Reilly's place in no time. As we come in the door, we heard Bridget moaning. Ma went to check on her. I stayed with Edward and Sean. Ma come back out quick.

"Edward, run and fetch water from the well. Sean, get the fire going good. Molly, bring me the water once it's boiling hot. Get clean cloths and scissors, too."

We started doing our jobs as fast as we could. Sean told me where to find the cloths and scissors. I brung the hot water in first and then the other supplies. Ma had Bridget lying in the bed with her knees up and out and her woman parts showing. I didn't know what to think about that. Ma told me to get one of the cloths and dip it in the water that was in a basin by the bed. I did just like she asked.

"Molly, put that cool cloth on Bridget's forehead and then take ahold of her hand."

I no sooner got ahold of her hand that the next pain started coming. Bridget cried out loud and squeezed my hand tight. I wanted to cry out, too, when she did that, but I had to be brave. Soon enough, the pain passed, and she loosened her grip on my hand. But then another one came.

Ma looked at her private parts and said, "Push, Bridget, push!"

I was afraid the poor woman was dying 'cause she started screaming so loud.

"I see the baby's head," Ma said. "Push again!"

This time, Bridget squeezed my hand so tight, I shouted out right along with her.

"I got the head and the shoulders. Push one more time!"

Bridget pushed again, and the baby come flying out of her. Ma caught it before it fell on the floor. She looked at it and smiled.

"You were right, Bridget. You have a fine baby girl!"

The baby started hollering after Ma patted her hard on the butt. After washing the scissors in the boiling water, Ma cut off the cord holding the baby to Bridget.

"Molly, you go tell Sean he has a beautiful daughter, but he's not to come in yet. I want to clean up the baby and Bridget first. You stay with your brother 'til I come to get you."

It wasn't but a few minutes later that Sean got his first look at his baby girl. She was round as she could be. She opened her eyes for a minute, and they was blue. She had pretty heart-shaped lips and a nice rose color to her cheeks. Bridget was sitting up in bed and holding her. She looked better than I expected after being in so much pain. She thanked me for holding her hand and hoped she hadn't hurt me none.

"Would you like to hold the baby, Molly?"

"Yes, ma'am."

Ma helped me get ahold of her in my arms, being careful to support her neck and head.

"What's her name?" Edward asked.

"We're naming her for my ma," Bridget said, "and for your ma. Her name is Anna Maureen."

Ma burst out crying after hearing that. She dried her eyes and then asked Edward and Sean to go outside so she could help Bridget nurse the baby. She told me I could stay. That's when I felt I done growed into a woman. After the baby drank her first milk from Bridget's breast, she fell asleep, and the menfolk come back into the room.

Bridget said, "I want to have my baby baptized, but there're no priest around these parts."

Nobody said nothing 'cause that was true.

"Let's do it now," Ma said.

"No!" Edward cried out. "She's too little to get dunked in the river. It's cold and dark outside!"

Ma's eyes got big, and then she smiled. "No, son," she said, "we can baptize the baby right here. I'll show you."

Ma had Sean fetch warm water and some oil. She took the oil and made a cross on the baby's forehead. Then she said, "This is how we baptize Catholic babies, Edward."

"Does it work as good as the Baptist way?"

"Yes, son, it does. Either way you do it, the baby is washed clean of sins and saved for Jesus."

I knew it was a sin when I kicked Jesse in the shin or told a lie, but I didn't see how Anna Maureen could have sinned yet. I asked Ma about that. She said it was a long story that she would explain to me another time.

"The next thing we do is pour the warm water over her head and say the proper words."

"Like Pastor Brown said when we got dunked?" I asked.

"Yes, Molly."

Edward said, "I know them words, Ma. Can I say them?"

Ma looked to Sean and Bridget, and they nodded their heads. "Go on ahead then, Edward."

Ma poured the water on Anna's head. Edward said, "I baptize you in the name of the Father, Son and Holy Ghost!"

The baby squinted her eyes and whimpered a bit, then got quiet. I figured that was 'cause she done got saved.

On the way home that night, Ma explained how Catholics believed that babies were born with a stain on their soul, called Original Sin 'cause of what Adam and Eve done in the Garden of Eden. That's why they had to be washed clean as soon as possible through baptism. Otherwise, if they died, they wouldn't go to heaven. That made no sense to me. Pa didn't punish me when my brothers did something bad, so why would God be mad at Anna Maureen 'cause of what Adam and Eve did. But I knew better than to argue with Ma.

Edward said, "Ma, can I ask you something?"

"Go on ahead," she said.

"Are you sure the Catholic baptism is as good as Pastor Brown's for saving souls?"

"Yes, Edward. I'm sure."

"Well then, I think I'm gonna do it that way when I become a preacher. It's a whole lot better than drowning young'uns in a river."

I knew then that Edward had gotten the call from Jesus to preach the gospel, and all of us would be better for it.

Chapter 10

"Moonshine in the Woods"

One Sunday at church, Pastor Brown preached about the evils of drinking whiskey.

"There are those living among us who make moonshine," he bellowed, "in the woods back behind their shanty. They're known to sell their vile brew to other sinners who will burn forever in the fires of hell!"

On the ride home, I asked Pa what moonshine was.

He said, "It's homemade whiskey that fools make in the woods under the light of the moon. That's why it's called moonshine."

"How do they make it?" asked Isaac.

"I ain't too sure about the particulars," Pa said, "but I hear tell they mix up cornmeal with sugar, malt and yeast, and then cook the mess 'til they think it's fit to drink."

"It's a dangerous brew," Ma said. "I've heard of people dying after drinking a bad batch."

"Who was Pastor Brown talking about making moonshine behind their shanty?" Edward asked.

Ma and Pa looked at each other. Then Pa said, "Ol' man Cole. He's a no-good lowlife."

"Miss June told me he gets drunk and beats his wife and young'uns."

"You stay away from anybody with the name Cole, Molly. Mark my words. Them young'uns will grow up to be just like their pa."

Edward waited 'til we was alone to tell me he didn't like what Pa said. "Jesse and Sarah ain't like that. They can't help who their pa is."

I told Edward he was right about Sarah and Jesse, but Roy and Charlie was just like their pa. A couple of days later, they proved me right.

From time to time, all the big boys, John and James included, went behind the schoolhouse during recess to sneak a smoke when Miss June wasn't looking. Nobody thought nothing about it 'cause it's just what boys do. But one day, the preacher's boys snuck off to the woods with Roy and Charlie, and I got a feeling they was up to no good. I followed them but kept out of sight. I saw Roy and Charlie pass a jug around and Matthew and Luke take a swig. When Miss June rung the bell to come in, they wiped their mouths and hid the jug. They come back and acted like nothing happened. But I reckoned they was drinking moonshine.

The next day, them boys did the same thing. They was acting silly when they walked back into the schoolhouse, but they got ahold of theirselves and stayed out of trouble that afternoon. The day after that, I snuck back into the woods to watch them again. This time, they really was acting the fool, dancing around and wobbly on their feet. It was then that I remembered what Ma said about what could happen if they got ahold of a bad brew. I'd never seen how boys act after drinking whiskey, so I got afraid they might be getting sick in their brains. I figured I better have a word with Miss June before something bad happened to them.

Miss June stayed in from recess that day. I found her alone at her desk. The young'uns were playing games outside, so I asked if I might have a word with her.

"Of course, Molly. What's on your mind?"

"Miss June, what happens to somebody's brain if they get ahold of a bad batch of moonshine?"

Miss June looked right surprised.

"A person can get very sick and even die from a bad brew. Why do you ask?"

I started to have second thoughts about telling Miss June what I seen. I didn't want to be a snitch.

"Something is bothering you, Molly. You can tell me."

"I'm afeared that some boys are drinking a bad batch of whiskey in the woods."

"What makes you think that?"

"I seen them pass a jug around after dinner for the last few days. Today, they was staggering around and not sturdy on their feet. I wasn't gonna say nothing 'cause it ain't right to tattle, but I got worried they might get sick from a bad batch of moonshine."

Miss June said, "All right, Molly. You did the right thing by coming to me. Let's keep this just between the two of us. I'll take care of it."

Just like the two days before, them boys got ahold of theirselves and come in when Miss June rang the bell. The next day, everything seemed regular. We had dinner and went outside to play. Them four boys snuck off just like before. Miss June had me stay next to her, so I couldn't follow them. She played outside with us, and when it was time to go inside, she didn't ring the bell. She just told us to take our seats.

Them boys still weren't back, but Miss June didn't say nothing. She got us busy doing our lessons. After a while, she told one of the big girls to go next door to the preacher's house and ask him to come to the schoolhouse.

Miss June had a word with him outside, and then had him come in to see what we was doing. He didn't say nothing. It got to be time for our afternoon recess, and we went outside just like always. After we played for a while, Miss June told us to go on back in. She and the preacher stayed outside. When we heard her ring the school bell, we crowded around the windows to see what was going on. Them four boys come staggering out of the woods, laughing and carrying on. They couldn't walk straight for nothing. See, they just kept on drinking that moonshine, waiting for Miss June to ring that dang school bell after dinner recess. They got so drunk, they couldn't tell how much time had passed.

Imagine the looks on Matthew's and Luke's faces when they saw Pastor Brown standing there with Miss June. "Go home, boys," he said in a calm voice that was even scarier than his mean, loud one. "I'll deal with you later."

Lord knows what happened to them boys after he got home, but my guess is they didn't feel like sitting down for a week.

As for the Cole boys, Pastor Brown took them by the collar and marched them down the road to their shack. He told them to never come back. When we told Pa, he said ol' man Cole better keep them boys in line, or they'd be run out of town and their shack burnt to the ground.

After that, Jesse and Sarah come to school by theirselves, except when they was too bruised to be seen. And school felt like a better place for having them bad boys gone.

Chapter 11

"A Handful of Days"

There are a handful of days that stay in your mind forever. Some are good days, some are bad, but you remember everything about them. Those are the days that you know what you ate for dinner or what you was wearing and doing. It was Friday, August 16, 1889. We ate beans and cornbread for our noon dinner. I was wearing a shirt and a pair of britches that Isaac had outgrown. Ma had on a pair of britches, too, and an old shirt of Pa's. Most of the time, we wore dresses, but that day we was working in the fields. I remember Isaac's shirt was green, and it scratched some. His pants was dark-blue and didn't fit me good around the waist 'cause they was too big.

Ma set out jugs of water for us while we was picking the tobacco plants. I took a break to get a drink, and that's when I saw Sean O'Reilly riding his horse up the path to our farm. I waved at him so he could see we was in the field. He was going so fast he had to reign his horse tight to get him to stop. He jumped down and started hollering for Ma. His cheeks was red as fire, and he was dripping sweat.

He had to catch his breath before he could get his words out. "Bridget … and the baby … are real sick."

"What's wrong with them?" Ma asked.

"They're burning up with fever."

"When did it come on?"

"Late last night."

Pa come over. "Have you ridden out to Doc's house?"

"I just came from there. Doc's wife said he's out tending to other sick folks and won't be back 'til after dark. Please, Maureen, I'm begging you to come help them!"

"I don't think that's a good idea," Pa said. "We don't know what kind of sickness she's got."

"Bridget's a sister to me, Jacob," Ma said. "I have to go."

I could see fear in Pa's eyes, but he didn't say nothing more to Ma. He looked over at my brothers, then pointed to John. "Hitch up the buckboard, John, and go with your ma. Look after her."

I figured Pa chose John 'cause he needed Joost and Jansen to help with the tobacco. They was bigger than John, and the rest of my brothers was too young to help Ma. I thought it only fittin' Ma take me, since I was ten years old and seen a baby born.

"Ma, can I go with you?"

Ma knelt down and brushed the hair off my forehead. "Not this time, Molly. I need you to look after Pa and your brothers while I'm gone, especially Edward. Can you do that for me?"

"Yes, ma'am," I said, even though I didn't want to.

"You're gonna have to cook the meals and tend to the house chores like I taught you. I know you'll do a good job."

Ma started to stand but then stopped. She looked me square in the eye and said, "You're a fine girl, Mary Molly Van Meter. I'm proud of you." She kissed my head and turned away.

I stood there with my mouth open. Ma had never said anything like that to me before, and it made me feel funny, but not in a good way. She said goodbye to my brothers, kissed Pa on the cheek, and climbed up on the buckboard with John. She turned and waved goodbye as they started down the path to Sean's house. I got back to picking tobacco, but my mind was filled with other worries, like what I could fix for supper to feed Pa and my brothers.

The next day, Doc Middleton paid us a visit just as we was eating our noon dinner. He had his horse hitched to the back of our buckboard. He asked if he could have a word with Pa outside. All of us crowded around the door so we could hear what he had to say.

"Jacob, I just come from the O'Reilly place. Bridget and the baby are not doing well."

"What's wrong with them?"

"They got diphtheria."

"Oh dear Lord," Pa cried. "How did they get that?"

"It started in Elizabethtown. They came down with it after they went to visit Bridget's sister."

"What can you do for it?"

"There's not much I can do for diphtheria. It's just got to run its course. Folks get high fevers and real bad sore throats. I fixed up a bottle of laudanum to help with the pain."

Pa lowered his voice. "I remember the sickness from when I was boy. Some people don't make it."

"I'm afraid that's right, Jacob. Sometimes a person's heart gives out from the stress of the illness."

"I appreciate you riding out here to tell me about them. When's Maureen coming home with John?"

"That's what I came to talk to you about. They can't come home 'til the sickness passes."

"But they're not sick."

"No, but I had to quarantine them together. I nailed the sign up today. Nobody can go in or out of the O'Reilly house 'til this passes, except to use the outhouse and get wood for the fire and water from the well."

Pa started to protest, but Doc stopped him. "Jacob, it's very important that Maureen and John stay right where they are and not leave the house. People around here are worried that the sickness will spread to them. It broke out in the Irish part of Elizabethtown, and folks got it in their heads that the O'Reillys are cursed 'cause they're Irish Catholic."

"How long before they can come home?"

"At least a couple of weeks. Maureen asked me to bring the mules and the buckboard home to you. She also asked to have Molly get clothes for her and John. I'll take them to her tomorrow."

"How are they gonna get along?" Pa asked.

"Don't you worry about that. I'll ride out to the O'Reilly place every day and check on them. I'll ask Albert Fry to get whatever supplies they need and have Isaiah deliver them. Isaiah's wife, Sally Ann, cooks for us. I'll have her cook up some meals, and I'll take them with me when I go to visit."

I fixed up a bag with clothes for Ma and John. I put her hairbrush in the bag along with a bar of soap. Doc took the bag, thanked me and left. We sat back down at the table and finished our dinner, but nobody had nothing to say.

Each day, I tended to Pa and the boys and did all my chores like Ma asked. Pa said I did a good job, but I could tell he wanted Ma back. That was OK with me. I was nowhere near as good as Ma at cooking or keeping our place clean.

When Sunday morning come around, I asked Pa if we was going to church.

"No, not today, Molly."

I was shocked when Pa said that. We always went to church.

I started to ask why not, but he turned his back on me and went outside, slamming the door behind him. After that, the days all started melting together. I kept thinking I'd see Ma and John coming up the path to our house, but two Sundays came and went without them.

The next Tuesday, Miss June paid me a visit. I was sweeping the house while Pa and the boys was seeing to the crop. She brung supper and cake and a big pot of chicken soup to take to Ma. She hugged me tight and said, "Don't you fret about your ma and John. Pastor Brown and I are praying for them every single day." Her words was meant to make me feel better, but I could tell by the look in her eyes that she was worried.

Miss June said she had to get back to Pastor Brown's 'cause she'd borrowed his buckboard. She promised to come back again in a few days. After she left, I ran down to the barn to ask Pa if I could take the soup out to the O'Reilly place.

Pa wiped the sweat off his forehead while he thought about it. "I reckon that will be all right, but you can't go in the house."

"I know, Pa, but I'll be able to see Ma and John through the window. That'll do me good."

"All right then, Molly. I'll have James hitch the mules and take you."

I was so happy on the ride to the O'Reilly place. I couldn't wait to see Ma and John. I was glad Pa asked James to take me. He'd been missing John something awful.

It was mighty quiet at the O'Reilly place. The wind wasn't stirring a lick, and even the birds were still. I saw weeds growing in the field with the tobacco. I wondered why Sean hadn't hauled the crop to the barn yet. Then I remembered he could only come outside to go to the outhouse, not to tend to his crop. I thought to ask Pa if we could bring the crop in for him, so it wouldn't get ruined. I started to think about who was feeding their chickens, but then I got excited to see Ma and decided to worry about that later.

James tied the mules to a post, and I fetched the pot of soup. We climbed up the steps to the porch. I went first. I knew better than to knock on the door. The windows were closed, and I wondered if they was hot inside. Bridget had sewed pretty lace curtains for their two front windows. The curtains were shut, too, so I had to strain to catch a look through the lace. I didn't see nobody through the first window. That was where Sean, Bridget and Anna Maureen slept. I moved over to the window on the other side of the door. Their house was like ours, with one big room with a wood stove for cooking and heating. I asked James to hold the pot of soup so I could cup my eyes for a better look. It took me a minute to see clear. I kept thinking I'd hear Anna Maureen, who was big enough now to run about, but I didn't hear nothing at all. First, I saw the wood stove. Then I saw Ma and John laying beside it. Ma was holding John close.

"What do you see, Molly?" James asked.

"I see Ma and John. I think they're sleeping on the floor. Sean's sleeping, too, on the other side of the stove."

"What?" James asked, his voice getting sharp. "Get out of the way! Let me have a look!"

I moved over so he could see. James dropped the pot of soup and banged on the window. "Ma! John!"

I started to fret about the soup as it spilled out of the pot and down the steps, but James was scaring me. I started calling out their names loud, too. But they didn't move.

James began screaming and knocking on the glass. "Wake up, Ma! Please! John!"

"What's wrong with them, James? Make them wake up!"

James fell down on his knees. Tears come out his eyes and spilt on his shirt. "They can't wake up, Molly. Ma and John … are dead."

Chapter 12

"Orange Glows"

Doc found us sobbing on the porch steps a short time later. He jumped down off his horse and looked through the window. Then he put one hand on my shoulder and the other on James'. "They're gone," he said. "I'm so sorry."

Pa knew something was wrong as soon as he saw Doc driving our buckboard up the path. He come up out of the field with my brothers when Doc brung the mules to a stop.

There was a tear crawling down Doc's cheek. "I'm so sorry, Jacob, but Maureen and John are dead. The O'Reillys, too."

Edward let out a scream and began sobbing. My other brothers started crying, too. Pa was the only one with dry eyes.

Doc said, "Bridget and the baby died after the first week. Sean and John buried them out back of the house. Sean got sick a couple of days after that, then your wife and boy."

"Why didn't you come tell me?" Pa asked.

"Because it wouldn't have done you any good. There was nothing you could have done to save them."

"But I could've come to say goodbye." Pa's voice cracked, and his eyes got wet after that.

"I'm so very sorry, Jacob. Maureen was a good woman, and your son a fine boy."

Pa wiped his eyes on the sleeve of his shirt.

"I want them to have a proper Christian burial," Pa said.

"We'll go see Pastor Brown right now and make arrangements. But ..." Doc hesitated. "We'll have to wait a day or two before we can take them out of the house."

"Why?"

"We have to make sure there's no way they can still spread the disease."

Pastor Brown decided to have the service for Ma and John on Friday. Word spread quick around Uptonville. Neighbors come to dig their graves in the church cemetery, and women started cooking up food to feed folks after the service. We planned to fetch Ma and John on Thursday.

Just before bed Wednesday night, I went out onto the porch and saw an orange glow in the sky. I smelt smoke and hollered for Pa.

He cried out, "For the love of God!" Then he yelled for my brothers, ran to the barn and hitched up the buckboard. All of us climbed in and rode out to the O'Reilly place. But by the time we got there, the house had burnt to the ground with Ma, John and Sean in it.

Pastor Brown come to see us early the next morning. Pa told him he was worried 'cause Ma and John didn't have a proper Christian burial. Pastor Brown told us to get down on our knees and pray.

"Dear Jesus," he said. "You died to save us from our wicked ways. Maureen was saved, as was John. They were denied their final resting place 'cause of the evil deed of another. We pray that you will have mercy on them and enfold them in your arms. We ask that you allow them to dwell with you in heaven for eternity. In your name, Jesus, we pray, and for your glory we give thanks. Amen."

When we got done, Pa asked Pastor Brown who would have done such a thing.

"I don't know for sure, Jacob, but I have my suspicions."

Pa looked the preacher hard in the eye and nodded his head.

Later, I asked Pa who he thought done it.

He said, "Ol' man Cole and his boys."

"Why do you think that, Pa?"

"No Christian man could have denied us a proper burial."

A fortnight passed before I saw another orange glow in the sky. I asked Pa if we should hitch the mules to go see where the fire was. He told me to get on back in the house and go about my business. Come to find out the Cole shack burnt up in a fire, but not with them in it. Don't know where they went or what happened 'cause Pa wouldn't speak about it. I didn't mind that Roy and Charlie were gone, but I felt sad about Jesse and Sarah.

Chapter 13

"Becoming a Woman"

I ain't too sure how we got through the next few weeks. Neighbors brung us food, and everybody said they'd do whatever we needed to get through this hard time. Thing was, no matter how much chicken and pie they brung, we never again would have what we needed 'cause Ma and John was dead.

During the first few weeks, Pa had an anger about him that was blacker than any storm cloud I'd ever seen. He blamed hisself for Ma's death. One night at supper, he pounded his first on the table and shouted, "It's my fault they're dead! I knew the O'Reillys were trouble the first time I laid eyes on them! I should've stopped your ma from taking up with them Catholics and going to their place when they got sick. If I'd done what I should, she and John would still be alive."

"You couldn't have known, Pa," Joost said.

"Besides, Ma was stubborn," Jansen added. "Ain't nothing you could've done to stop her."

"But I'm the man of the house!" Pa said. "I should've forbidden her to see them!"

"I should've gone with Ma instead of John," I said. "I would've been able to take care of her."

Isaac patted my hand. "There's nothing you could've done, Molly."

Edward said, "God just decided it was time for Ma and John to go home."

Nothing any of us said made Pa feel better, so we kept our heads down and didn't say no more to him that night.

Edward took Ma's death hard. I was afeared he would get sick and die, too. There was something heavy on my mind I had to ask him 'cause he'd got the call to become a preacher.

"Was God mad at Ma? Is that why she's dead?"

"Why would God be mad at her?" Edward asked.

"'She wasn't supposed to be Catholic no more, and then she baptized the baby. Maybe God don't like Catholics, so He sent the diphtheria to kill them."

"That's not what happened," Edward said. "God may like Baptists better 'cause we save sinners for Jesus, but He loves everybody, even Catholics."

I wasn't too sure Edward was right. "I don't like God right now. Ma was the kindest person I know. She was only trying to help Bridget and her baby 'cause they was sick. I think God was mean to let them die."

Every time I looked at James, I wanted to cry. No matter what I fixed for supper, he wasn't having none of it. He couldn't sleep good, either. John was the other half of him and he was gone forever. I was hoping James would get back to his old self when we went back to school in the fall.

One day, I went out before sunup to get eggs from the hens and milk the cows. When I come in, I found a note on the table addressed to Pa. Then my brothers come downstairs, and James wasn't with them, and I got a sour feeling in my belly. Pa sat down at the table and stared at the note.

"Want me to tell you what it says, Pa?" Isaac asked. Pa nodded, and we all listened as Isaac began.

I'm sorry to leave you, Pa, but I got to live my dream.
I'm going to a place called West Point, Kentucky, where

*I can get work on a riverboat. I got to see the world.
Not just for me, but for John. I don't know when I'll see
you all again. I love you, Pa, my brothers and Molly,
too. Forgive me, but this is what I got to do.*

James

Nobody said nothing when Isaac finished reading. I served up breakfast and waited 'til they was done to sit down and eat my eggs. I didn't want Pa or my brothers to see me cry. That morning, I felt like my heart had cracked in two. Ma was gone, and now both of my middle brothers was, too. I didn't know how we was gonna make it without them.

The only thing that kept me going was knowing school was starting soon. I couldn't wait to spend my days with Miss June and learn new things. The Saturday before school began, I was talking with Isaac and Edward after supper about what we needed to do to get ready. Pa heard us talking. He said, "I need to have a word in private with Miss June after church on Sunday."

Pa didn't say nothing to us as we drove home from church that day. He waited 'til we finished our noon dinner, then told Joost and Jansen to get to their chores so he could have a word with Isaac, Edward and me.

"There's no easy way to say this," Pa told us, "so I'll spit it out. Molly, you can't go to school no more. With your ma gone, you got to be the woman of the house. Edward won't be going to school, neither. He can help you with house chores when he's not needed to work the crop."

There was fear in Isaac's eyes when he asked, "What about me, Pa?"

"You get to finish the eighth grade 'cause Miss June thinks you're smart enough to become a teacher."

"Pa," I pleaded. "Don't do this! I can keep up with my chores and go to school, too. Give me a chance. I'll show you. You'll see!"

"No, Molly. Not another word about it."

"What about me, Pa?" Edward pleaded. "I want to be a preacher like Pastor Brown. I gotta go to school."

"Isaac's gonna teach you both at home, and I told Miss June she could come around every few weeks to make sure you was learning good." Pa had a tender spot for Edward since Ma had favored him. He patted his shoulder and said, "If God wants you to be a preacher, son, He will find a way to make it happen."

With that, he got up from the table and went outside, leaving the three of us to sort out our feelings.

I felt a boiling rage coming over me like I'd never had before. Pa had taken away the thing that mattered most, and I wanted to bawl my eyes out. But for the first time in my life, I was too mad to cry.

Isaac said, "I'm so sorry, Molly. I know how much you love school. I promise to teach you everything I learn. Trust me."

The whole rest of the day, Pa wouldn't look me in the eye. I figured I'd show him. I fixed up his plate for supper. But before I carried it out, I spit on his food. I did that for the rest of the week with every meal I fixed. It made me feel better 'til the evening I looked up to see him in the doorway.

He didn't say nothing. He took his plate, sat down and ate his supper. My brothers ate theirs, too, and then he sent them outside. My food was getting cold 'cause I still waited to eat 'til they got done, just like Ma did. Pa didn't get up from the table. He sat there, staring down at his lap. I knew I done wrong.

"I'm sorry for spitting on your food, Pa."

He slowly lifted his head. There was tears coming out his eyes. "I miss your ma, Molly. I don't know how I'm gonna make it without her."

"Oh, Pa. I miss her, too."

"You're strong, Molly, like your ma. That's why you got to see to us instead of going to school." Pa laid his head down on top of his arms and sobbed his heart out. I went over and put my arms around him 'til all the sadness he'd stuffed in his heart come out.

"I know it ain't fair," he said, "but you gotta be the woman of the house now."

That made me think of something.

"Does that mean I'm in charge of the house, Pa, like Ma was?"

"Yes, it does."

"Does that mean I get a say in how things are done?"

He nodded.

"Then here's how it's gonna be. I'm not gonna wait 'til you and my brothers get done eating before I do. I'll serve up your plates like always, but then I'm gonna sit down beside you, so we all eat together."

I didn't have to wait 'til my first monthly come on to become a woman. I become one that night. I made up my mind to do what Pa wanted and care for him and my brothers the best I could. But when I went outside before bed, I looked up at the stars and made some promises to myself. I was gonna learn every dang thing I could from Isaac and Miss June, so I'd be smart 'stead of ignorant. I was gonna wear britches whenever I wanted, and when it come time to hang the tobacco sticks to dry, nobody was gonna tell me to stay off the beams 'cause I was a girl. Whether Pa liked it or not, we was gonna run the farm as equals. No difference between the boys and this girl, except for the cooking and house chores I had to do. I wasn't sure what would become of me as the years went by, but there was one thing I knew for sure that night. I was never gonna eat cold eggs again.

ELIJAH

Chapter 14

"The Attic"

My first memory is of the attic in a boarding house, where my mother and I lived. It had no windows or much room to walk around. We had a small bed, two chairs, a table, a bathtub, and a slop jar. When it got hot, we couldn't sleep good at night. We got some fresh air from the holes in the pitched roof above our heads, but every time it rained hard, we got wet. The attic was cold in the winter so we slept under blankets and snuggled up close to keep warm. But I remember the attic as a happy place because I had my mother, Julia.

I was born in Elizabethtown, Kentucky, on March 4, 1866, when my mother was eighteen years old. Her eyes were the blue of a clear summer's sky. The color of her hair reminded me of dark polished wood. Her lips were soft on my cheek.

My mother was smart. She taught me my letters before I was four and read stories to me every day. She sang songs when she put me to bed at night. Her voice was soothing and helped me fall asleep.

I never thought to ask why we lived in the attic of a boarding house, where she cooked and cleaned for the boarders. All I knew was how glad I was every night when she climbed up the stairs to our place. I had to stay by myself while she worked, and I spent a lot of time lying on our bed and looking out at the sky through the holes in the roof. I wanted to go outside and feel the sun on my face. I lived for Sunday afternoons when my mother was free, and we could go for walks or to have a picnic at a park nearby. I wanted to play with the other young'uns there but Mother said we had to keep to ourselves. I asked why people sometimes stared at us, then frowned and turned away.

She said, "Never you mind about them, Elijah. Some people just have a sour disposition and no manners."

Memory is a funny thing. Some things I remember with ease, like feeling safe beside my mother in the bed and how good she smelled after a bath. Yet, there are some things I can't call to mind no matter how hard I try. I don't remember hearing her laugh.

One memory is hard to shake. I might not recall all the details because I was only seven years old, but I will never forget how I felt. Nellie and Howard, who owned the boardinghouse, were decent folks. Nellie took us to a church sale the Sunday before I started school for the first time. My mother wanted me to have proper clothes to wear, but she didn't make enough money to buy things new. Nellie told her not to worry because even though the clothes at the sale had been worn before, they were presentable and clean. And the money from the sale went to the church to buy new Bibles.

I wanted to go to school in the worst way. By then, I could read a little and I was ready to learn new things. Besides, going to school meant I got out of the attic and could play outside.

Nellie told me to pick out whatever I wanted and she would pay for it. We found several things, but I liked a red shirt the best. Red was my favorite color, and the shirt fit me good. My mother said I looked handsome. We were having a grand time finding nice things for me to wear … until Nellie went to pay for them.

A finely dressed woman stood with her husband and son at the table where you gave your money. The boy was bigger than me and had a mean look about him. The woman was thanking people for coming to support the church. When it came our turn to pay, the woman looked at my mother and me. Then she held a hanky up to her nose and wrinkled up her face like she smelled a dead mouse.

"That's the Simpson whore with her bastard son," she said in a loud voice to her husband and turned away from us.

My mother didn't say a word but gripped my arm tight, so even though I didn't know what *bastard* and *whore* meant, I knew those things weren't good. Nellie paid for my clothes, and we got out of there fast. On the way home, we didn't talk much. Tears were falling from my mother's eyes, and my heart felt heavy.

"Never you mind that awful woman, Julia," Nellie said. "Money doesn't buy class."

When we were alone, I asked my mother why that woman called her a whore and me a bastard. She said, "Elijah, I need to tell you about your daddy and me."

I didn't know much about my father, other than his name was Robert Fry and everyone called him Bo.

Mother said, "Bo Fry was a fine-looking man, with dark eyes and black hair that he wore slicked back, away from his face. Nobody knew much about him because he didn't come from Elizabethtown. He just showed up one day looking for work."

I couldn't picture the man, but I could tell by looking at my mother that she had a sharp image of him still in her mind.

"I met your daddy in the general store one day, right after he came to town. Most of the young men I knew were long gone, serving in the war. It was nice to have a conversation with a fella my age. He was nothing like the boys I grew up with in Elizabethtown. He was what you call *worldly*."

"What's that mean?"

"It means that he'd been to places and done things that I knew nothing about. I liked hearing his stories. I was tired of people like my father who did nothing but go to work, come home and live in the same house their whole lives. Bo was different. He seemed exciting and adventurous."

My mother had a look on her face that I'd never seen before, like she was talking to me but her thoughts were off somewhere else.

"Bo had a way of looking in my eyes that made me feel special. I know you don't understand what I'm talking about, Elijah, but one day you will."

Mother told me that people around town didn't think highly of Bo Fry because he didn't fight in the war. In Kentucky, it didn't really matter which side you were on, Union or Confederate, as long as you took up arms for whichever cause you believed in.

"Bo got a job working at the tavern right down the street from here. He called on me before going to work at night. My folks didn't take to him at all. They didn't think he was a suitable match."

"Why not?"

"They wanted me to marry a man who had money and morals. Morals means doing the right thing, Elijah, being good instead of bad."

I understood that. My mother taught me to always do what I thought was the right thing. Turned out that Bo Fry had no morals. He drank too much and gambled away what little money he made. He had a wild streak and a wandering eye. But my mother loved him anyway and thought she could change him over time. Besides, eligible suitors were scarce in those days. A lot of young men who went to war didn't come back. Those that did were most times crippled, or not right in the head after all the bloodshed they'd seen.

"I asked my father for his blessing to marry Bo, but he wouldn't hear of it."

George Simpson owned the bank in Elizabethtown. George and his wife, Emma, had only one child, my mother. They expected her to marry well and do what she was told. George made it clear that she would never have his blessing to marry Bo Fry. He forbade her to ever see him again.

My mother had trouble getting her voice out of her throat when she started speaking again. "Not too long after that, I found out I

was having you. My folks didn't want anything more to do with me
after that and told me to leave their home.

"Because of me?" I asked.

Mother reached over and took my hand. "No, baby. They weren't
mad at you. I let them down."

I didn't understand, but I nodded so my mother thought I did.

"I moved in with your daddy, and you came along a few months
later. I loved you from the moment I saw you, Elijah. Bo did, too.
But then one day, he just up and left, and I had to figure out how
to take care of you by myself."

My mother went to school to get book learning, but she didn't
know nothing about working for somebody else. She'd been raised
to be a lady, so she could marry a man with morals and money like
her folks wanted. Now she was on her own with a baby to raise
and she had to find a job. She went all over town looking for work,
but nobody would have anything to do with her. They wanted to
stay in George Simpson's good graces, just in case they needed a
loan from his bank one day. The only two people who didn't give
a damn what other people thought were Nellie and Howard. They
hired my mother and made sure the boarders were respectful of
her.

There was still something I didn't understand. I asked her the
question a second time. "Why did that woman call you a whore
and me a bastard?"

"She was judging us because your daddy and I didn't get married
in a church."

My mother sat me on her lap and held me so close I could feel
her heart beating. "People can call us any names they want, but it
doesn't matter a lick. You're the best thing that ever happened to
me, Elijah, and I love you with all my heart."

Chapter 15

"Shaming Me"

The next morning, my mother walked me to school. I wore my red shirt with blue pants and carried my dinner in a pail. The school was just down the road from the boardinghouse, so it took us no time to get there. Mother knelt in front of me, licked her fingers and smoothed down my hair. She pinched her lips together and looked me in the eyes, so I knew she had something important to tell me.

"Elijah, we're not like other families. There's just you and me. But that's all right because we have enough love between us to fill up the whole boardinghouse."

Julia rubbed my shoulders and fiddled with the collar of my shirt.

"Because you and I are ... different ... special ..., you're gonna have to try extra hard to be good so nobody thinks less of you."

She waited for me to say something, but I didn't understand what she was talking about. She sighed, then stood and kissed the top of my head. "Mind your manners and always do the right thing like I taught you. I'll be here at four to walk you home."

My mother held on to my hand another moment before letting me go. I walked through the gate to the little white schoolhouse with lots of windows. When I turned around, she was still standing there, holding a hanky to her eyes. I was thinking about the windows and being able to look outside whenever I wanted. Then I saw our teacher standing on the steps to meet us. Mr. Rooney had squinty eyes, and his lips turned under in a frown.

Once we sat down in our seats, he showed us his cane and told us that he would use it on any boy who didn't mind good. I guess the girls didn't have nothing to worry about because they were better behaved than the boys.

I got along fine until we had dinner and went outside for noon recess. Mr. Rooney had the girls play on one side of the yard and the boys on the other. He left the girls alone so he could keep a sharp eye on the boys. Right away, that boy from the church sale, whose name was Gus Meade, got up in my face. He rubbed his fingers on the collar of my red shirt.

He turned around to his friends and said, "I gave this shirt away 'cause I didn't like it no more. Elijah Fry wears my hand-me-downs. He's not good enough to have new clothes."

One of them said, "Why don't you have something new to wear like us? Ain't your daddy got no money?"

Gus started laughing. "He's a little bastard boy who ain't got no daddy."

My cheeks got hot, and I started for him, but before I could hit him, a hand gripped my shoulder.

"What's going on here?" Mr. Rooney asked.

"Nothing, sir," Gus said. "Nothing at all."

"Is that correct?" he asked me.

I gritted my teeth.

"Answer me, boy," he said cuffing my head with the back of his hand.

I remembered my manners. "Everything is fine, sir."

"Let's keep it that way. Understood?"

I came to understand a lot of things that first day of school. Gus shamed me in front of his friends, and that stuck in my craw. I wanted to hit him so bad that I hurt, but I knew if I did, I'd get caned for sure. So instead, I found a place to go inside of me where I didn't have nothing to do with nobody and I could think whatever thoughts I wanted, even if they were mean and spiteful.

After that, I hated that red shirt. My mother went looking for it a few days later. I told her I didn't know what happened to it, but I did. I made sure nobody would wear that red shirt again.

Mother came every afternoon at four to walk me home. She was happy when I told her what I learned that day. She asked what games we played after dinner. I told her lies about the good times I had with the other boys. Truth was, I didn't have nothing to do with any of them. But that didn't stop them from tormenting me every day, coming up behind me and calling me a little bastard boy.

You'd think a mean boy might get better over time, but that wasn't the way with Gus. Something about me rubbed him raw. I didn't understand it. He lived in a fancy house, not an attic. He wore brand-new clothes and not somebody's hand-me-downs. He ate fresh food whenever he wanted, not just the scraps the boarders left behind. But I had one thing he didn't, and maybe that's why he hated me. I was smart. Even though he was two years older than me, I could read a book before he even learned his letters.

Just before Christmas, we got our grade cards. I earned good marks in all my subjects, and my mother was proud. I couldn't make out the note Mr. Rooney had written on my card, but whatever it said made her mouth turn down. After that, she never asked me again about the games I played at school. I heard her tell Nellie that Mr. Rooney said I was a troubled boy who stayed to himself, probably due to my low station in life. I figured it had something to do with being a little bastard boy and being different, like my mother said.

Chapter 16

"Rage"

The day I turned eight years old, I saw the man in the black suit for the first time. I was sitting on the schoolhouse steps by myself, eating out of my dinner pail, when I noticed him staring at me. He wore a wide-brimmed hat, so I couldn't see his face good. Mr. Rooney went over to the gate and had a word with him. Both of them looked my way for a spell before the man walked away. I only saw him a time or two after that, but I always wondered who he was and why he stared at me.

As dumb as he was, Gus knew better than to pick a fight with me at school. Mr. Rooney was a twisted sort. The only time I ever saw him smile was when his cane whacked flesh and a boy wailed.

But when Mr. Rooney wasn't looking, Gus took every chance he could to make fun of me or my clothes. He never called me by name, only *little bastard boy*. I spent a lot of time thinking about how I was gonna make him pay. I wondered just how much I could make him bleed.

Right after I turned ten, I heard my mother tell Nellie that she was worried about me. I had stopped caring about school and learning new things. Mother decided right there and then that she was gonna save what little money she made so we could move away from Elizabethtown and make a new life somewhere else. She began telling me stories about places we might go where nobody cared who you were or where you came from, only if you were a good person or not. I liked those stories. I told myself it didn't matter a lick if I had friends at school or not, just as long as I had my mother.

On the first day of January in 1877, Mother made me a promise that we would leave Elizabethtown that year. As it turned out, we did, but not the way either of us imagined.

As a little boy, I didn't notice things that come on gradual. I thought I was just getting too big when my mother told me I couldn't sleep in the bed with her no more and she fixed me a place with blankets on the floor across the room. I didn't know she wasn't eating until her hug felt bony and her chest looked caved in.

One night, she sat up coughing into her hanky for hours. I knew then that she must be sick. I wanted to stay home with her, but she made me go to school. She said she'd be fine, but I couldn't shake my worried feeling. That was the same day that Gus made a big mistake.

At four o'clock, my mother didn't come to meet me like usual. I got scared but didn't want to show it. I walked through the gate with the other boys and started for the boardinghouse. All I could think about was the blood I'd seen on her hanky when she coughed. I hadn't gotten very far before I heard footsteps close behind me and the voice I hated.

"Little bastard boy!"

Realizing that I was away from school where Mr. Rooney couldn't see, I turned around and spit in his face. He looked shocked.

When he caught his breath, he shouted, "You son of a whore!"

A rage took over me like nothing I'd known before. It come up from the bottom of my belly, through my chest and out my eyes until I couldn't see nothing but black, like a dark night sky before a storm. The next thing I knew, I was on top of Gus, pounding him with both fists. He hit me back as hard as he could, but I didn't feel a thing. A couple of passersby finally pulled me off him. By then, his eyes were swollen shut, and he had bloody goo all over his face.

I learned something about rage that day. When it's out of control, you don't know what you're doing. As you come out of it, everything feels like a swirling blur and gets all mixed up together. When my head cleared, I heard Gus screaming, other boys yelling, and a woman shouting to fetch Gus' pa. I found myself sitting on the ground, staring at my bloody hands.

A woman sat down beside me. It was Nellie.

"What happened, Elijah?"

No words come out of my mouth.

"It's my fault for not getting here sooner," she said, patting my arm.

I saw a man with a black bag kneel down beside Gus. Then Gus' father came charging toward us. He was spitting mad.

"You crazy little bastard! You damn near killed my son!"

A man got ahold of him and pulled him away from me. "You're scum and don't belong living around God-fearing folks!" he yelled.

Nellie said we had to get home. When we got there, she told me to sit outside with her for a few minutes before going up to see my mother.

"The doctor came to see your mother today, Elijah. She's got consumption."

I didn't know what that was. "Did he give her medicine to make her better?"

"He said the only cure is rest and fresh air."

When I got sick with fever, the doctor gave me a bad-tasting medicine. Rest and fresh air sounded much better. Nellie washed me downstairs before I went up to the attic, but my knuckles were swollen and bruised, and Mother took notice.

"Did you get in a fight, Elijah?"

After months of keeping it inside, I told my mother about Gus

Meade calling me a little bastard boy and making fun of me every day. I told her I beat him up because I couldn't take it no more.

"I may be a bastard boy, but nobody calls you a whore! I'm sorry if I shamed you, but I did the right thing."

That night, I didn't sleep on the floor. I crawled in bed beside my mother and held on to her tight. I never wanted to let go.

A few days later, the man in the black suit came to see us. He stood at the top of the stairs and took off his hat. My mother stared at him a moment before she said, "Father?"

"Hello, Julia. We have to talk."

I sat in a chair beside my mother and watched them stare at each other.

"Elijah, this is your grandfather."

I'm sure my mouth was hanging open. So that's who the man in the black suit was! I'd never met any of my kin before, and I was excited. I stood and stuck my hand out for a shake like my mother taught me. But my hand just hung limp in the air because my grandfather wouldn't touch me.

"Go sit on the floor," he ordered. "I'm here to speak with your mother."

I did what I was told and sat in the corner near the bed. I felt the rage coming over me again, but I stuffed it down and went inside to my quiet place instead.

"Two people paid me a visit—the constable and the doctor," my grandfather told my mother. "Let's talk about you first, Julia." He paused and looked my way. "Then we'll deal with him."

"My son's name is Elijah."

The big man paid her no mind.

"The doctor tells me you have tuberculosis." He looked around our attic. "I'm not surprised, living in a place like this."

"What choice did I have? You turned me out." My mother started to cough. My grandfather looked away when he saw the blood on her hanky.

"The only cure for tuberculosis is rest, proper food and fresh air.

I've arranged for you to go to a sanitarium where you will get the care you need to get well. Your mother and I will see to everything."

"Will you see to Elijah, as well?"

"Your son is in a great deal of trouble."

He turned and stared at me. "Mr. Meade wants to press charges against you for assaulting his son."

Mother said, "Gus Meade tormented Elijah from the day he started school. He got what he deserved."

"I've had a number of conversations with Mr. Rooney. He tells me Elijah is a disturbed boy, not unlike his father. If Meade presses charges, your son will go to the delinquent boys' workhouse in Louisville until he turns sixteen. Is that what you want, Julia?"

"Of course not!" My mother started to cry.

"Then listen to me. I have another option. I've located a relative not far from here who is willing to take him. Did Bo ever mention his older brother Albert?"

"No, he never said anything about his family."

"Why does that not surprise me?" he said with a frown. "Albert and his wife, Pearl, own a general store in Uptonville. From what I hear, Albert is a good man. Your son needs firm guidance, now more than ever. Since they have no children of their own, they can tend to him proper."

I spoke up. "I don't want to live with strangers."

"You have no say in the matter," my grandfather said gruffly. "Julia, let me make this perfectly clear. The only choice you have is to live or die. Your son can go stay with his uncle or rot in the workhouse. It makes no difference to me."

"How can you be so cruel, Father?"

"You disgraced your mother and me, Julia, but you are still our daughter, so we will see to your health. Your only chance for recovery is the sanitarium in Lexington. Don't you want to get better for your son?"

My mother told me to come to her. She took me in her arms and held me close.

"Do you promise I'll get Elijah back as soon as I'm well?"

The man who was my grandfather nodded. "I will come around first thing in the morning to take him to Uptonville. See that he is packed and presentable. I will arrange for a second carriage for you and your mother to travel to the sanitarium. We are agreed, then?"

Chapter 17

"Safe With Us"

Early the next morning when my grandfather came, I was ready. Nellie helped get my belongings together and saw to it that I had a bath and clean clothes. I wore my best black pants, a white shirt and polished shoes. My hair was combed and my face scrubbed. I suppose I was presentable. My mother insisted on coming outside to see me off, even though there was a cold chill in the air.

My grandfather told his driver to take my bag. "Come along," he said to me.

I grabbed ahold of my mother. "Don't make me go! I want to stay here with you!"

Tears started falling down her cheeks and mine.

"You have to go, Elijah. Otherwise, I can't go to the sanitarium and get better."

"Promise you'll come get me."

My mother looked me square in the eye and said, "I promise. Now you go and be a good boy. Remember to always do the right thing like I taught you."

My grandfather sat beside me in the carriage. He told the driver to proceed. I turned around and waved to my mother one last time as the horses picked up speed. All too soon she was gone.

I tried hard not to cry on the twenty-mile ride to Uptonville. I felt scared and sad. I'd never been apart from my mother except to go to school. I hadn't been anywhere during my ten years of life but the boardinghouse, park, church sale and school. There were streets in Elizabethtown I'd never seen, with all kinds of shops, houses, buggies and people. Once we left town, the countryside went on for miles. There was one farm after another with men working in the fields. I didn't know what to make of any of it. What I did know was that I didn't like the stern-faced man sitting beside me.

He asked me a question. "What do you plan to do with your life, Elijah?"

I told him the truth. "I want to grow up to be a good man and take care of my mother proper."

He nodded and didn't say another word. That was the only talk I ever had with my grandfather.

When we got to Uptonville, my insides started shaking. Unlike Elizabethtown, this town had only three buildings on its main street—a train depot, a bank and a store. The sign above the store read: *Fry's General Store*. The driver brought the horses to a halt and a scrawny man appeared, followed by his short, fat wife. My grandfather told me to get out of the carriage, then he came to stand beside me. He shook hands with the man, who then bent down to have a look at me.

He said, "Welcome, boy. We're happy to have you here. I'm your Uncle Albert, and this here is your Aunt Pearl."

The woman put her arms around me and pulled me to her. I didn't know what to make of her. She was all round and soft, not bony thin like my mother. My grandfather took an envelope from the inside pocket of his suit coat and asked to have a word with Albert alone. Pearl took me by the hand and led me inside the store to have a look around.

The place had a pine-wood floor and was almost as big as our one-room schoolhouse. Every nook and cranny was filled with things for sale—farm tools and grain, yard goods for sewing and all kinds of dry goods like flour, sugar and coffee. There was a contraption on top of the counter that caught my eye. I asked Pearl what it was.

"That's a cash register. It's where we keep money and make change when folks buy things. Your Uncle Albert will show you how to use it."

Albert and Pearl made their home in several rooms in the back of the store. It wasn't nothing like the houses I'd just seen in Elizabethtown, but it was a whole lot nicer than the attic.

Our little house, as I came to call it, had a sitting room with a red-velvet couch and a wood stove for heating. Pearl cooked up supper in another room that had a pantry and a second stove. Albert and Pearl had their own bedroom with a tub for bathing, and they'd made up a special room just for me. I'd never had a place to myself before, but now I had a brass bed with a quilt on top, a dresser for my clothes, and a pitcher and bowl for washing.

When I first saw that room, my insides stopped shaking. I couldn't believe they had gone to all this trouble for me. It was a feeling I'd never known before.

Pearl fixed up a big supper that evening with beef, potatoes and gravy. I'd never tasted such good food, and there was so much of it.

"Slow down, son," Albert said. "Don't make yourself sick!"

I could tell right off that Albert and Pearl were kind, and that stayed true for the whole time I knew them. They had nightclothes for me to wear and warm water in the bowl with a cloth to wash my face. Just before bed, they said they wanted to pray with me. When they bowed their heads and put their hands together, I did, too. I didn't tell them I'd never prayed with my mother.

"Gracious Lord," Albert said, "we give thanks for this fine boy, Elijah Fry, who's come to stay with us for a spell. Let him know your love, Lord, and help us teach him to walk your path of righteousness. We give thanks for your bounty in the name of our Lord Jesus Christ. Amen."

I got in bed, and Albert tucked the quilt around me. Pearl kissed my forehead and said, "You sleep well, Elijah. Your Uncle Albert and I are glad you're here." They blew out the candle and shut the door.

I lay in bed a long time that night. My belly was full for the first time I could remember, and I felt warm under the quilt on my brass bed. I liked Albert and Pearl because they made me feel wanted.

But then I started thinking about my mother. I kept seeing her face and feeling her arms around me. I tried to get her out of my mind but I couldn't. I remembered the sound of her cough and the hanky in her hand that was red with blood. I called out in the dark for my mother.

Pearl came right to me. She picked me up and held me like a baby.

"It's OK, darling. You love your ma. You go ahead and cry for her."

I let loose and sobbed my heart out. Pearl just held me. Then she tucked the quilt back around me and kissed both my cheeks.

"You're safe here with us, Elijah. We won't let nothing bad happen to you."

Chapter 18

"Honesty and Integrity"

The next morning, Pearl fixed up a breakfast of eggs, bacon, cornbread and jam. After I cleaned my plate, Albert said he wanted to explain the house rules.

"Our rules are pretty straightforward, son, but we expect you to follow them to the letter. First, you are to be respectful to your aunt and me at all times. Do like we tell you and mind your manners when folks come in the store. You will have chores to do every day and you are to do them well. Understood?"

"Yes, sir," I said.

"There's one more thing," Albert said. "Honesty and integrity are two of the most important qualities in a man. We expect you to practice both of them."

I must have had a puzzled look on my face because Albert asked if I understood what he meant.

"Honesty means telling the truth," I said. "But I don't know that other word."

"Integrity means you are a man of your word and you can be counted on to follow through with what you say. Can your Aunt Pearl and me count on you to always tell the truth and be a man of your word?"

"Yes, sir. You can. But I don't want to get in trouble for telling the truth."

"Why would you get in trouble for that?" Pearl asked.

"'I got in trouble once for telling a girl she was ugly and her brother was stupid. What I said was true, but I had to stand in the corner for saying it."

Albert smiled and then coughed behind his hands. After he cleared his throat, he said, "The most important thing is that you are always honest with your Aunt Pearl and me. We'll work on learning when to speak your mind and when to hush."

Albert and Pearl made me feel welcome, not just that first day but every day after that. They protected me, too. They said they were fond of me and didn't want me getting in trouble like I did in Elizabethtown. Only a few months were left before school let out for the summer, so they were going to teach me at home. I was happy to hear that. I hated even thinking about going to school after having Mr. Rooney as a teacher and being made fun of every day. I reckoned my mother would come to get me long before the new school year started.

Albert and Pearl were serious about teaching me. Pearl was pleased that I could read but surprised I'd never been to Sunday school and didn't know anything about the Bible. So every evening before it got dark, she made me sit close beside her while she read Bible stories. I didn't much care for the stories but I did like sitting next to Pearl, because she was warm and soft. She smelled good, too, and that reminded me of my mother.

During the day, Albert showed me how to run the store. He taught me how to make change when folks paid their bills. He said I had a knack for working with numbers. He told his customers that I was his nephew and that he and Pearl were tickled pink I was staying with them. Every time he said that, I felt warm inside.

Albert had a colored man named Isaiah who worked in the store some afternoons and on Saturday. Isaiah, his wife and son lived on Doc Middleton's farm and saw to chores and cooking there. Isaiah was honest and a man of integrity.

Every few days, I asked about my mother. Albert always said he hadn't heard nothing but not to worry because she was getting proper care. He promised to let me know as soon as he got word about her.

One evening after supper, we were warming ourselves by the stove before reading Bible stories. It had been a cold, rainy day, so the fire felt good.

Pearl said, "Elijah, I know you're ten years old, but I don't know when your birthday is. Do you?"

"Yes, ma'am," I said. "I was born March 4, 1866."

"Why, my heavens!" Pearl said. "You're gonna turn eleven in just a few days."

"Am I? When's that?"

"Today is Tuesday, and you turn eleven on Sunday. Now isn't that something! What did you do with your ma when it was your birthday?"

Hot tears stung my eyes. I missed my mother something awful, so I tried not to think about her much, but that question put her right in front of my mind.

"We didn't do nothing, ma'am, because my mother had to work every day, and we didn't have money for extra things. But she made sure I got a full plate of supper on my birthday, even if she had to go without."

Pearl's eyes got big when I said that. I saw a tear spill out, but she didn't say nothing. The next Sunday morning, like every Sunday, Albert and Pearl took me to a little church not far from the store. I didn't much like going but I didn't make a fuss. We always came straight home to have our Sunday dinner. Pearl made a habit of cooking everything ahead of time, except that morning. On the way home, I was hungry and wondered what we would eat. Well, when we walked into the store, I saw a bunch of people, and they all looked at me and yelled, "Surprise!" They had a long table with benches set up in the middle of the room. And on it lay big platters of fried chicken, greens, potatoes and a butter cake.

Albert introduced me to Doc Middleton, his wife, Madeline, and their three daughters—Martha, Miriam, and little Mary, who was just seven years old. Mary was the prettiest of the three girls, but she was bashful and clung to her mama's skirt. She had big eyes, and when she looked up at me, she twirled a curl around her second finger.

Isaiah Jackson brung his wife, Sally Ann, and their boy, Henry. Even though Henry was three years younger than me, he was bigger and stronger from working in the fields.

I ate so much dinner I thought my belly was gonna explode. Then Albert said, "Why don't you young'uns go outside and play awhile before we cut the cake. It'll do you good to get some fresh air on this nice sunny day."

The Middleton girls didn't want nothing to do with me or Henry, so we wandered off by ourselves. We kicked rocks around the dirt for a spell. When we got tired of that, we went over to a grassy place across from the store and leaned up against a big oak tree.

I'd never been around a colored boy before, and I couldn't help but stare at him. Henry didn't take kindly to that.

"What you looking at?" he asked.

"I'm looking at you," I answered. "I've never seen a boy with brown skin up close."

Henry shoved his hand in his pocket.

"Can I ask you something?"

"Suppose you can," Henry said. "You going to anyway."

"Are you a slave?"

I thought Henry was gonna fall out then and there.

"I ain't no slave," he said. "I is a free boy!"

"But your mama's colored and cooks for Mrs. Middleton. Doesn't that make her a slave?"

"My mama ain't no slave," Henry said, standing up tall. "My daddy, neither. Don't you know nothing? The war done been over for ten years. We is all free. We gets paid for the work we do. We ain't slaves no more."

"Were you slaves before?"

"Like I told you, I was born a free boy. But my mama and daddy were slaves. And their mama and daddy before them."

"Did they belong to the Middletons?"

"No, my granddaddy belonged to Andrew Jackson. Do you know who he was?"

"No. Who's that?"

"He was the president of the United States," he said proud. "My granddaddy was named for him since Mr. Jackson owned him. He gave my granddaddy to Doc Middleton's daddy 'cause they was good friends. My granddaddy was only a boy, but he was big and strong like me, and they needed help to plant tobacco. The Middletons owned our family after that 'til we got free."

I tried to understand what Henry was telling me, but I couldn't make sense of it. Then I thought how hard my mother worked cooking and cleaning for Nellie and Howard. We didn't have money to buy things and barely got enough to eat. It felt like we had been slaves, too.

While we were talking, a man rode up on horseback. He tied his horse up to the rail in front of the store and went inside. He looked familiar, but I couldn't place his face.

When we went inside, Albert and the man were talking together behind the counter. Albert saw me and leaned in closer to the man, whose back was to me. They were talking low, so we couldn't hear what they were saying. The man handed Albert an envelope. Then he turned to leave. I looked him in the face and remembered where I'd seen him before. It was on the ride from Elizabethtown with my grandfather. He was the man sitting up front driving the carriage.

I got shaky in my legs.

"What did that man want?" I asked Albert. "Is it about my mother?"

Albert put his hand on my shoulder. He started to say something, but then he stopped. He looked down at the floor and then back up to me.

His voice sounded funny, but his words were good. "Your ma's doing fine. She wanted you to know she was thinking about you on your birthday and she loves you very much."

"You mean she had that man ride all the way here to tell me that?"

I couldn't believe my mother, as sick as she was, sent a message to me on my birthday. I had a big smile on my face. This was the best birthday I'd ever had.

"Come on now, let's have some cake," Pearl said. "We got us a party going on. Sit on down, Elijah. Let me cut you the first piece."

I ate every bit of that first piece of butter cake and then had a second one. I got presents from Albert and Pearl—nice new clothes and books, too. I'd never gotten presents before then. I thanked them from the bottom of my heart. I missed my mother for sure. But I went to bed that night feeling happier than I could remember because my mother loved me and so did Albert and Pearl.

Chapter 19

"The Watch"

Ikept that warm feeling for near on a week. Then everything changed.

One night at supper, Albert and Pearl were quiet. Usually Pearl was a talker. After we ate, Albert put more wood in the stove and asked me to come sit with them a spell. Pearl started patting my knee. I knew something was wrong.

"Son, there's no easy way to tell you but straight out. Your ma didn't make it. She tried real hard to get well, but she was too sick. The consumption killed her. We're so sorry."

My ears heard Albert's words, but my brain couldn't make sense of them.

"That can't be right!" I said. "Who told you that?"

"I'm afraid it's true, Elijah. Your mother passed away."

"But she promised to come get me!"

I ran to my room. Pearl started to come after me, but Albert told her to leave me be. I lay down on top of the quilt, staring at the ceiling. I started thinking about the holes in the attic roof and sleeping next to my mother in our little bed. I kept seeing my mother's face and feeling her lips on my cheek. I remembered the last time I hugged her tight. I begged her not to send me away. She promised to come for me, but now she never would. She died.

Later that night, Albert and Pearl came in to check on me. I kept my eyes shut so they'd go away. I tried to sleep, but too many questions whirled around in my head.

What was to become of me? What if Albert and Pearl didn't want me no more? Where was I gonna go? Would they send me to the workhouse after all? Why did my mother die and break her promise?

The next morning, I got up but couldn't eat my breakfast. Pearl said, "Elijah, your Uncle Albert and I have something important to say."

I set down my fork. I thought I knew what was coming and I didn't want to cry. They were going to send me to the workhouse.

"Elijah," Pearl said, "we always wanted a son, but God didn't see fit to give us one 'til you came along. Your Uncle Albert and I want you to be our boy."

Albert said, "We'll take real good care of you, son. I promise you that."

I stared at them with my mouth open. This was not what I expected. They weren't sending me away. They wanted me to be their son. I felt hot waves of relief spread over me. I picked up my fork and cleaned my plate.

It took me some time to let them love me like they wanted. But after a spell, we became a family. Yet as the months went by, one thing kept weighing heavy on my mind. I asked Pearl about it.

"I'm starting to forget things, Aunt Pearl. I can't see the attic as plain as I used to. What if I forget what my mother looked like or how she smelled?"

Pearl said, "Let's put your memories of your mother and your life together down on paper. We'll work on it every day as part of your lessons. Thataway you'll keep your mother always in your heart."

That's what we did and what you are reading now—my life story, up to the point I didn't want to write about it no more.

The next few years went by quick. I never did go to school. Pearl did a fine job teaching me at home. I got to where I could read and write as good as if I'd completed the eighth grade. And Albert taught me everything I needed to know about adding sums and making change. I especially liked the days when Isaiah brung Henry with him to work at the store. There was something about Henry Jackson that I liked from the start. He was like his daddy and my Uncle Albert. He was honest and had integrity.

On my sixteenth birthday, Albert gave me a special present. He said he wanted to have a talk with me, man to man, now that I was grown. He reached in his pocket and took out the watch I'd seen him use every day to tell time.

"Elijah, my pa gave me this watch when I became a man. He's the one who taught me to be honest and have integrity. He said there comes a time at least once in your life when you have to tell a lie for the sake of someone else."

"What do you mean?"

Albert looked uneasy. "You'll know it when it happens, son. I want you to have my pa's watch so you'll always remember to be honest. But if there comes a time you have to lie, you give the watch away, like I'm giving it to you."

Just before handing me the watch, Albert looked me in the eyes and said, "I should have given this to you a long time ago, but I wanted to wait until you were grown enough to understand."

I looked at the watch he placed in my hand and started to ask if he'd lied to me about my mother sending me a birthday wish. But then I decided to let it be. I treasured that watch. Every time I looked at it, I thought about being a man who was honest and had integrity. I planned to keep that watch until the day I died.

Chapter 20

"The Middletons"

Inever did grow tall, but I filled out good because of Pearl's fine cooking. Hauling deliveries for Albert made me strong, too. I didn't make friends easy—it was hard for me to trust people after those years of being made fun of at school. The only boy I came to trust was Henry.

Every chance I got, I went out to the Middleton farm. I liked walking through the fields with Henry, feeling the sun on my face and the wind in my hair. That's when I felt free. Most times when I worked inside the store, I felt like a rooster that couldn't bust free of its coop.

The summer after I turned sixteen, Doc asked me to work for him, setting and harvesting tobacco plants. Isaiah was ailing, and Doc thought I could help Henry. He promised to pay me a good wage, if Albert could spare me. Albert thought it was a fine idea for me to learn about growing tobacco.

I took to the work natural. It was amazing to watch a seed grow into a plant that could be harvested and sold for money. And if truth be told, I didn't mind being around the Middleton girls, especially little Mary.

Over time, I come to know a lot about the Middletons' history. Doc's given name was Gavin, and his kinfolk came from Scotland back in the 1700s. Folks said he was a good-looking fella when he was young, but age was already setting in when I came to work for him.

When the Civil War broke out, Doc decided to help the Union soldiers. He marched with the Kentucky boys in 1862 and treated the wounded after battles. He came home after the Battle of Perryville because he couldn't take it no more. Instead he built a house in Uptonville to treat soldiers when they needed a long convalescence but he was never quite himself after the war.

Martha, the oldest of the Middleton girls, wanted to be a doctor like her daddy, but that wasn't fittin' for a lady in those days. From the time she could sit up straight in the buckboard, she made house calls with Doc. She got real good at delivering babies. She didn't faint, no matter how much blood she saw.

A couple of years before I started working for Doc, he made up his mind to find another sawbones to help him. He'd had pain in his joints since the war, and over time it got worse. His hands started cramping up to where he couldn't cut on folks no more, so he sent out a notice to the medical school in Louisville looking for just the right person.

A young man by the name of Nathaniel Patterson, who hailed from Cincinnati, jumped at the chance to work with Doc. His family was rich and expected him to return home once he finished medical school. Nathan, as he liked to be called, didn't want no part of that. There were already plenty of fine doctors in Cincinnati. Nathan wanted to go somewhere he could really make a difference.

At first, Doc wasn't sure that he'd like the rich kid from Ohio, but Nathan had a kind way with folks and didn't put on fancy airs like society people were known to do. He knew a lot about mixing up medicines, and he could saw a man's leg off without puking his guts out. That's what made him a good sawbones.

Once Nathan moved to Uptonville, he and Martha took to each other like they were born to be together. It was no time before they got married. Right after they came back from their wedding trip, they moved into the house in Uptonville that Doc had built for wounded soldiers. It was plenty big and set back aways from the main street of town.

They had living quarters on the first floor and six rooms upstairs for folks who needed round-the-clock care. Nathan set up another room at the back of the house where he and Martha could cut on somebody, if need be. During the day, they used the front room to see patients.

Miriam, the middle girl, wasn't as pretty as Mary or as smart as Martha. She was plain-spoken, which got her in trouble. I once heard a woman say that Miriam had both sharp features and a sharp tongue, neither of which was pleasing to behold. But she had a soft heart and stood up for people who couldn't fight for themselves, so people forgave her for being plain and contrary.

Martha was always looking out for Miriam. She wanted her sister to find a good husband like she had, but Uptonville didn't have many eligible suitors. One Sunday, Martha invited the Middletons to join her and Nathan so Miriam could meet Herbert Smith, the nephew of the first president of the L&N Railroad. Herbert worked for the railroad and had come to Uptonville to figure out how they could do a better job of hauling tobacco to market while serving passengers.

Martha asked her mother if Sally Ann could fix her special fried chicken, mashed potatoes, greens, and berry pie. Sally Ann was happy to help with the matchmaking. She made cornbread and white gravy, too, because chicken just wasn't as good without all the fixin's.

Martha had Herbert sit next to Miriam. But those two were an unlikely pair. Miriam thought Herbert was a snob because he just sat there all stiff without saying much at all. From time to time, he looked at Miriam, then away real quick. Miriam didn't like that one bit, because she reckoned he thought she was ugly.

They might have all just sat there in queer silence if Doc hadn't asked about the railroad. Herbert was more than happy to oblige. His eyes took on a sparkle when he talked about the L&N. He told Doc all about the lines of track from Louisville to Nashville and how they were expanding now to other cities, like Cincinnati. Doc recalled how important the railroad had been for the Union during the war. Herbert talked about the damage the rebels had done to the track and what it took to get the railroad running again after that.

Miriam asked Herbert what he thought his future might hold with the railroad.

"I don't know yet, Miss Middleton," he said. "I have to prove myself first, but I'm up for the challenge."

"What challenge is that, Mr. Smith?"

"Two things come to mind. First, I got to get to know the people we serve, so we can do our job better. Second, I want to do more for the men who work for us. I don't think we're paying them enough to support their families. I want to make that right."

Miriam nodded her head in approval.

When Sally Ann brung out her platter of fried chicken with all the fixin's, all talk was put on hold. Herbert started out eating real polite, but soon his manners went out the window. He dug into his food like he hadn't had a good meal in years, and from the puny looks of him, the Middleton women thought that might just be true. When he smacked his lips, Miriam smiled, and Mary giggled behind her hands.

Things might have ended there, but Herbert did something unexpected. When Sally Ann came in to take away the dirty dishes, Herbert stood, bowed to her and said, "Ma'am, that was the finest dinner I've had in years, and I thank you for your trouble."

He sat down, took more helpings of everything and started eating again. Everyone else sat there with wide eyes and open mouths. The Middletons loved Sally Ann and held her in high regard, but nobody in these parts ever treated a colored woman with that kind of respect. After that, it was Miriam who looked at Herbert from time to time and smiled.

Miriam and Herbert got married the following summer and settled down in Louisville. Miriam kept her sharp tongue, and she didn't get no prettier with age. But that didn't matter a lick to Herbert. They both had a love of people and a need to treat them good.

Chapter 21

"Twisted Curl"

Mary was four years younger than me. I didn't see much of her until I started working for Doc. Mary was twelve then. She was pretty but shy. Also, she was dainty like my mother, and that made me want to protect her, especially when she looked at me with her big eyes and twirled a curl around her finger. I was a man of sixteen and couldn't have much to do with a girl that young. Henry would tease me about how I perked up every time the *young'un* brung us lemonade. I told him to shut his mouth and tend to his own damn business. That just made him laugh.

Mary didn't go to the schoolhouse in town because she had such a hard time being around strangers. Doc hired a man and his wife to tutor her at home. Mr. Montgomery taught Mary reading, writing and arithmetic, while his wife taught her about art, music and literature. Literature means fine old books. Mary liked music and got to where she could play nice tunes on the piano. On a nice day when the windows were open and I was working outside, I could hear her making music.

By the time she was sixteen, Mary had learned all she could from the tutors. Her mother wanted her to go on to a finishing school, but Mary had no desire to be away from home, so Mrs. Middleton fretted about what would become of her until Nathan came up with an idea that pleased everyone.

Nathan was an only child. His father, Duncan Patterson, owned factories up and down the Ohio River that made iron. He died of a heart ailment when Nathan was in medical school. His mother, Clara, was left with a fortune, but she was lonesome. Nathan thought Mary would be a fittin' companion for his mother. He also believed his mother would be good for Mary and help her become more at ease with people.

The Middletons thought this was a wonderful idea. Getting Mary to agree was a challenge, but when Nathan told her all about the fine art museum and opera house they had in Cincinnati, Mary got excited to go.

A lot of folks turned out to say goodbye when she boarded the train in Uptonville for Cincinnati, including Albert, Pearl and me. I tried to freeze a picture of her in my mind as she stood on the platform before boarding the train. She wore a dark-blue dress and coat, and her hair was fixed with curls around her face. Her cheeks were pink from the cold, and that made her look especially pretty. It was her shy smile that I liked best of all. Her lips looked like a heart when she held them together. Sometimes when I couldn't sleep at night, I imagined kissing those lips.

Mary was away from Uptonville for near on two years. Mrs. Middleton read Mary's letters to Sally Ann, who then told Henry all the news. Henry couldn't wait to pass it all on to me. Clara Patterson was a short, plump lady with a big heart. Mary liked her because she didn't act all uppity even though she was a well-to-do lady. After they got to know each other, Mrs. Patterson surprised Mary with a trip to Europe. Mary wrote that they had a fine time aboard ship, dressing up in ball gowns and eating supper with the captain every night. There was music and dancing, and every afternoon they took tea outside on the deck.

Henry said one day they went to the Queen Victoria's palace in London. Another letter told about big mountains they saw called the Alps. Henry told me the Alps were hills made out of rock instead of dirt and were so tall that they almost touched the sky.

Henry couldn't remember the fancy French words that Mary wrote about Paris, so I didn't learn much about that place. After all this time wearing ball gowns and going to palaces, I reckoned Mary would never want to come home to the farm.

When she was in Cincinnati, Mary turned eighteen, the age to think about getting married and having babies. Mrs. Patterson wanted her to meet a rich man who could care for her proper and she started making arrangements for her to come out in the spring. I asked Doc what that meant, and he said Mary would be going to a ball to meet eligible suitors once she learned how to do the waltz. I figured that, being as pretty as she was, she'd have her pick of Cincinnati suitors. But that wasn't what the good Lord had in mind.

Two weeks before the ball, Mrs. Patterson collapsed on the floor in the drawing room. She couldn't move or talk. The doctor came and said she'd been struck down from apoplexy. I think they call it a stroke now. He told Mary it wouldn't do any good to send her to the hospital because there wasn't anything they could do to help her get better.

Mrs. Patterson didn't die right away, but she couldn't do nothing but lay in bed and look out the window as she got weaker and weaker. Finally, the doctor sent a message to Nathan to come right away because the poor woman had only a few days to live.

After Mrs. Patterson's funeral, Mary had no reason to stay in Cincinnati. She came home with Martha and Nathan as soon as they closed up the house and got his mother's affairs in order.

Mary grieved a long time for Mrs. Patterson. Nathan showed her letters that his mother had written him about how much it meant to her to have Mary around. She said Mary gave her a reason to live after her husband died and and her son moved to Uptonville. And for that she would always be grateful. In return, Mrs. Patterson helped Mary come out of her shell and meet all kinds of new people.

Chapter 22

"A Worthy Suitor"

In her last letter, Mrs. Patterson told Nathan that if anything happened to her before Mary had her coming-out in Ohio, he should see that she met proper suitors in Kentucky. Nathan got that letter just a week before his mother fell ill. It was like she knew she was gonna die.

It wasn't long before a steady stream of fellas came calling. One was a man by the name of Carlton Helmstead, whose kin owned acres of rich farmland near Elizabethtown. Helmstead wasn't like Nathan who made his own way. He told Mary he'd never have to work a day in his life on account of all the money his grandfather left him.

Helmstead was taller than me and had light brown hair. I couldn't tell you what color his eyes were because the only time I got close enough to see them, I was too mad to notice. What I remember most about him were the fancy lace shirts he wore and his high, polished boots.

For months, he came roaring up the path in a carriage drawn by four highbred horses. He and Mary would have tea with her mother in the drawing room or drink lemonade on the porch by themselves. Sometimes when they were sitting outside on the swing, I heard her laughing. I didn't like it, but there was nothing I could do about it.

Henry told me that Mrs. Middleton thought he was a worthy suitor, but Doc had his doubts. Sally Ann was good at reading people and she didn't like Carlton Helmstead a lick.

Well, on this particular day in late August, Henry and me were starting to bring in the tobacco crop. We were hot and dirty when we came in to have our noon dinner. Sally Ann cooked up fried catfish, taters and greens, and we ate at a little table under a big oak tree, not far from the main house. We were minding our own business when Mary and her beau decided to walk down to the pond. They had to pass by us to get where they were going.

Mary looked wonderful in her bright-yellow dress. I couldn't help but notice how she'd grown from a pretty girl into a beautiful woman during the two years she spent in Cincinnati.

Minding our manners, we stood when Mary stopped to say hello.

Henry said, real pleasant, "Nice to see you, Miss Mary."

"You too, Henry."

"Henry, I'd like you and Elijah to meet Carlton Helmstead from Elizabethtown. Carlton, these are my friends Henry Jackson and Elijah Fry."

Henry wiped his hand on his pant leg before sticking it out for a shake. I kept my hand to myself because there was something about the dandy that rubbed me raw. And I was right because that fella didn't take Henry's hand. Instead, he wrinkled his nose as he looked first at Henry and then at me.

Two memories from when I was a boy flashed through my mind. The first was of Mrs. Meade sniffing at my mother and me, like we were rotten meat. The other was of my grandfather refusing to shake my hand.

Helmstead said low, "Come along, Mary."

For a minute, Mary didn't move. She didn't seem to take kindly to the way her beau was acting.

Helmstead leaned in to her and said, loud enough for us to hear, "Where I come from, whites don't mix it up with niggers."

Mary stared at him with her mouth wide-open. The Middletons

never used that word, and she didn't like hearing Henry called that. She wasn't the only one who was shocked.

I asked, "What did you say?"

Helmstead turned to me with pure hate spewing out his eyes. He didn't say nothing but held tight to Mary's arm tight. She was looking at him like her belly hurt. He repeated himself, a little louder. "I said *come along*, Mary!"

He nudged her hard as he gripped her arm. She stumbled because she didn't expect him to shove her. He jerked her back to him.

"You're hurting me!" she cried, trying to break free.

When Henry heard that, he started for him, but I waved him back and moved forward myself. "Let go of her *now*!"

That fool stared at me like I was nothing but mule dung. Worst of all, he wouldn't let go of Mary.

I felt the old rage come over me. I grabbed his arm and yanked him away from her. Then I hit that man first on the jaw with my right hand and then on his nose with my left. But I didn't stop there. Pow ... pow ... just like I had with that Meade boy. He staggered back and fell. I grabbed him by the shirt collar and pulled him to his feet to pound him all over again. It felt so good, I couldn't stop. I didn't come back to my right mind until I heard Mary screaming and Henry got ahold of me. Helmstead was sprawled out on the ground moaning.

Henry kept his arms tight around my chest and jerked my head around to the front porch where the Middletons stood frowning. They'd come running when they heard Mary scream.

Mary didn't fall to her knees bawling for Helmstead like I thought she would. Instead, she stood over him and said, "Don't you ever come back here! I never want to see your hateful face again!"

She marched her pretty little self to the porch and told her folks what happened. Mrs. Middleton cupped her hand over her mouth and hurried inside with Mary. Doc stayed put.

Helmstead struggled to his feet. "I'll get you for this, you bastard," he spat at me. "And you too, nigger," he yelled at Henry.

He staggered to his carriage, his white lace shirt torn and covered in blood.

Doc watched him drive away and went in the house without saying a word.

"Well, I done it now," I told Henry. "Doc won't want me around no more."

I got on my horse and rode to town. I kept replaying what happened in my mind. I wasn't sorry for what I'd done because that man disrespected Mary and called Henry a nigger. My hand hurt like hell.

Albert was surprised to see me in the middle of the day. I told him about the fight and he called for Pearl to tend to my hand. It was swelling up bad.

"I'm sorry if I shamed you," I told Albert and Pearl. I'd come to love them, and I never wanted to hurt them.

"There's no shame in standing up for people you care about, Elijah. Go get cleaned up, and we'll talk more later."

Pearl heated up some water and washed off my hand. I put on fresh clothes and let her bind my hand in a clean cloth.

Albert stuck his head in the door. "Come here, son."

I followed him into the store. Henry was standing there.

"Oh, Lord," I muttered to myself. "This can't be good."

"Doc sent me to fetch you. He wants to have a word with you."

"You coming with me, Henry?"

"You go on, Elijah, and have your talk with Doc in private," said Pearl, who'd come in from the back. "I'm gonna fix Henry some tea and cake. I'll send him along later."

I tried not to think about things too much on the ride to the farm because there was nothing I could do about it.

Sally Ann opened the door and said, "Doc wants to see you in the library. You mind yourself, Elijah, and Henry, too. I scared of that Helmstead fella. He's an evil, hateful man."

"Don't you fret none, Sally Ann. I'll look out for both of us."

I'd never been in the library before. It had a fireplace and soft comfortable chairs. The shelves were filled with leather-bound books.

"Sit down," Doc ordered.

I sat, bracing myself for the worst.

"You have a mean punch."

"Yes, sir. I've been told that."

"I think you might of broke the man's nose, maybe his jaw, too."

"I think you're right about his nose. Not too sure about his jaw."

"Did you knock out any teeth?"

"Don't know for sure, but he was spitting blood. I might have broke his cheekbone because it felt like mush after I hit him."

"Mary told me what happened. What do you have to say for yourself, Elijah?"

It took me a minute to answer. I wanted to be respectful of Doc, but I aimed to tell the truth.

"Well, sir, I'm not sorry for what I done. I wasn't about to let that man hurt Miss Mary or get away with calling Henry a nigger. But I know that I've caused you trouble, and I don't blame you for not wanting me around no more."

"Don't go telling me what I think, young man. I'll speak for myself."

I hung my head, feeling even worse.

"Listen to me, Elijah. I thank you for what you did. I wouldn't have tolerated him calling Henry a nigger. And if I'd seen that bastard shove my Mary, I would've laid him out myself. Now let me have a look at your hand."

Doc unwrapped the cloth and felt the bones around my swollen hand. I winced but didn't say nothing. He got a proper bandage and some white cream, then rewrapped my right hand.

"I don't think you busted any major bones, but you messed your hand up good. You've got a bad sprain, and it's gonna hurt like hell for a while." Doc grinned, then said, "But it ain't nothing compared to what you did to Helmstead. His face won't ever be right again. Serves him right, the sorry bastard."

I grinned back at him.

"Let me ask you something, Elijah. What do you want to do with your life? Run the store?"

It took me no time to answer. "No, sir. I'd like to have my own place like you got here so I can grow tobacco and provide for a family."

"I understand," he said. "There's nothing compared to having your own land and watching a crop grow. That's a fact."

"I like the heat of the sun on my face and the feel of dirt in my hands when I'm working."

"Then that's what you're meant to do, Elijah."

Doc stood. "I'd shake your hand, but you wouldn't want me to."

"Yes, sir."

"I don't want you bringing in the tobacco until that hand heals up good. Let me have a look at you again in a couple of days. In the meantime, take it easy and tell Pearl to feed you good. Soak your hand in warm salt water at least twice a day to bring down the swelling."

"I will, Doc. Thank you."

I started to leave, but he stopped me.

"Mary wants a word with you on the porch."

"Oh, Lord," I muttered again.

Mary was sitting by herself in the porch swing. My stomach knotted up being close to her alone.

"Doc said you wanted to see me."

"Sit with me for a few minutes."

I sat down in the swing beside her.

"How bad is your hand?"

"Doc doesn't think it's busted, but I messed it up good."

"I should think so," Mary said. "I was afraid you were gonna beat Carlton to death."

I looked her straight in the eye and said, "I probably would've if you hadn't started hollering."

"Why did you do it?"

"He wouldn't take his hands off you when you told him too."

"I thank you for looking out for me."

I asked Mary why she had a funny look on her face.

She said, "You're not the same boy who saw me off at the train depot a few years ago."

That was true. I was twenty-three, after all. But I didn't know exactly what she meant.

"You're a fine man, Elijah Fry. That's plain to see."

I wasn't too sure what to say next, but it felt good just to be around Mary. Then she said something that scared the tar out of me. "I'm ruined because of you."

"What do you mean?"

"Why, the story of what happened to my beau will spread all over Kentucky like a fire gone wild. No man in his right mind will call on me now. Not with you around."

My leg started twitching. "I'm sorry for that."

Mary looked at me with her big eyes as she twirled a curl around her finger.

"I guess we'll have to invite you to Sunday dinner since nobody else will be coming around. Would you want to come?" she said, looking up at me kinda shy.

"Yes, ma'am, I would," I said.

"Then stop calling me *ma'am*. My name is Mary.

Chapter 23

"More to the Story"

After that, we started seeing each other regular. I don't mean when I was working in Doc's fields. I called on her in the evenings, after I'd gone home to clean up, or on Sunday afternoons. It felt natural being with Mary. She reminded me of my mother with her kind ways and sweet demeanor. That was a blessing and a curse. Before I asked for her hand in marriage, I had to tell her something. It took me a long while to work up the courage. I picked the right time and place. The evening was warm, and we had the porch to ourselves.

"Mary, spending time with you these past months has meant the world to me. I like the way we can talk about anything."

"I do as well, Elijah."

"You are the only one in the world who understands the shame I felt being called a little bastard boy and my mother a whore."

"I'm honored that you shared that with me."

"You remind me of my mother."

"That's a high compliment."

"My mother was a wonderful woman," I said. "And you are very like her. That's why my mind is uneasy."

"I don't understand."

"Mother was a beautiful, educated woman. She could've had

any man she wanted, but she loved someone who wasn't worthy of her. And look what happened to her!"

"You are nothing like your father!" she said.

"But I haven't been to the Alps or Paris. I haven't even been out of Uptonville since I came here as a boy. I'm a plain man who likes to grow tobacco. Why would you want to be with me when you could do so much better?"

"I want to be with you because of your heart, Elijah. You speak the truth, and I can count on you."

"Albert and Pearl taught me to be a man of my word."

"A good heart means a whole lot more to me than lace shirts or polished boots."

During the months we'd spent time together, I'd gotten to know Mary well. When she got nervous, she still played with her hair, like when she was a child.

"I'm not like my sisters, who enjoy being around people. It takes me a long time to warm up to strangers."

"But don't you miss the grand life you had with Mrs. Patterson?"

"I miss her for sure, but not that life. Here with you, I can be who I really am, not just pretending to be someone else."

"I don't want you to wake up one day and wish you had a different life."

"Well then, you better love me good and take care of our children."

That was all I needed to hear. I asked Doc for Mary's hand in marriage that very night. A few weeks later, we celebrated our engagement. Albert and Pearl came, along with Nathan and Martha. Everyone had a good time at supper. Afterward, Doc asked to have a word with Albert and me in the library.

He poured each of us a glass of brandy and toasted the marriage. I hadn't had a drink of liquor before that night. I drank it straight down like Doc did. It burnt my throat so bad that tears filled my eyes.

"Elijah," Doc said, "the more I get to know you, the happier I am with Mary's choice for a husband. You're a hardworking man of integrity, and I admire that more than anything else."

"Thank you, sir."

"I have only two things to ask of you, son. The first is that you treat Mary well. She's most precious to me. You love her good. Understand?"

"Yes, sir. I promise."

"The other thing I ask of you is to raise your children to be good Christians by making sure they go to church. Will you do that for me, Elijah?"

"Yes, sir. You have my word."

"Albert and I have something important to tell you."

Doc went first. "You told me you want a place of your own someday where you could grow tobacco and raise a family. Well, I'm deeding you forty acres of my farm to get started. It's some of the best land I own for growing tobacco. The plot sits right next to the house where the Jacksons stay, so Henry can help you tend the crop."

I was so surprised I couldn't find enough words to thank Doc. Then Albert spoke. "Elijah, you've made Pearl and me real happy being the son we always wanted. Now I got something to tell you. Remember the man who brung you to us?"

"Yes, sir, my grandfather. He never came to see me after that."

"Pearl and I never understood why he acted the way he done. But, be that as it may, he did look after you in his own way. He gave us money to help raise you, starting the day you arrived. He sent money regular after that, up 'til he died a few years ago."

"I'm glad he done something right, so you could raise me up proper. I thank you for that."

"Well, you see, there's more to the story. We didn't use that money to raise you. That was our job as your ma and pa. We put it away for you."

For a moment, nobody said nothing.

"We counted it up last night after Doc told us what he had a mind to do. The way I figure it, you got enough money to build a fine house and barn on the land Doc give you. So maybe you can find it in your heart to forgive the old man.”

They both looked at me, but all I could do was smile and shake my head. Doc refilled each of our brandy glasses and held his up for one last toast.

“Here’s to a good life for you and Mary.”

Chapter 24

"My Dark Place"

We had a good life while it lasted.

Thomas was our firstborn. He came the year after we got married. By then, we had our house and barn built and we'd brung in our very first tobacco crop. I was pleased about that and grateful for Henry's help.

One day I asked Henry if he thought about getting married. He said there was a colored girl he'd fancied once, but Isaiah died before he could do something about it. Now he had to look after Sally Ann and help Doc and me with our crops. That didn't leave much time for courting.

After Isaiah died, I helped Albert in the store whenever I could. I noticed that Pearl wasn't as hearty as she used to be. She spent a lot of time in her chair and got short of breath when she was up and about. Nathan told me that Pearl had a bad heart, probably from being portly all her life.

Our second son came along the next year. He was a fat, fine-looking baby, and Mary done good during her long hours of labor. We named him Daniel. I felt blessed. We had two fine sons, good crops of tobacco, and we were happy together. I didn't worry no more about Mary wanting a different life. She loved being a wife and mama, and our life suited her well. But the year we found out she was having a third baby, right after we buried Pearl, everything changed.

It was a miserable winter all around, unusually cold for Kentucky. Lots of folks were getting sick with pneumonia. My boys were fine. They were staying up at the big house with the Middletons because Mary was having a hard time carrying this baby. Then a month before it was due, Mary caught the pneumonia.

I took her to the little hospital to stay until the baby came, so Nathan and Martha could look after her good. Every evening, I went to see her. She started coughing just like my mother done and a fear took over me that wouldn't let go. I couldn't bear the thought of losing her the same way.

When her pains started, Nathan sent Albert to fetch me and Doc. After a while, he came out of her room to talk to us.

"Elijah, Mary's too weak to push the baby out. If we don't do something quick, she's gonna die and the baby, too."

My mind went dark, and I couldn't understand what Nathan was saying. I knew it was bad when Doc's face turned pale.

Nathan said, "The only way to save the baby is to take him from Mary now."

"What do you mean, take him?"

"I have to cut her open."

"Will she be OK once you do that?"

Nathan put his hand on my shoulder. "No, Elijah. Chances are, Mary won't make it. She wants to see you first."

Mary had a gray color to her pretty face, and the curls on her head were wet with sweat. I knelt down beside the bed and wrapped a curl of her hair around my finger. I could barely hear her when she tried to speak. She whispered, "I love you, Elijah Fry. You made me happy. Be a good father to our children."

I promised her I would, but then I just laid my head down and started sobbing. Doc came in to say his goodbye. Then Nathan carried her downstairs to the operating table. Martha held Mary's hand while Nathan had her breathe in some medicine on a cloth so she wouldn't feel any pain. Then he cut the baby right out of her belly. Mary died a few minutes later. The date was April 11, 1894.

Martha wrapped the baby in a blanket and brung him to me.

"You have a fine son, Elijah. Would you like to hold him?"

I couldn't bear my sadness, so I asked Doc to take him.

"What do you want to name him?" Martha asked.

"Mary liked the name Benjamin."

Martha said, "We need to keep Benjamin here with us until we're sure he's healthy."

"How you gonna feed him without Mary to nurse?" I asked.

"We got something new here called formula," Nathan told me. "It's a powder that you mix with warm cow's milk. He'll be fine."

The next day, Henry and me dug a grave for Mary up on the hill overlooking the house. I reckoned she could watch over our young'uns when they played outside.

I went to my dark place for a long while after we poured the dirt on top of Mary. I didn't care nothing about the farm or raising tobacco. And for a time, I didn't pay my boys much mind. First, I'd lost my mother, then Pearl. Now my Mary was gone. I'd promised to take care of her and I failed. All I wanted was to crawl inside the grave with her. I would've, too, if Albert hadn't come to see me a few weeks later and put things plain.

"You have a choice to make, Elijah. You can give your sons to the Middletons to raise or you can do what Mary wanted and be the father they deserve."

I'd grown up without a daddy, and I didn't want that for my boys. I got up, put my pants on, and got back to work. We settled in and got by the best we could. Everyone pitched in to help, but the sadness in the house stayed for a long, long time.

MOLLY

Chapter 25

"Unexpected Turn"

Have you ever watched a turtle cross a road? When you live your life from day to day, time moves along at a turtle's pace, and nothing much seems to change. Yet when you look back over the span of a decade, you can see you're not in the same place no more. I kept the promises I made after we lost Ma and John, and I became the woman of the house. I cared for Pa and my brothers. I wore britches most of the time, worked alongside my brothers growing tobacco, and ate my meals sitting next to Pa at the table. Most important, I learnt all I could from Isaac and Miss June so I'd be smart 'stead of ignorant. More days than not, I felt satisfied with my life. Joost and Jansen grew into fine men. They liked farming better than anything and had a knack for growing hardy crops of tobacco. Joost took a wife. Her name was Elizabeth. Pastor Brown married them, and I cooked up a fine wedding supper afterward. Joost saved most of the money he made from the tobacco crops, so he bought some acreage next to our farm and built them a little house.

Jansen was still backward with women, but I had hopes he would find a suitable wife in time. Even though he was shy, he was a kind man with a big heart.

We had no idea what happened to James 'cause he didn't write us letters. Isaac went on to high school to become a teacher. He got a position in Elizabethtown but promised to come teach at the little schoolhouse when Miss June got too old to keep up with the young'uns.

Edward followed the path I could see for him since before Ma died. Pastor Brown took a shine to him after his sons left home 'cause they didn't want to be preachers. Right after Edward turned sixteen, Pastor Brown invited him to live with him and Mrs. Brown, so he could learn about saving souls for Jesus. The pastor was getting up in years, and his wife was none too spritely. He told Edward he was grooming him to take over our little church just as soon as the Spirit of the Lord came upon him.

Well, that done happen one hot day in June. Pastor Brown invited folks from all over Hardin County to come to a revival, which lasted several days. Edward, who'd just turned twenty, spoke on the last day. He got so full up with the Spirit that he fell to his knees trembling. Tears spilled out his eyes when he begged people to get saved for Jesus. Right afterward, Pastor Brown baptized ten people down at the river, and he knew Edward was ready to take the pulpit. From that day forward, my brother was known as Pastor Van Meter, and the little church was his.

I couldn't help but remember getting in a sweat as a young'un when Pastor Brown got going about burning in the fires of hell. Edward had a gentle way about him and a good voice for preaching. When I listened to him in church, I felt like I was sitting in a soft puffy cloud just waiting for the gates of heaven to open.

As for me, I didn't get no prettier with age, and I still couldn't do nothing with my hair. I grew nearly as tall as my brothers, but they filled out while I stayed skinny as a stick. My skin turned brown from being in the sun, and I had hard places on my hands from hoeing tobacco. I didn't have much hope of getting a good husband, so I made up my mind just to live out my days the best I could.

Thanks to the good Lord and Miss June, my life took an unexpected turn. Not too long after Edward started preaching,

Miss June asked me to come teach Sunday school with her. She promised to work with me 'til I could handle the lessons alone. I was excited to teach Sunday school, but I didn't own but two hand-me-down dresses. Miss June and Elizabeth told me they could fix that straightaway. Joost bought Elizabeth one of them newfangled, foot-pump sewing machines so she could make curtains and clothes. Elizabeth said she'd sew up some pretty new dresses for me, and Miss June offered to pay for the cloth and thread. That's how the three of us come to pay a visit to Albert Fry's store.

I didn't get to see Albert but a few times a year. He was a pleasant man who always inquired about folks, but he stayed powerful sad after the death of his wife. Miss June struck up a conversation with him while Elizabeth and me looked over the yard goods.

"How's Elijah doing with the boys, Albert?"

"Most days he does pretty good, Miss June, but he doesn't leave the farm much except to help me out sometimes. Are my grandsons learning good at school?"

"Thomas and Daniel are bright and well-behaved. They are both quick learners and do fine work. I look forward to having Benjamin in another year or two."

Albert smiled. Then his brow creased. "There's something that's been bothering me."

"What's that?" she asked.

"Elijah promised Doc he'd raise the boys as good Christians, but he hasn't done nothing about that since Mary died. I tried taking them a time or two to my church here in town, but they didn't cotton to it. They said the preacher was boring and they didn't learn nothing."

Miss June nodded. "They're right. I could barely keep my eyes open when I heard the man preach one time. The flies on the ceiling were more interesting. Why don't you bring the boys to our little church?"

Throwing me a look, she said, "Molly's going to be the new Sunday school teacher. Believe me, it's never boring when Molly's around. I think all three of your grandsons would like her a lot."

That's how I come to meet the Fry boys and their daddy. Mary had been dead five years by the time I met Elijah in 1899, when he was thirty-three and I was nineteen.

Chapter 26

"Sad Eyes"

Thomas, the oldest Fry boy, was eight. He was tall and thin with light-brown hair. He reminded me of Doc 'cause he was smart and serious. He liked reading books better than playing outside. It took a lot to get him to let loose and be silly. Daniel was the exact opposite. He was seven when I first met him. I didn't know Mary, but Albert said he resembled her quite a bit with his curly dark hair and big eyes. He was the wild one of the bunch. I had to stay on him to pay attention during Bible lessons 'cause he was always talking or telling jokes. All the young'uns liked being around him 'cause he made them laugh. He was a handful, and that's a fact, but I liked his spirit. Daniel had spunk like me.

Benjamin was the shy one. Albert said he took after Elijah in looks but like his ma in temperament. He was a small boy with a slight build and a look of sadness most of the time. I figured that was on account of having no ma. I held him on my lap every chance I got.

Sometimes Albert stood in the back of the room when I was teaching lessons. You could tell he had a powerful love for the boys and they for him. They called him Pappy. After they'd been coming to Sunday school for several weeks, Albert asked if I'd do him a favor.

"Molly, would you mind staying for a while after Sunday school and look after the boys? Their daddy came to church with us today, and he wants to have a word with Pastor Edward. His wife will be gone five years next Sunday, and Elijah still feels bad for not giving her a proper Christian burial. He thought maybe Pastor Edward might offer up a prayer for her during service and say a few words about her passing."

"That's a fine idea, Albert."

"Doc's been ailing some, and Elijah hoped it might ease his mind to know he finally done the right thing by Mary."

"Well, you tell Mr. Fry to take his time with Edward. I'd be pleased to mind the boys."

After lessons, the four of us read stories and played games for near on an hour. Then we sat down at a little table to have some lemonade and cake. I asked each of them to tell me about theirselves.

Thomas said, "Well, ma'am, since I'm the oldest, it's my job to look after my brothers. They're decent boys, even though they don't mind too good."

I had to stop myself from grinning.

"What's your favorite thing to do, Thomas, besides reading books?"

"I like spending time with my granddaddy 'cause he's a doctor. I want to be a doctor like him and my Uncle Nathan when I get growed."

"I expect you'll make a fine doctor one day. Daniel, what do you like to do best?"

Daniel got a mischievous look in his eye. He smiled big and said, "I like coming to Sunday school to see you."

All of us laughed 'cause we knew he was telling a story.

Benjamin was too little to know what he liked or what he wanted to be when he growed up, so I asked him a different question. "Benjamin, I know it's your birthday next Sunday. Are you gonna have a party?"

I'll never forget the look on that little boy's face. His eyes opened wide and he asked, "What do you mean?"

Thomas said, "Our pa is always sad on that day, so we just stay quiet and think about our mama. We go visit her grave up on the hill. I still remember her some."

"Mama died bringing Benjamin into the world," Daniel added, "so we don't celebrate his birth none."

My heart started pounding. I looked at that sweet boy, and tears just rolled down my cheeks. I couldn't imagine growing up believing that you weren't worth nothing on account of your mama died giving you life.

Benjamin squinted his eyes like he was gonna blubber, too. I got out of my chair and picked that little boy up and put him on my lap. I held him and rocked him in my arms.

"Listen here, Benjamin Fry," I told him. "You're a fine boy. And we're gonna celebrate the fact you got born. Your mama loved you. And she's real proud of you now."

I held that boy tight and just let him cry. I asked Thomas and Daniel to come in close. "Listen to me good, boys. It's not this baby's fault that your mama died. The good Lord loved your ma so much that He wanted her to be with him in heaven. So He took her, but he gave you Benjamin to be your brother 'cause he was his special angel. So don't none of you blame him for your mama's death. Hear me?"

A man's voice startled me.

"You listen to her, boys. She's right."

I looked up and saw Albert standing in the back of the room with a man I hadn't seen before. He was a mite shorter than Albert but had a sturdy build, brown hair and a weathered face.

Thomas and Daniel ran over to him.

"Elijah," Albert said, "I'd like you to meet Miss Molly Van Meter. She's the Sunday school teacher I've been telling you about. Molly, this here is Elijah Fry, the boys' daddy."

Elijah came over to me and bowed respectfully. "I like what you told my boys, Miss Molly. And you're right. I'm ashamed for not thinking that way myself."

He knelt down in front of Benjamin, who was still curled up on my lap. It was then that I noticed his eyes. They were a nice shade of brown mixed with specks of green, but they looked sad like Benjamin's.

Elijah patted Benjamin and said, "Son, you deserve a fine birthday party, and that's exactly what you're gonna get. We got a whole lot to celebrate 'cause my life just wouldn't be the same without you."

Well, all three of them boys looked at their pa with open mouths.

"What you saying, Daddy?" Daniel asked.

"I'm saying that I'm powerful glad Benjamin was born, and it's high time we let him know that. So let's have a party. I'll ask Sally Ann to cook fried chicken with all the fixin's and a chocolate cake for dessert. How would that be?"

They all said that would be just fine.

Albert said, "You deserve a present, Benjamin. I got something special in mind from the store."

Little Benjamin's face lit up. He got down off my lap and ran to give Albert and his pa big hugs. All three of them boys looked pleased. I was tickled for the young'uns, but when I stood up, my legs wobbled, and I felt peculiar. I'd been holding Benjamin on my lap for a spell, so I figured that was the cause. But when Elijah stuck out his hand for a proper introduction, my palm started sweating.

"I'd like to thank you, Miss Molly, for what you told my boys. You're right. It's time I stop mourning Mary and think about my son. That's what his mama would want. I'd be pleased if you would join us next Sunday for the party."

Before I could answer, Albert said, "I'll take you right after Sunday school and bring you home afterward, Molly."

I might have said no if it wasn't for the Fry boys staring at me and nodding their heads yes. How was I gonna turn them down?

"Please come, Miss Molly," said Benjamin, pulling on my dress.

Well, my heart done melted on the spot, and I said, yes, of

course, nothing I'd like better. And so it was that, a week later, I went with Albert after Sunday services to celebrate Benjamin's fifth birthday and the first party he ever done had.

Albert, Elijah and me was sitting on the front porch after dinner, watching the boys play with the ball and jacks that Albert got Benjamin for his birthday. It was a nice warm day, and the boys were having a great time playing outside. Our bellies were full up with fried chicken, yeast rolls, mashed potatoes and chocolate cake. I hadn't liked the taste of chicken ever since I first saw one get its neck wrung. But Sally Ann's special fried chicken made me forget all about the poor critter and just enjoy my food.

When Elijah excused himself to go play with the boys, I asked Albert why Doc and his wife hadn't come. He said they was still grieving for Mary, but I wondered if maybe they didn't take kindly to another woman being in Elijah's house.

After a while, Elijah came back to the porch and sat down. Benjamin was having a high time, laughing and carrying on like little boys are supposed to do. His daddy looked pleased. He lit up a pipe and watched the smoke curl above his head. Then he started telling me about his first birthday party after he come to stay with Albert and Pearl.

"Why, it seems like yesterday that Sally Ann cooked fried chicken for my birthday dinner. It was as good this evening as it was then."

Albert chuckled. "I'll never forget the look on your face when we walked into the store after church and all them people were there for your party. You didn't know what to make of it."

"Who came to your party?" I asked.

Elijah said, "Isaiah and Henry were there with Sally Ann. Doc, his wife … and their girls."

He looked off in the distance, puffin' on his pipe. I knew he was thinking about Mary. Albert and I stayed quiet, and it wasn't long before he was back talking again.

"I'd never had a party before. We were poor, and my mother had to work all the time. I came to stay with Albert and Pearl when she got sick with consumption. We got word she died not too long after my birthday."

My voice was a mite rough when I spoke. "It's hard to lose your ma when you're a young'un. I lost my ma when I was ten. Ain't nobody can take her place."

"Pearl did a fine job of filling in the holes I had in my heart," Elijah said. "I came to love Pearl as my ma and Albert as my pa. And I felt blessed to have them in my life."

Chapter 27

"Yellow Teeth and Crazed Eyes"

Remember how I said there are times in your life when something so important happens you never forget the details of the day? For me, the last day I saw my ma alive was one of those. July 29, 1899, was another. I was teaching Sunday school by myself now, on account of Miss June was feeling too tired. That afternoon was so hot, all of us was dripping sweat by the time the children went home. Elijah had started coming to church regular, and most times we'd talk a spell when he came to get his boys. That day, he had to take Thomas home right away 'cause Doc wanted to spend time with his oldest grandson. Albert said he'd bring Daniel and Benjamin home later, after they'd had their Sunday dinner at his place.

Just as they was fixin' to leave, Edward asked Albert to come back inside the church 'cause he had supplies to order. Albert told the boys to play in the churchyard 'til he got done. Instead, they wandered off to the cemetery, back behind the church.

I was sweeping up my room when the sound of the boys screaming carried through the open windows. They sounded real scared. I took off running toward the cemetery with the broom still in my hand.

First, I saw the dog—a big mangy critter with matted black

hair and slobber dripping from his mouth. I spotted the boys a few feet further on. Daniel had Benjamin up against a headstone and was trying to shield him. The dog kept creeping closer and closer to them, growling and pawing the dirt. Daniel was hollering for the dog to get away, and tears were rolling down his cheeks. Then the dog crouched and bared his teeth. I hitched up my skirt with one hand and charged the dog with my broom, getting between him and the boys just as he started to pounce.

I saw his big yellow teeth and the crazed look in his eyes as he tore into my leg where I'd been holding up my skirt. He ripped into my flesh like I was a raw piece of meat. Blood began spewing everywhere, and I fell back to the ground with that dog on top of me. I remember pain and screaming, and—just before everything went black—a gunshot.

When I woke up, I found myself in a strange bed. I started to sit up but fell right back on the pillow. The room was spinning, and I felt sick. A man and a woman were standing by my bed.

"Where am I?"

"It's all right, Molly. I'm Dr. Patterson, and this is my wife, Martha. You're at our hospital in town."

I tried to speak but I felt too weak. I closed my eyes and went somewhere else. I don't know how long it was before I come around again. No light came through the bedroom window, so I knew it was night. Nathan and Martha, as I would come to call them, was sitting in chairs on either side of the bed, their eyes closed and their heads nodding a little. My leg hurt something awful. I must have let out a cry 'cause they got up and started looking me over good.

"You had us worried, Molly," Martha said.

Nathan put his instrument on my chest. He moved it around some so he could listen to my heart and lungs. Martha wiped off my forehead. I couldn't remember much after the dog got ahold of me, but I worried about Benjamin and Daniel. Maybe the dog got them once I couldn't fight him off no more.

"Are the boys OK?"

"They're doing fine, thanks to you."

"Thank the Lord! Did somebody shoot a gun?"

"Yes. Edward and Albert heard the commotion and hurried out of the church. Albert grabbed his hunting rifle from his buckboard, then ran to the cemetery. He fired the first shot up in the air, and it startled that dog so he let go of you. Then he shot him dead before he could attack you again."

"How did I get here?"

"Edward brung you," Martha answered. "Albert took the boys home to Elijah, then fetched your pa and brothers. All of them waited downstairs 'til we made them go home to get some sleep. You got a lot of folks who care about you, Molly."

Everything was a blur. The only thing I knew for sure was that Benjamin and Daniel were fine, but my leg felt like burning hot coals was cooking my skin.

Nathan sat down beside my bed. "That dog tore your leg up real bad. You lost a great deal of blood. We cleaned the wound, but I can't sew it up yet because we've got some things to watch out for."

"What do you mean?"

"Molly, you got bitten by a wild dog. We don't know what diseases he might have carried. Was he foaming at the mouth?"

"I remember his big teeth and crazy eyes. He did have a lot of spit coming out his mouth."

"I'm worried that the dog might have had rabies."

"I know about rabies. There's nothing you can do about that."

"Well, a man named Pasteur developed a vaccine for rabies. I'm trying to get ahold of some. We don't have any here, and there's none in Elizabethtown. I sent a messenger to my brother-in-law in Louisville to see if we can get some from the hospital there. We should know by tomorrow."

I knew of people who died of the rabies, and it wasn't an easy death. Folks would foam at the mouth and get crazy in the head. Some had convulsions before they died, and their loved ones were helpless to do anything. But the rabies wasn't all they was worried about. Nathan said, "I also got to watch you real careful to make sure you don't get gangrene in that leg."

I'm not a learned woman, but I'd heard about men losing their legs during the war on account of the gangrene.

"I thought that only happened if you got shot."

"I'm afraid you can get gangrene anytime a wound gets infected, especially when the blood supply is compromised."

I wasn't sure what the word *compromised* meant, but I knew it didn't sound good.

"Is that what happened to me?"

"We don't know yet."

"We need to keep you here so we can look after you," Martha said. "Nathan's a fine doctor, and he'll do everything he can to make sure your leg heals up proper."

Then she patted my arm and told me not to worry. Well, that was easier said than done. They left me alone to look in on their other patients. I closed my eyes and prayed to Jesus to save my leg if he could. I gave thanks that it was me who might get the rabies and the gangrene, and not one of the Fry boys.

Chapter 28

"Alcohol, Acid and Powerful Conversations"

Through the rest of the night and into the morning, Nathan and Martha stayed with me. When the pain got too bad, they gave me morphine, which helped me sleep but gave me bad dreams. I kept seeing Nathan with a saw in his hands getting ready to cut off my leg.

During the next day, Martha tried to get me to take some soup, but my stomach was too sick from the morphine. I was burning up with fever, so she kept a cold cloth on my forehead.

Late in the afternoon, the downstairs bell rang. I closed my eyes while they went to see who was there. When I opened them, they was standing with another man at the foot of my bed. The stranger wore a white shirt and black waistcoat and was holding a box. I could tell by the looks of him that he was someone important.

"Molly, this is my sister Miriam's husband, Herbert Smith."

Nathan took the box over to a table and opened it. Martha came to stand on one side of my bed, while Herbert stood on the other.

Martha said, "When the rider we sent told Herbert what had happened to you, he got ahold of the head of the hospital to see if they had the rabies vaccine."

Herbert spoke up. "I can't tell you how relieved I was, Miss Van

Meter, when he told me that they had a single vial of Pasteur's vaccine. I brought it here myself on the train because I didn't trust anybody else with it."

"Why did you go to all that trouble for me?"

"What you did to save my nephews was beyond brave. I wanted the chance to do something for you."

I thanked him from the bottom of my heart. Then Nathan asked Martha and Herbert to leave so he could give me a shot of vaccine. I expected it to hurt bad, but compared to the pain in my leg, it was nothing.

Nathan told me it would take months before we knew for sure whether I got the vaccine in time, or if I would get the rabies. In the meantime, he needed to make sure I didn't get the gangrene, so he asked Doc Middleton to come by.

The next day, Doc stood looking over me. During the war, he saw a lot of the gangrene. I could tell it pained him to look at my leg. "I want you to know how grateful Madeline and I are for what you did to save our grandsons. We will forever be in your debt."

He took my hand and patted it gently. "Molly, the only way I know to prevent you from getting gangrene is to clean the wound out every single day with a mixture of acid and alcohol to kill the germs. It's mighty strong stuff, and it's going to burn like hell every time we do it. We can't keep giving you morphine 'cause you'll get addicted to it. So the only time we can give something for the pain is if you can't stand it no more, and you'd rather I go ahead and take your leg off." He stopped, and we just stared at each other for a moment. Then he patted me again and said, "I'm so sorry you have to go through this."

When they began cleaning out the wound every day, I thought I was gonna die. That acid and alcohol burnt my wound clear through 'til it was bubbling. I tried to be brave and not scream out, but tears kept rolling down my cheeks 'til I thought I might drown from them. I kept telling myself to hang on. I'd be better soon, and then I could get back home to help Pa and my brothers. But as the days went on, my leg didn't heal up good liked we hoped. I kept getting infections that they had to dig out and clean.

The six weeks I spent with Nathan and Martha were some of the worst times of my life. But the Lord intended that something good come out of my suffering. And I'm here to say that it did.

The nights and mornings was the hardest. I had trouble sleeping sound on account of the pain wakin' me up. And I had to use a slop jar 'cause I couldn't get to the outhouse. The mornings when Nathan and Martha cleaned and dressed my leg were near unbearable. But in the afternoons, when I was feeling better, I got to visit with folks. Miss June and Edward come regular. Even Isaac come from Elizabethtown to see me.

Martha was so kind. She bathed me and fixed my hair before people come to call. She even got me some fancy nightdresses to wear so I'd look presentable. I liked the time we spent together. I asked her to tell me stories about growing up with Miriam and Mary. I especially liked hearing about Mary, since was real fond of her boys. I come to understand why Elijah loved her so much.

Pa visited when he had time to spare, which wasn't very often. I worried about how he was doing without me to cook and clean for him. Well, to my surprise, he said he was getting along just fine. Joost's wife, Elizabeth, come every day to tend to him. And Jansen had finally found a woman he fancied and wanted to marry. Her name was Caroline, and she was raised in Hardin County just like us. Pa told me that Jansen and Caroline was thinking of living right there on the farm so they could help out with chores. That pleased me something fierce 'cause that meant I didn't have to worry about Pa so much.

I got to tell you, I had some powerful conversations with people during that time. It all began with Thomas Fry.

Once I wasn't so crazy with pain, Albert brung the Fry boys to see me. All three of them ran to my bed and hugged me tight.

"Are you all right, Molly?" Daniel asked. "We've been worried sick about you."

"I'm doing fine. Don't you fret none."

"That dog would've killed us if it wasn't for you. Benjamin wakes up at night hollering sometimes."

"Why is that?" I asked.

"I keep seeing him tearing into you," Benjamin said. "I thought he was gonna kill you for sure."

"Well, I was a mite tougher than that, wasn't I? Let's put that mangy critter out of our minds for good. Tell me what you boys have been doing."

After we visited for a while, Thomas asked if he could have a word with me alone. That boy was a straight shooter like his granddaddy, so I was curious about what he had to tell me.

He said, "Miss Molly, I'm troubled by what happened this past year at school. I need your help figuring out what to do before school starts again."

I asked him to tell me about it.

"Well, it began late in the spring when the weather got warm. I don't know what was troubling Miss June, but she wasn't herself. After dinner, when it got hot, she'd fall asleep at her desk."

Poor Thomas looked pained. He stopped talking and stared down at his shoes. "Go on, Thomas. You can tell me," I said.

"I'm not proud of what we done, but sometimes we pulled the pins out of her hair bun when she was sleeping. And that wasn't the worst of it. A time or two, we all just went outside to play in the woods 'til it was time to go home. I don't know what Miss June thought when she woke up and found us all gone. She never said nothing to us 'cause we all would've got in trouble, her included."

What Thomas was saying broke my heart, but I tried to stay steady.

"Do you think Miss June is ailing?" I asked.

"I think so, ma'am," he replied. "Sometimes she seems weak as a little kitten and she don't talk so good."

"What do you mean?"

"Sometimes her words get all slurry like she's been drinking moonshine. But we all know she's a good Christian woman who doesn't drink a drop."

I thought about the times I'd seen Miss June lately, when she was almost too weak to walk and her words come out funny. I wanted to think she was just getting old and bothered by the heat. Now I felt mad for not looking deeper.

I said, "We better find out what's wrong with Miss June and see what we can do to help her."

Thomas nodded. "I love Miss June," he said. "She's good to us, and I don't want to see her suffer none."

Then he hugged me around my neck.

"I love you, too, Miss Molly," he said.

Oh, I just held that sweet boy close 'cause nobody done told me that before and meant it like he did.

Chapter 29

"Choices"

That night, when Martha and Nathan come to look in on me, I asked them to sit a spell. I wasn't too sure how to ask them since it wasn't none of my business, but Miss June was so important to me. So in my usual way, I just spit it out.

"I got to tell you both something. The happiest days of my life was when I was going to school with Miss June. And about the saddest time was when I couldn't get book learning from her no more."

I told them how Miss June made sure I got lessons and come to see Edward and me as often as she could. In fact, if it wasn't for Miss June, I wouldn't have been teaching Sunday school the day I saved the boys from that awful dog.

Nathan and Martha listened politely, but I could tell they wondered what I was going on about. "I know Miss June is ailing and I reckon you know it, too. Would you tell me what's wrong with her, so I can help? I love that woman like she was my ma."

Nathan and Martha looked at each other in a way that said they knew exactly what was wrong with Miss June. But was they was gonna tell me? Then I saw Martha nod her head and Nathan cleared his throat.

"What I'm about to say, Molly, has to remain between us."

Suddenly I wasn't sure if I wanted to hear more.

Nathan got to it. "I've been seeing Miss June for a couple of years now. She came to me when she started feeling some muscle weakness in her legs that made it hard to walk straight. At first, I didn't know what to think because I hadn't seen patients with symptoms like this before."

Martha said, "Then one day, she came to the clinic because she wasn't talking clearly. We worried she might be having a stroke like Nathan's mother, but that wasn't it at all. When Clara had the stroke, she didn't get better. Miss June's symptoms seemed to come and go."

"I read every medical journal I could get my hands on," Nathan said. "And the closest thing I can figure is that she has a neurological disease that's called *Sclérose en plaques*. If what I suspect is true, Miss June won't get better. She'll get along for awhile, but one day she won't be able to talk or get around."

I asked if he had some medicine he could give her.

He said, "No, there's no treatment. The disease affects her brain and spinal cord. She's going to die an early death, and that's a shame because she has no one to look after her."

I wanted to bawl my eyes out. I thought about what was gonna happen to her if I didn't do something. Finally, I said, "You better see to it that I get well then, so I can take care of that dear woman for the rest of her days."

I lay awake a long time that night thinking about Miss June. I remembered the talk I had with Edward after Ma died, when I told him I was mad at God and didn't like Him much. Over the years, I made peace with my faith. No matter how much you wish it weren't so, sometimes bad things happen to good people, like Ma and Miss June. And you wonder what God was thinking. There are other times when you know He was right there with you, like helping me keep the boys safe from that crazy dog.

I prayed hard that God would find a way for me to care for Miss June. I never could pronounce them fancy words that Nathan said. But I came to learn later that they called Miss June's ailment multiple sclerosis. It's easier just to say the MS.

A few days later, Miss June come calling. I was pleased to see her, but my heart hurt 'cause of what Nathan told me. It must've been a good day for the MS 'cause she spoke plain and was of a mind to talk about all kinds of things.

She told me about her kin in Louisville. Her ma and pa had been settled in their graves for many years, and she didn't have no brothers or sisters. She didn't go back there no more 'cause she'd been living in Uptonville so long that people in Louisville forgot about her.

"Do you feel at home here?"

Miss June said, "Yes, Molly, I do. I've loved every day teaching at the schoolhouse, but my time there is drawing to an end."

I knew why, of course, but I wasn't supposed to let on. So I said stupid things about how she was still a young woman who could teach awhile longer.

"No, Molly. It's time for Isaac to come home and take over. I might stay on a few weeks just to make his transition easier."

I couldn't bear to ask what she would do after that. I wanted to take care of her myself, but I knew Pa wouldn't hear of it. He'd growed even more stubborn in his ways. Miss June read me like a book.

"Don't fret, Molly. I've had a good life in Uptonville. I have memories to last me a lifetime. Why, do you remember the day Pastor Brown's boys got drunk in the woods? I'll never forget the look on their faces when they saw their pa standing with me outside the schoolhouse."

Both of us laughed at the thought of them fools staggering out of the woods, thinking it was just after dinner.

Miss June leaned in closer to me. "I never liked Pastor Brown's boys a lick. And ... a good licking is what they finally got!"

We laughed some more. Miss June told me she always kept a special place in her heart for Jesse and Sarah Cole. None of us knew what happened to them after their shack burnt down and they left town.

That afternoon, we talked like never before. Knowing how good Miss June was with young'uns, I'd always wondered something.

"Do you miss not having babies of your own?"

"More than you can possibly imagine!" The force of her answer took me back.

"Molly, I don't think I'm gonna live many more years, and it makes me sad to think I'll spend my final days alone. I never met a man to love, but I pray you do. You don't get to choose who you love. God does that. You only choose if you'll love that person or not."

Chapter 30

"Why Me?"

The following Sunday, I got a surprise that would've knocked me off my feet if I wasn't sitting down. It was August 27, and I'd been at the little hospital for a month. Other patients had come and gone, but I was still stuck there. I was feeling lonesome. I missed teaching Sunday school and being with the young'uns. I read my Bible that morning and ate a bite of dinner. I was hoping somebody had come calling when Martha hurried into my room. She got my brush and started running it through my straggly hair. She told me I had a visitor. He was downstairs having a word with Nathan.

"Well, who is it?" I asked her. "And why are you making such a fuss?"

"It's Elijah."

The room suddenly felt hot, and I asked Martha for a sip of water. Then I looked up and saw him standing in the doorway holding a big bunch of wildflowers.

"These are for you," he said, sticking out his arm. "The boys picked them this morning."

"Thank you, Elijah. They're beautiful."

"I'll fetch a vase," Martha said.

Elijah sat down in the chair by my bed.

"How are the boys?" I asked.

"They're doing fine, Molly. Albert's minding them so I could have a word with you. I'm sorry I haven't come to see you sooner."

"I figured you was busy," I said. But I'd wondered why he hadn't come before.

"To tell you the truth, Molly, I wasn't sure I could come back here after what happened to Mary."

"Of course, Elijah. I understand."

"Albert's been telling me all about your leg and what they got to do to keep the gangrene from setting in. I'm sorry you're having to go through this."

I started to say something, but he made me hush.

"Let me speak what's on my mind," Elijah said. "This may be the only time I get it right." He cleared his throat. "To begin, I want to thank you proper for saving my boys from that dog. What you did was very brave, and I'm sorry that you've been suffering on account of it."

I forced myself to stay quiet when he stopped to take a breath.

His voice was thick when he said, "Molly, I will always be grateful to you for showing me I still got enough heart left to love my boys."

I blinked hard so I didn't cry.

Thanks be to Jesus that Martha come in then with a vase. She didn't stay but a minute, but it gave me time to get ahold of myself. I thanked Elijah and told him how fond I was of his sons. I thought that would be the end of our talk. But he didn't move out of his chair.

"That was the easy part of what I came to tell you," he said, breathing kind of hard. "I respect you, Molly, and I want to be honest with you. Mary was the love of my life. I don't reckon I'll ever love a woman the way I loved her."

My mind began bouncing around in my head.

"My boys love you, Molly, and I got fond feelings toward you. I was wondering ..." He cleared his throat again. "I was wondering if we might keep company to get to know each other."

"What do you have in mind, Elijah?"

Oh my, that poor man got red in the face and started rubbing his hands together.

"I told you I lost my own mother when I was not much older than Thomas. I don't know what would've become of me if it hadn't been for Albert and Pearl."

I nodded my head to keep him going.

"I don't want my boys growing up without the care of a woman. I'm a fittin' daddy, but I can't take the place of their mama. I was wondering if we could spend time together to see if you might want to marry me and help me bring up my boys."

I could've fallen over with a whisper of wind. And for once in my life, my mind was working harder than my mouth. I thought about my visit with Miss June and what she told me about love. *You don't get to choose who you love. God does that. You only get to choose if you'll love that person or not.*

I didn't know yet what to make of Elijah Fry, but I had a tender place in my heart for his boys, so I said, "Elijah, I'd like you to come and see me while I'm still here so we can talk more. If I don't get the gangrene or the rabies, I think it would be fine to keep company. But I don't want to be in no hurry, and I want to do it right."

Elijah nodded his head, and the red went out of his cheeks. But my heart started pounding, and my hands began to sweat.

As summer began giving way to fall, I wondered if I would ever go home. My leg was doing better, but Nathan said I wasn't out of the woods yet. Elijah come to see me regular. After tending to the crop, he'd clean up and have supper with his boys, then come to sit a spell before nightfall. He didn't stay long, but he was a welcome sight at the end of an endless day of doing nothing.

Elijah talked a lot about his mother and how much he missed her. He talked some about Bo Fry, though he had no memory of the man hisself. "But I learned a lot from my father, Molly."

"You did?"

"I learned not to be the kind of man he was. I learned to honor my obligations instead of running from them. Most of all, I learned how to be a good daddy to my boys. I became the man I am because of what he wasn't. And for that, I thank Bo Fry."

I had to ponder that for a spell. I reckon we all got things that hurt us bad. Some folks just give in to the bad feelings and never move on. But a few blessed souls, like Elijah, take something out of their pain to make their own lives better.

Elijah didn't just talk about hisself. He wanted to know about me, too. I told him about growing up with Pa and my brothers after Ma and John died. I got sad talking about James. I hadn't seen him since he was a boy. He'd be a full-grown man now, and I couldn't picture what he looked like. I told Elijah that I hoped James was happy and that he was having a good life. I couldn't bear to think that he might be dead or that I'd never see him again.

"Do you know where he settled, Molly?"

"When he left, he said in his note that he was going to West Point, Kentucky, but we never heard a word from him after that."

I always felt kind of empty when Elijah left at night, but I spent a considerable time going over what he said in my head and slept better for it.

Martha seemed pleased that Elijah was coming to visit me regular. I was surprised 'cause she loved her sister Mary. I worked up my courage to ask her about that.

Martha said, "Mary could have had any number of rich suitors, but she saw something in Elijah that she valued more than money or social standing. Watching him with his boys and now with you has made me appreciate what she saw in him. Elijah Fry is a fine man, Molly, and worthy of your time."

"But why me, Martha? Elijah is a hardworking man with three fine sons. Couldn't he have any woman he fancied?"

Martha sat down beside my bed.

"Do you have any idea what a wonderful woman you are, Molly?"

I looked her in the eye. "Look at me, Martha. There's nothing pretty about me. Even my own ma, God bless her soul, didn't find me pleasing to look at. Your sister Mary was a beautiful lady. And Elijah is a good-looking man. Why would he want to spend time with me?"

Martha spoke gently. "Molly, I think the world of you. To tell you the truth, I admire you more than you can imagine."

"Why's that?"

"You've suffered more pain with your leg than most people do in a lifetime. But you've never complained. You just gave thanks that it was you instead of Daniel or Benjamin."

She took my hand and squeezed it. "There's no one I'd rather have as mother to my nephews than you. And Elijah Fry would be forever blessed to have you as his wife. Now that's all I'm going to say on the matter because I don't want to blubber like a baby. But I'll dance at your wedding, sure enough, as will Nathan, who loves you nearly as much as I do."

Martha tucked the covers around me, kissed me on the forehead and left me to my own quite amazed thoughts. I started to get teary-eyed 'cause of the good things she said about me. Then I thought of something that made me laugh out loud—that part about dancing at my wedding. Baptists didn't cotton to no dancing, even at weddings. But it sure sounded nice.

Chapter 31

"Worth It"

The third week in September, Nathan finally gave me the news I'd been hankering for.

"Molly, I feel confident your leg is gonna heal up just fine with no more infection."

"What about the rabies?"

He pursed his lips and took a moment.

"I don't think you're going to get rabies, but there are cases where it shows up months after a person's been bitten. I can't guarantee you're in the clear, but the more I read about the vaccine that we gave you, the better I feel."

Martha said, "What do you say we get you cleaned up proper and then take you home."

I was so happy, I couldn't say nothing for the tears rolling down my cheeks. Martha helped me bathe, then Nathan come to dress my leg a final time. Martha surprised me with a new blue dress she'd ordered from a catalogue. Riding back home in their buckboard, I felt like a queen in a carriage.

When we got there, Pa and my brothers was waiting. Nathan helped me down and onto the front porch. My leg pained me some, and I was weak from being in bed for weeks. But I didn't mind 'cause it felt so good to be home. I stood still a minute just breathing in the smell of earth before going inside.

The home place looked neat and tidy. I thanked Elizabeth for that.

Jansen grinned and said, "You might want to thank my wife, too."

"Your *wife*?" I said, grinning.

Caroline was standing behind Jansen, so I hadn't seen her yet.

"Molly, I'd like you to meet Caroline."

I welcomed her into the family with a big hug.

My brothers' wives were quite different. Elizabeth was a pretty golden-headed girl with soft green eyes. She was well suited to Joost in looks and temperament. Caroline was more timid, like Jansen, but she seemed real sweet. She had brown hair like me, but she was shorter and plumper.

I asked when they'd gotten married.

"We went to Elizabethtown a couple of weeks ago," Caroline said. "I don't have much kin, so there wasn't no need for a big wedding."

Caroline invited Nathan and Martha to stay for tea. I sat back in my chair amazed at the changes while I'd been gone. Inviting folks to tea of all things! Why, if I closed my eyes, I would think our little farmhouse was now a country manor. I didn't mean to laugh out loud with everybody staring at me. I was just happy to be home.

While we was drinking our tea, Nathan said he needed to talk about my care. I tried to tell him that it wasn't necessary, but Pa shut me up like I was a schoolgirl.

"Let the man talk, Molly."

"Yes, Molly," Nathan said with a jolly smile. "I intend to lay down the rules in front of everyone, so there's no way you can ignore them."

He set his cup on the table and looked at all of us real serious.

"I know Molly is a workhorse, but you got to keep her down for a while. She can help with the cooking and house chores, but I do not want her in the tobacco fields."

My mouth fell open so wide, it's a good thing there was no flies in the house. "What do you mean I can't go in the fields? That's where I belong, especially now during the busy season."

"Not this year, Molly. We got to let your leg finally heal up proper. Remember, I couldn't stitch it shut because of the infection. Now we have to give it time to close and scar over. We can't take a chance of the wound getting infected from working in the soil. Mr. Van Meter, may I have your word that you'll keep your stubborn daughter inside the house and out of the field?"

Pa looked at me hard and nodded. "You have my word."

"That's what I needed to hear," Nathan said, finishing his tea and then standing. "We'd better be going, Martha. Molly, I'll ride out to see you in a few days, and I expect you to be inside resting or doing light chores. Understood?"

I guess I had no choice.

Caroline and Jansen made their bed upstairs in the snuggery where my brothers used to sleep. My room was just down from Pa's. I had my bed and dresser with a wash bowl and slop jar. I had a curtain I could pull when it was time to dress or sleep. After being gone so long, I couldn't wait to sleep in my own bed.

Elizabeth and Joost stayed over at their little place but took most of their meals with us. Caroline and Elizabeth put supper on the table. It was plain to see that my brothers' wives were now in charge, and I was like a maiden auntie come to visit.

I thought it might take a few days before I let Elizabeth and Caroline know just which Van Meter woman was in charge. I laugh every time I think about that now, 'cause that never came to pass.

I waited 'til after supper on Sunday to ask Pa if I might have a word with him in private. It was a pleasant evening for late September, so we went out to the porch. I sat close to him in an old wicker chair. I looked him over good. He was fit and well but aging some, and that bothered me. He had wrinkle lines all around his eyes from working in the hot sun, and his hair was now more gray than brown.

"What you got on your mind, Molly?"

"Well, Pa, there's a man who's asked me to keep company with him. His name is Elijah Fry."

"Yes, Molly," Pa said nodding. "I know the man."

He stayed quiet for a few minutes, just gazing at the tobacco field. I knew better than to prod him.

When he looked at me, his eyes was full of kindness. "Molly, Elijah come to see me before he called on you the first time."

"Why did he do that?"

"He wanted my permission to court you."

"What did you tell him?"

"I said he had my permission to ask you about keeping company, but he was to mind your decision if you said no."

Well, now. That surprised me.

"I thank you for telling him that, Pa. Elijah's a good man, and I'm tender towards him. But I'm worried."

"What for?"

"What if he wants to get married? I'd feel awful to leave you."

It wasn't often that Jacob Van Meter smiled. But I'll never forget the grin that my pa plastered all over his face after I said that.

"Molly, my dear girl. Have you had a look around lately? I don't have just one of you naggin' me to eat my supper and clean my boots before coming in the house. Now I got three women fussin' and frettin', and that's at least two more than I can stand!"

We both started laughing so hard, I was afraid I might pee myself.

Pa took my hand and patted it. "My girl, you've taken fine care of me all these years since your ma died. I'm grateful, and I know your ma would be real proud of you. But time's come for you to have a life of your own and find what happiness you can on this earth. So you go on and keep company with Elijah. And if you decide that man is worthy of you, I'll walk you down the aisle and give you to him myself."

That night, I went to bed feeling warm in my soul, and that felt better than any quilt. I closed my eyes to sleep, but hot tears slid down my cheeks. It wasn't 'cause I was sad. No, sir, it was 'cause all my years staying on the farm to care for Pa and my brothers counted for something. I never got to finish school, but I kept my promise to my ma, and for the first time ever, I believed it had been worth it.

Chapter 32

"Treasured Birthday Dinner"

During the next few weeks, I healed up good and settled back into life on the farm. No matter what fuss I made, Pa wouldn't let me help with the crop. I had to stay inside and do women's work with my brothers' wives. It wasn't so bad except when they teased me about Elijah. I got all red in the face, and that kept them going about how I must be sweet on him. I told the hens to leave me alone and find something better to do. But I did smile inside when they fussed over me for having a beau.

Elijah come over one evening and we sat on the porch for a spell. I liked being outside in the fall 'cause when the sun went down, it got cool enough to catch your breath. I also liked the sound that creatures made at dusk, as they bid goodbye to summer and prepared for winter.

Elijah asked if I would take Sunday dinner with Albert, the boys and him. I said yes and asked what I could cook up to bring.

He said, "Molly, we want to take you out for Sunday dinner to the hotel in town. Albert says the food's real good, and there's plenty of it."

I said I'd be pleased to have dinner with them on Sunday. What I didn't say was that I'd never eaten in a hotel dining room before. It scared me some to think about it.

The next day, I told Elizabeth and Caroline the news. Oh, Lord, you would've thought I got invited to meet President William McKinley! They started frettin' over what I was gonna wear. Elizabeth said she had a pretty rose-colored dress that would look nice with my eyes. She was tall like me but more filled out. When I tried it on, it hung on my body like a rag strung on a clothesline. Well, that didn't stop the two of them none. They started nipping and tucking something fierce, and soon they'd sewed that dress up to fit me. I thought that was real generous 'cause that meant Elizabeth couldn't wear it no more.

I fretted to myself all week. Finally, on Thursday, I told Caroline and Elizabeth, "I hear you got to use fancy silverware to eat your meal at a hotel. I don't know how to do that."

On the farm, we ate simple with plain utensils and didn't worry about our manners.

Caroline said, "I'll show you how it's done after we feed the menfolk their noon dinner."

Sure enough, after we got the dishes done up, we pretended we was at the hotel having Sunday dinner. We didn't have no linen or fancy silver, but Caroline set the table best she could with dishes and tin drinking cups. She put our eating spoons and forks on one side of our plates and the knives on the other. We didn't do that when we ate our meals.

"How do you know how to do that?" I asked.

"I had to eat thisaway when Jansen and me had our wedding dinner at the hotel in Elizabethtown," Caroline said. "It was so grand I'll never forget how everything looked."

Elizabeth pretended to be the waiter, and Caroline made sure I used the knife and fork proper before setting them down on my plate. She took an old rag and told me to pretend it was something called a napkin. I poked it down the top of my dress in case I spilt something. She grabbed it back and said I couldn't do that. No, ma'am, them ladies at the hotel put the cloth in their lap. That didn't make no sense to me. You was more likely to spill something on the front of your dress before your lap, so what was the use of setting it there?

On Sunday morning, Elizabeth come over early. We fixed up ham and eggs for the menfolk and hurried them out to the barn just as quick as we could. Then she and Caroline fussed over my hair and my dress 'til it was time to go teach Sunday school.

I only had six young'uns that morning, and three of them were the Fry boys. Thomas, Daniel and Benjamin were wearing nice shirts and pants. They smelt good and their faces was clean. We all looked at one another and tried not to giggle 'cause we was so dressed up. The other three young'uns in my class didn't know what to think. I sat prim in my chair that morning when we talked about Jesus. I was telling the story of how he turned five loaves of bread and two fish into enough food to feed five thousand people.

The young'uns asked me how he done that. All I knew was that it was a miracle. I laughed to myself, thinking that those folks in the Bible story got to sit outside and eat their fish and bread with their fingers and didn't have to worry none about napkins and silver.

Right after preaching, Elijah and Albert come to my room. Elijah tipped the brim of his hat and took me by the arm to his buckboard. Albert had the boys ride with him down the gravel road to town.

When we got to the hotel, Elijah helped me down like I was a delicate little lady. I could hear his boys giggling behind us when he took my arm and said I looked pretty in my rose-colored dress.

The hotel wasn't very big. It looked more like a rich lady's house, with white shutters and fancy ironwork. Albert said it had eight rooms for guests to stay in. Just inside the doorway was the lobby, with red-velvet chairs for people to sit in when they took tea in the afternoon. Now ain't that something? I couldn't understand why people would stop to have tea during the day. Didn't they have chores to tend to?

The dining room was the grandest room in the hotel. Right

in the middle was a big round table with a sign on it that said: *Reserved For The Fry Party.*

The table was set with a white cloth, china plates and fancy silverware, just like Caroline said. The prettiest flowers I'd ever seen floated in a glass bowl. They weren't like the wildflowers that sprung up on the farm. I wondered where they got them.

When I got ready to sit down, my heart started thumping. I didn't want to do nothing to shame Albert or Elijah. Then Daniel did the sweetest thing. He held out my chair so I could sit and kissed my cheek. He sat down beside me and held my hand. Elijah took off his hat and sat on my other side, with Benjamin next to him. Thomas and Albert took the other chairs, and once we got settled in, all of us laughed out loud. See, we felt out of place 'cause we was simple folks. But it was easy to get over when we shared that feeling together.

I wondered why we was going through all of this fuss when I could've just cooked something up for Sunday dinner. Then a man dressed up in a black suit and white shirt came over to the table.

"Welcome to the Uptonville Hotel," he said. He turned to me. "Happy Birthday, Miss Molly." I almost fell out of my chair! Then Elijah, Albert and the boys all wished me a happy twentieth birthday, too. My real birthday would be on Tuesday, but this was close enough. The man said his name was Jamison and he'd be our waiter. He told me that Albert and Elijah had selected our meal beforehand, so there was nothing for me to do but enjoy myself.

I don't remember ever having a Sunday dinner that tasted as good as that one. We had beef that was cooked slow in a red wine sauce. I was scared at first to eat something cooked in wine. But Albert told me not to fret 'cause the alcohol had been cooked away, so all that was left was this sweet-tasting brown gravy on the meat. That beef with wine sauce was so tender, you could cut it with a fork.

We also had honey-sweetened carrots and new potatoes in garlic. Oh my, every morsel of food sang its own sweet song in my mouth. I had to mind not to smack my lips or suck my fingers. When my plate was empty and Jamison carried it away, I actually felt sad.

But then we had apple pie for dessert. I got to tell you, I am a fine cook, but I never tasted a pie that good. To top it all off, Jamison brung me my own special little chocolate cake and candy to take home. I ain't never felt so special, before or since, and I will treasure the memory of that birthday dinner 'til the day I die.

After we finished dinner, Thomas brung out a card that he'd made with his brothers. All of them had written their names the best they could under the word love. My heart done melted on the spot.

We finished our coffee, and Elijah paid the bill. Benjamin looked wore out from all the excitement. He got out of his chair and climbed up on my lap. Daniel, who was still sitting beside me, leaned in real close so no one else could hear.

"We love you, Molly. Please be our ma."

Tears come up in my eyes. I kissed his head and whispered that I loved him, too. I couldn't promise to be his ma 'cause his daddy hadn't asked me yet, but I let that little boy know that I loved him just as fierce as if I was his ma from the beginning.

Chapter 33

"The Agreement"

Elijah gathered up the flowers and sweets, then asked if I might ride out to his place for a visit before he took me home. Albert told the boys he was taking them back to the store for a rest.

It was a fine afternoon in October. The sun warmed our faces, and the sky was a bright shade of blue. I told Elijah how much I'd loved my birthday dinner and thanked him for his trouble. After that, we didn't have much to say. Elijah puffed on his pipe, and I enjoyed the ride.

As we come up the path to his place, I noticed that Elijah was sweating under the brim of his hat. He took it off and wiped his forehead with the sleeve of his shirt. I wondered why he was so warm, since there was a bit of a nip in the breeze.

He brung the horses to a halt right in front of the house. But he didn't make a move to get down. Instead he said, "Molly, I'd like to have a talk with you if you don't mind."

My heart dropped down a few inches.

The question he asked next made no sense. "You've only seen my house once, when you came for Benjamin's party. I thought maybe you might like to go inside and have a good look around, if you think it would be proper?"

Well, I didn't worry a whole lot about it being proper 'cause I knew I could take care of myself and run out quick if he tried to kiss me. But to tell you the truth, I had no worries about that. Elijah Fry was a gentleman who had morals.

He helped me down and up the stairs of the porch. I liked the porch a lot 'cause it circled clear around the house. You could tell straightaway that it was built sturdy and well. Whoever had put a hammer to the nails had put their heart and soul into every stroke.

There was a stone fireplace in the front room with comfortable chairs around it. The wooden eating table was just off to the left and had benches on either side. Elijah's house was nicer than Pa's 'cause it had a good-size kitchen with a potbelly stove, cupboards and a pantry, as well as a table to wash up dishes and fix food.

It was a fine home, not fancy but well-thought-out. Elijah's sleeping quarters was on the main floor, but we didn't go in there 'cause that wouldn't be fittin'. A sturdy ladder led to the loft, so the boys could climb to their beds at night just like my brothers had.

When we got done looking around, Elijah asked me to sit with him on the porch. He was still sweating a mite, and I asked if he was all right.

"I'm OK, Molly, just a mite nervous about what I got to say."

He filled his pipe with tobacco and lit it. "Molly, we've been keeping company just a few weeks. But I think we've gotten to know each other pretty good."

He breathed in deep a couple of times like he just couldn't get enough air to fill his lungs.

"My boys love you, sure enough. And during these past few weeks, I've come to have real tender feelings for you. So I was wondering ..."

Then he stopped and didn't say no more. I just sat firm in my wicker chair and gave him time to gather his thoughts. He blew them words out in one breath.

"I was wondering if you would marry me."

He didn't give me a chance to answer. "I had a talk with my

boys, and we want you to be part of our family, if you're agreeable. We could get married in the spring before we plant tobacco or go ahead and get married now. Thataway, we could settle in before Christmas and celebrate the birth of Jesus as a family. My boys told me they would like that a lot."

Now it was my turn to have trouble breathing. I don't know why Doc come to mind, but that was the first question I done asked.

"Have you talked to Doc about this?"

Elijah nodded. "Yes, we had a talk a couple of days ago. We came to an agreement if you said yes."

I wasn't sure what he meant by an *agreement*, but I didn't ask. I trusted that it would be all right. I had no idea how hard it would be to fulfill that agreement when the time came.

I stayed quiet to myself for a few minutes. My mind was swirling around with all kinds of thoughts. Then I said, "Let me ask you something, Elijah."

"Of course, Molly. Go ahead."

"You got plenty of room here in the house to make another bedroom, right?"

He looked at me queer, like he thought I meant I wanted to sleep separate from him. It took me awhile to find the right words to say what was in my heart. Finally, I found the courage.

"I would be honored to be your wife, Elijah, and a mama to your fine sons. I love them with all my heart. And I think I could come to love you that way, too. But there's someone else I love."

He looked at me real strange then.

"I come to find out that Miss June has something called MS and is not expected to live a long life. I told Nathan to make me well so I could care for her 'til the day she died. That's on account I love her like my own ma. I would be willing to marry you before Christmas if we could build a little room for Miss June. She's been alone for most of her life, and I want her to know the love of a family before she dies. Would you be of a mind to do that?"

Elijah puffed on his pipe and smiled. "Molly, I know how much

Miss June means to you. You have my word that our home will be her home as long as she lives."

I got to tell you, my heart swelled with love for this man when he told me that. And the very next day, he started building a room in the house just for her. That's when I knew I wanted to be his wife and mama to his children, those already born and those that might yet come.

Chapter 34

"Three Surprises"

Pa asked if I would like to wear Ma's wedding dress. Ma put it away real careful after they got married, so it didn't fall apart. He told me that he hadn't offered the dress to Elizabeth or Caroline 'cause it was saved for me. That touched my heart, and I told him I would be honored.

When I saw the dress, I got worried 'cause my ma was a beautiful woman with a full round figure. It had beads and lace on the front, and it was just about the prettiest dress I'd ever seen. I could picture Ma wearing it on her wedding day. She must've been a vision of loveliness. Caroline and Elizabeth were hens on fire to fix that dress to fit me proper. I was scared spitless when they started cutting it up like they was butchering a hog. They wouldn't let me see nothing 'til they got done and I tried it on. It looked every bit as beautiful as it had when Ma wore it, and it fit my bony body just like it was supposed to. With the scraps they cut off, they sewed me up a hat to wear and fancy bloomers for underneath.

We was planning a small wedding dinner in the meeting hall right after the nuptials. Everybody pitched in to help. I was told to stay out of the way 'cause it was to be my special day. That weren't easy for the likes of me, but I just fanned myself and did like they told me. Albert ordered all the food, and Elizabeth, Caroline and

Sally Ann did the cooking. I knew we would eat ourselves silly, and after that maybe I'd have a nice round figure for my wedding night.

Elizabeth and Caroline sat me down to talk about what to expect. What they told me made me weak in the knees. I'd seen horses and mules mate, and one time I'd even helped deliver a foal. Watching the act between farm animals didn't bother me none. But now it would be me and Elijah doing those things in our bed. I didn't want to think about my wifely duties, so I prayed to Jesus that I'd know what to do when the time come.

One afternoon about a week before the wedding, Elijah come over. He seemed real pleased with hisself. He made a point to tell me that Albert had ordered him a new suit to wear. He must've wanted me to know that he wasn't gonna wear the same one he wore to wed Mary. I hadn't given it much thought, but I did feel relieved when he told me that.

He took ahold of my hand and said, "I'm real glad we're getting married, Molly. I'm gonna get my hair trimmed and get a proper shave right before our wedding so I look nice for you." He kept smiling real big. "What else you got on your mind?" I asked.

"I got three surprises for you on our wedding day. The first one will come during our nuptials. The second I got planned for our dinner afterward. And the last surprise I'll have waiting for you when we get home."

The way Elijah looked at me made me feel warm inside. I knew then I didn't have to fret none about our wedding night.

On my wedding day, I got up early like always, but I wasn't allowed to help with breakfast. I took my bath the night before, so I didn't have much to do 'til it was time to go to the church. Elizabeth and Caroline wrapped my dress up in quilts and laid it flat in the buckboard. Pa asked me to ride with him so we could visit along the way. Joost and Jansen and their wives brung all the food they'd been cooking. Everybody bundled up good. We could tell by the smell in the air that snow was coming soon.

On the ride to church, Pa said he wanted me to have a good life with Elijah. He thanked me again for taking care of my brothers and him. And then he told me, "Molly, something has been troubling me a long time. I'm sorry I didn't let you go to school after your ma died. I hope you can find it in your heart to forgive me."

He took the reins in his right hand and covered my hand with the other. He looked me in the eye and said, "You were stronger than any of us, Molly, and I had to lean on you to get us through. I'm sorry for that."

Tears filled up my eyes. My pa never asked nobody to forgive him for nothing. I told him that I forgave him. But I didn't let go of his hand.

Pa carried my dress into the Sunday school room. Then he kissed me on the cheek and went outside to stand with my brothers. Caroline and Elizabeth brung tea and cakes for us to have while I was getting dressed.

Caroline showed me a picture of a lady with a fancy rolled-up hairdo. She wanted to fix my hair with pins to look just like it. I let her twist and roll my hair to her heart's delight. After that, she brung out a little pot of red goo. She put some on her finger and rubbed it on my lips and cheeks. I didn't want to look like no hussy on my wedding day, but Caroline said I needed some color on my pale face.

Then they tied a corset over my fancy bloomers and helped me into my dress. They pinned my wedding hat on top of my rolled-up hair. Then they stood back and looked me up and down. I thought about my first day of school when Ma done the same thing to make sure I was presentable. Ma was none too pleased with my looks that day and I feared they thought the same thing.

But Caroline smiled and said, "You look beautiful, Molly." And I knew she meant it.

Elizabeth said, "Now sit down here and don't move 'til it's time to go."

Then Miss June walked into the room, and my heart fluttered.

She was wearing a starched purple-flowered dress. She looked at me and dabbed her eyes with a lace hanky.

"Oh, Molly, my sweet Molly. I've been dreaming of this day for years."

I asked her to stay with me 'til it was time. She sat down and patted my hand. I'd been waiting 'til Elijah had her room ready to tell her the surprise. Now I begged her to look at me and listen careful. "Miss June, I love you like you was my own ma."

She said, "We're like the yellow yoke and white of an egg. Good together and hard to separate."

That made me smile. "There's something I want to ask you on my wedding day, and I'd be obliged if you said yes."

"What is it, Molly?"

I wasn't supposed to know how sick she was, so I told her something else that was true. "Miss June, Elijah's boys are a handful, and I don't know nothing about caring for them. Now that you're not gonna teach school no more ..."

I had to swallow hard to get out what I wanted to say. "I was wondering if you might come live with us and help me tend to the young'uns proper. It would mean the world to me and Elijah."

Well, that dear woman looked at me like she'd been struck down from lightning. She couldn't find her words. Then she put the hanky to her eyes again and said, "Oh, Molly. There's no place I'd rather be and nothing I'd rather do than help you with your family. If you truly want me ... then the answer is yes!"

We hugged and carried on 'til Elizabeth and Caroline started clucking that I was gonna ruin my dress. I was happier than I can tell you. I really was scared about raising them boys proper and maybe having more babies with Elijah. Having Miss June to help made me feel like I could do it.

The wedding was set for eleven o'clock, but folks started coming well before then. I watched them through the window and got shaky in my belly.

Doc and Mrs. Middleton was standing with Nathan and Martha.

I felt honored that they'd come 'cause I knew they must remember the day that Mary wed Elijah. I heard Mrs. Middleton was having sad spells and didn't want nobody coming to see her. I hoped that being around these good folks might lift her spirits some.

Sally Ann and Henry stood off to the side of the church, talking to Isaac and a man standing with his back to me. I don't remember ever seeing no colored folks at our little church before, and I wondered if Henry and Sally Ann felt uneasy.

Caroline and Elizabeth made me step over to the side of the window 'cause it was bad luck for folks to see the bride on her wedding day before the groom did. When they saw Elijah coming up the road with his boys, they made me get away from the window all together.

Then everybody went into the church 'cause the wedding was about to start. Joost and Jansen came to fetch their wives and Miss June. Pa come and said, "Molly, I wish your ma could see how pretty you look in her dress. Elijah Fry better treat you good 'cause he's marrying the finest woman I know next to your ma."

When Pa and me entered the church, everybody stood. I stared straight ahead, feeling weak in the knees. Elijah looked mighty handsome in his wedding suit, with his hair trimmed proper. Pa gave me a kiss when we got to Elijah. Then he sat down in the front pew beside Miss June, Albert and the boys. Thomas, Daniel and Benjamin was all dressed up and smiling from ear to ear. Elijah took me by the arm, and we turned to face my brother Edward.

He looked every bit the preacher with his straight-combed light-brown hair, vest, suspender britches, and the spectacles Nathan had gotten him. His voice was gentle, but he looked at us stern when he told us that Elijah was to keep faithful to me and I was to submit to him. I wasn't too sure what that meant but I nodded my head. When I heard I was to honor and obey him, too, I smiled to myself. I knew I could honor Elijah 'cause he was a good man. But I didn't take kindly to obeying nobody. We'd have to talk about that later on.

Remember about the three surprises Elijah had for me? The first one come when he placed the wedding ring on my finger. He looked me straight in the eye and said, "My beloved Molly, this ring belonged to Pearl, and I know she would want you to have it. She was a wonderful ma to me, just like you'll be to my boys."

My breath went clean out of my body when he put that lovely pearl ring on my finger. And, from then on, every time I looked at it, I thought of Pearl, and my heart felt warm.

After Edward declared us husband and wife, we walked down the aisle holding hands and went to the meeting hall. We sat at the center of a long table, facing everyone else. Albert, Pa, Miss June and the boys sat with us. I looked out and saw everybody I loved, even Henry and Sally Ann, who was sitting with the Middletons.

Before we started to eat, Edward offered up a prayer. Then Elijah stood and faced me. Everyone stayed quiet.

"Molly, I told you I had a surprise to give you at our wedding dinner. So before we start to eat, there's one more person who has come to join us."

The door opened, and I saw the man I'd seen earlier with Isaac, Henry and Sally Ann. At first, I just stared. He had a full beard and a stocky build. When he took off his hat, I noticed his hair was red with flecks of gray. As he started toward me, I saw his brown-green eyes. It was the eyes I recognized after all these years. My hand flew to my mouth.

"*James!* Is it really you?"

Well, he raced to my table and scooped me up in his big, strong arms. He held me tight, and I cried. Then I asked him how he'd come to be here.

"Elijah came to West Point right after you said you'd marry him. He found me and told me how much you missed me. When he asked me to come to the wedding, I told him I would, as a surprise for you, if it was OK with Pa."

I come to learn that everybody but me knew about Elijah's

surprise. As a matter of fact, James had come a few days early to make peace with the family. He stayed over at Isaac's little place near the schoolhouse so I wouldn't see him. Pa and my brothers made up with him there. I was so overcome with joy that I grabbed my husband and kissed him right on the mouth. Everybody laughed 'cause now that we was married, it was OK to kiss him.

Elijah pulled a chair up to our table so James could sit by me while we ate our dinner. He told me that he was a riverboat captain, and had a wife and two daughters in West Point.

"Why did you stay away all these years?"

"Molly, I lost my way when John died. It took me a long time to find myself again. By then, five years turned into ten and then fifteen. After so long, I didn't think I'd be welcome here no more."

Well, thanks to Elijah Fry, from that day on, our family felt whole once again—except, of course, for Ma and John.

I can't tell you how content I felt on the ride from the church to my new home. It had just started to snow. The boys were staying with Albert, so we could have the place to ourselves for a day or two. Henry and Sally Ann had left right after dinner to start a nice fire and to bring the nightdress Elizabeth and Caroline had made for my wedding night.

As we come into the house, Elijah asked me to close my eyes for the final surprise. He led me across the living room to the fireplace and said, "Open your eyes, Molly."

There set the finest wood rocker I ever saw. I sat right down and tried it out. It creaked on the floorboards as I rocked back and forth.

Can you hear it now? It's been rocking and creaking that way since my first time sitting in it on our wedding night. Elijah paid nearly three dollars for it, a lot of money in them days.

He pulled up a straight-backed chair and sat down beside me.

"Albert and I ordered this rocker out of the Sears and Roebuck catalogue."

I come to love that catalogue. You could find just about anything you wanted in them pages. Then after you was done with it, you could use the pages to wipe yourself in the outhouse.

"How did you come to get me a rocker?" I asked.

"I remembered the way you rocked Benjamin back and forth that day at the church when you was comforting him about his birthday. You didn't have a proper rocker, but that didn't stop you! I got this chair for you to rock our babies because I want to have babies with you, Molly Fry."

He stood and took me by the hand and led me to our room. There was something I had to ask him before we took to our marriage bed.

"Elijah, what if I can't have babies? Would you still want me to be your wife?"

My husband looked me gentle in the eyes as he started taking the pins out of my hair. He said, "Yes, Molly, I would." And I knew he meant it.

Let me just say I needn't have fretted about having his baby. Nine months later, Nathan and Martha delivered our firstborn child, a girl who was just as sweet as she could be. She had a fine head of hair when she come out and a wail to set a body's teeth on edge. She was plump and red-cheeked and a pure pleasure to behold. Why, she started suckling at my breast an hour after she was born. We named her Viola 'cause she reminded us of pretty little violets that grow wild in the springtime, and we wanted her to know how special she was.

I held Viola close right after she was born and rocked her in this here rocker … and every baby that come after.

MOLLY and ELIJAH

Chapter 35

"Hot Dry Dust"

Two more babies come right after Viola. We had a son named Clifford the following year and then a daughter, Irene. I don't know what I would've done without Miss June. For a while, all I did was put another young'un on my breast right after one got done sucking. When one baby started wailing, so did the other two. We just had to laugh 'cause there wasn't a quiet corner in the whole house. Most times when we sat down for supper, I had two babies on my lap and Miss June had the other. It's hard to get a good mouthful of food with babies squirming all over you. Truth was, we didn't mind, though there were times we couldn't walk straight after too many nights without sleep. I come to find out there wasn't nothing sweeter in the world than rocking my babies to sleep in my rocker with my husband sitting nearby.

Elijah and Henry worked the fields together, just like they done when they was boys. Doc told Henry that in return for helping with the crops, he could have the house he lived in with Sally Ann and use of ten acres 'til Doc died. The money Henry made from the sale of his tobacco and part of ours provided him and Sally Ann a good living. That first year, on the day the crops sold and he was paid his fair share out of the proceeds, Henry stopped by and announced this was the happiest day of his life.

"I'm proud to grow and sell tobacco," he told me. "Reminds me that I'm a working man and no man's slave."

Henry had grown into a big, strong man with thick arms and sturdy legs. I liked sitting on the porch and watching him and Elijah working in the fields. It made me sad, though, that Henry had no wife and young'uns of his own. The colored gal he fancied just before Isaiah died married another fella and moved away. I asked him once if he didn't want to find a good wife. He just shook his head no. "I got my hands full up, Molly, working the land and looking after Mama. If the good Lord intends a woman for me, then He'll just have to bring her here. Otherwise, this is just the way it's gonna be."

Once Irene come, I stopped having babies for a while. Elijah and me was grateful 'cause it gave us time build on to the house and settle down with our six young'uns and Miss June. Life moved along like a gently flowing stream 'til the day in 1906 that turned our world upside down.

It was the time of year that was hot and dry in Kentucky, good for growing tobacco but not for quenching thirst. I didn't do good in the heat that summer, and I wondered if I might have another baby on the way. I hadn't said nothing to Elijah 'cause I wanted to be sure before I told him. I couldn't keep the house swept clean for all the dust the south wind blew in. Everything we touched felt like grit. It hadn't rained in weeks, and Elijah feared we was in for a nasty drought.

Viola turned six that year. She was a feisty little thing who was like me in thinking she could keep up with her older brothers. She didn't much like being confined to the house when she could be running through the tobacco fields chasing after Benjamin. Clifford, at the age of five, followed his daddy around like a hound dog and never stopped asking about what he was doing.

Irene was three and just learning to talk good. She was shy around most people and hung on to Miss June's skirt most days. It warmed my heart to see the bond the two of them had. Miss June was just about the finest grandmother I ever seen. She was kind and patient with all the children, but Irene was her favorite. Miss June put that baby on her lap every afternoon to read her a story. The first word Irene said was "MiJu" for Miss June, and that's what all the young'uns called Miss June thereafter.

By the summer of 1906, Elijah's boys were near on grown men. Thomas was fifteen and took after Doc with his slender build and serious nature. The two of them seemed to spend all their spare time together reading every book Doc had on the subject of doctoring.

"I reckon you want to grow up to be a sawbones, just like your granddaddy," I told Thomas one day. But he corrected me.

"Nobody says *sawbones* anymore 'cause doctors now have to do a whole lot more than cut off arms and legs. They have to learn all about diseases and how to treat folks proper so they can live longer."

At fourteen, Daniel had curly dark hair and big blue eyes. Elijah said he looked like Mary. He was a charmer to be sure, and I saw how silly girls acted around him. Elijah worried some 'cause he didn't want Daniel growing up to be like Bo Fry.

Speaking of Bo, Elijah come home from town one day with news about his father. A man come from New Orleans to tell Albert that his brother was dead. Seems he got caught in bed with another man's wife, and the husband shot him dead away. I asked Elijah how he felt hearing the news.

"Molly, Bo Fry was never a daddy to me, so I got no good feelings for the man. But after the way he treated my mother, I think getting shot naked in bed was a fittin' way for him to die." After that, we never spoke about Bo Fry again.

Benjamin was twelve that July day in 1906. He was tender-hearted, and he and I was just about as close as any ma and son could be. Oh, how I loved that boy and treasured the time we spent together. I knew I'd be losing him to manhood soon.

I was proud of all three of them boys. They was fine big brothers to Viola, Clifford and Irene. The young'uns required most all my time and Miss June's. But the boys never complained. I wanted to do something special for them so they'd know how much I loved them. School was starting soon, and I told the boys I'd buy them new clothes. That's what we was doing in town on that awful day.

Chapter 36

"Missing Pearl"

Thomas, Daniel and Benjamin went to the same country schoolhouse that I had. They loved my brother Isaac and learnt from him good. They could've gone to the school in town, but they wanted no part of any other teacher.

I have to tell you about my brother Isaac. He stayed tall and skinny like me, with sharp features, but he was as kind as the day was long. He loved teaching young'uns how to read and write. He kept Miss June and me entertained with endless stories about their escapades. Now there's a word for you. *Escapades*. Isaac taught me that word, and it means what things they did that was daring and adventurous.

Isaac was in no hurry to get married. All he could think about was being the best teacher in Hardin County. He was like Miss June that way. I was getting worried 'cause my brother was near on thirty years old. Miss June told me not to fret; God would bring him a suitable wife when the time was right. And that is just what happened.

Her name was Lela Howard. In 1905, her daddy, George Howard, bought the Uptonville Hotel and was making fancy changes to the place. Isaac and Lela met when they was both at Albert's store, buying supplies. Lela's ma died when she was a young'un, just like mine, so we had a bond.

Lela helped her daddy run the hotel, but that didn't stop her from keeping company with Isaac. When he wasn't teaching school, he'd work right alongside her at the hotel. That's what he was doing on that particular Saturday 'cause the hotel was especially busy.

When I told Elijah I wanted to take the boys to town, he said it might be nice if we spent the night with Albert. Thataway, we could take our time picking out what we wanted and be in no hurry to get home before dark.

Albert was tickled to have us stay. The boys had a good time going through the Sears and Roebuck catalogue and choosing new shirts and pants. I loved looking at the fancy gadgets and spent so much time on each page that the boys started to get restless. I sent them over to the hotel to see Isaac and Lela. Albert and me sat down in the front room for a good visit while they was gone.

Albert was getting on in years, but he took good care of hisself. His mind was as sharp as the point of a nail. I knew he missed Pearl something dreadful. He showed me a picture in a pretty wood frame that he kept by his chair, a real nice likeness of him and Pearl together on a bench outside the store. He said he liked sitting in front of the wood stove of an evening and holding it, thinking about the good times they had together. "I had that made a year before Pearl died. A fella came to town with a covered wagon filled with picture-making supplies. It cost me near on ten dollars, but it's been worth every cent."

He looked at the picture real tender and wiped his eyes on the sleeve of his shirt. "I'll tell you something, Molly," he said, setting the picture back on the table. "There's nothing I own that means more to me than this here likeness of my Pearl."

I liked spending time with Albert, but I thought it would be good to get him thinking about something other than his lost wife. "How did you come to start up your store in the first place?" I asked.

"I grew up on a farm about thirty miles from here," Albert

said, "but I knew I didn't want to be no farmer. I set out to find another way to make a living. I come to meet Larsen Upton, whose kin owned several hundred acres of land they wanted to sell to homesteaders. Once the farmers came, they needed a way to get supplies. The Uptons built the store in 1856 and helped me get started. It's been a good business ever since."

Albert got a faraway look in his eyes. "Why, when Elijah first come to stay with us, this town only had my store, the bank and the train depot. Next come the blacksmith shop, and then the Uptons built the hotel in 1885. After that come the tavern and boarding house."

Albert told me all about the man who built the barbershop next to the tavern in 1902 and about his wife who fixed up ladies' hair in a back room of the same building.

"Nowadays, they even got a telegraph at the train depot, and there's talk about running a telephone line in town."

Albert said he was mighty impressed with Lela's daddy and the changes he was making to the hotel. "They got fancy kerosene lanterns that they light of an evening in the dining room. They say it makes the place feel warm and cozy. You know what Mr. Howard's got planned for next year? He's gonna put toilets inside the hotel, so folks don't have to use slop jars or the outhouse no more."

I was shocked. "Toilets inside the hotel! How they gonna do that, Albert?"

Albert couldn't say how it was all gonna work, but he knew they was building water closets for the toilets and some kind of steam pump for water that would go into a contraption on the roof. It was more than I could grasp. "I never thought I'd live to see Uptonville booming the way it has, Molly. I wish Pearl was here to enjoy it with me."

Chapter 37

"Burning Rubble"

The sun was just beginning to set when Benjamin come running into the store. Isaac and Lela wondered if the boys could join them for supper. "Lela said to tell you that they cooked up way more food than they need tonight 'cause of a meeting in the hotel. And there's more than enough for you and Albert, if you would like to come. Otherwise, we'll bring you a plate after we get done eating."

I told Benjamin to go on along but not to make a bother of hisself once they done ate their supper. Albert warned him to keep away from the hotel guests. When Benjamin was gone, I asked him what he meant.

"There's some bad people come here from Elizabethtown to stir up trouble."

"What kind of trouble?"

"Them men don't like colored folks," Albert said. "They say that ever since coloreds got freed, they been trying to take the country away from white folks. They're asking men around here to join them to make sure that doesn't happen."

A shiver ran down my back. I didn't understand none of this. Henry and Sally Ann wasn't trying to take over nothing. Henry worked hard every day alongside Elijah, and there wasn't a sweeter soul on the face of the earth than Sally Ann.

Albert frowned and spit a wad in his spittoon.

"Elijah knows the fella who's causing the ruckus."

"Who is he?"

But before he could say more, we smelt smoke and heard people yelling. We ran outside and I saw smoke coming out of the front windows of the hotel, two doors down from the store.

"Oh, sweet Jesus!" I cried out, thinking of my boys and my brother being in there. We ran to the hotel just as Lela come out of the door with the boys beside her. I grabbed them tight.

"What happened?" I asked. It took a minute for Lela to catch her breath.

"We were eating supper in the front room when we heard shouting coming from the dining room. My daddy told us to stay put while Isaac and him went to see what was happening. We heard glass breaking, and then I smelled smoke. Isaac came running and told us to get outside quick. Now he's helping my daddy get everyone else out."

Men were starting to run out of the hotel. Most of them was coughing bad. Some fell into the dirt, and a couple of them was bloodied up bad. Lela and the boys helped me move them across the road to the train depot. I told Thomas to run and fetch Nathan.

There must've been twenty men who come out of the front door of the hotel. Two colored fellas ran out the back, but I didn't see Isaac or Lela's daddy anywhere. Just then, we heard crashing sounds and saw that the fire was spreading. One of the men took charge. He shouted for people to find buckets to collect water. Albert told everyone to run quick to the store to get whatever they needed. Then the man, whose name was Johnny, had them form what he called a fire brigade.

Them buildings in town was built to stand together, so if we didn't put the fire out quick, they'd all go up in flames. Albert didn't have enough buckets for all the townfolk who come running to help. Johnny told some of the men to fetch water from the town well and pass buckets on to the people at the end of the line. They'd pass them up as fast as they could, and the men in front would throw the water on the fire. Then young'uns would run the empty buckets back to the well. We kept moving them buckets just as fast as we could, but I was afeared it wasn't fast enough.

By now it was starting to get dark, and all we could see was the color orange taking over the hotel and lighting up the street. Oh, how I prayed that Isaac would come staggering out. I knew if he didn't get out soon, it would be too late. I caught sight of Albert outside his store. He had a look of pure dread on his face. If the fire spread, it would get to his store right after the bank.

Just then, Lela started screaming, "Isaac! Daddy!"

My brother tumbled into the street carrying a man in his arms just as the hotel caved in on itself. Nathan ran to them right away. Isaac was sick from the smoke, and the other fella was burnt bad. Turns out, he wasn't Lela's daddy.

Nathan said most of the folks who got out of the fire was gonna be OK. But Isaac, the man he rescued, and four other people was in bad shape. He asked me to come help him and Martha care for them at the hospital. We brung Lela, too, 'cause we knew she couldn't do nothing about her daddy. There was no way he could get out now.

A few men helped us carry the injured to the hospital. The rest kept trying to put out the fire even as it began to eat up the other buildings.

We worked clean through the night tending to those poor souls. Nathan wasn't sure the burnt men would make it. But Isaac come 'round to hisself a few hours later. Nathan thought he would get better in time if he didn't have no complications from breathing in so much smoke. Lela promised she'd take good care of him. Then she broke down and sobbed her heart out. She knew that her daddy was dead, and the hotel and boardinghouse were gone.

I went outside to get some air. The sun hadn't come all the way up yet, and I could still see flashes of fire in the sky. It wasn't raging no more, so I knew the town was gone. A thick cloud of smoke hung low in the air. I began coughing and started to turn away, but I saw a man walk through the smoke toward me. My eyes were tearing, and it took me a moment to see who it was.

"Oh, Elijah!" I cried, running into his arms. It was the first time all night I'd felt safe.

"I'm sorry I didn't get to you sooner. I was with the boys."

"Are they OK?"

"They worked the line most of the night. They're exhausted." Elijah paused for a moment to catch his breath. Then he said, "Is Albert with you?"

"No," I said. "I figured he was with the boys."

"They haven't seen him since the fire started spreading. They thought maybe he'd come here with you."

I took Elijah's hand and said, "Let's go look for him. Last time I saw him, he was standing outside the store."

As we started walking, I got dizzy and thought I was gonna faint. But I stayed on my feet. We walked down what had been the main street of our town. Piles of burning rubble lay where the hotel, store, bank, blacksmith shop, boardinghouse, tavern and barbershop had stood. The fire brigade had done all it could, but the fire was too strong. At least they kept the fire from spreading across the street to the train depot or around the block to the hospital.

All during the night and into the morning, folks from surrounding farms come to help. They must've seen the orange sky and made their way to town. Pa, Joost and Jansen were among them. Doc and Henry, too.

We had to wait 'til afternoon, when the fire died out, to search the pile of bricks and wood for Albert. I told Elijah to look by the wood stove, and that's where he found him. He'd gone into the store to save the thing that mattered most to him, and he died right there, holding on to the picture of him and Pearl.

Elijah was overcome with grief and anger. I tried to get him to go home with me and the boys, but he wouldn't hear of it … not 'til he found out what caused the fire that killed his pa. We went back to the hospital to see what Isaac could tell him.

"What do you remember about the fire?" Elijah asked.

"We were eating supper when we heard a ruckus coming from the dining room," Isaac said in a hoarse whisper. "Mr. Howard and I went to see what it was about. When we got there, men were cursing and shoving each other. We tried to break them up. Then we saw a man in the center of the room holding Jerome up by his collar and jerking him hard."

"Who's Jerome?" Elijah asked.

"He's the colored boy who works in the dining room. I could tell he was scared. The man holding Jerome was slurring his words and saying ugly things."

"What things?" I asked.

"He called me a nigger lover. I tried to reason with him, but he wouldn't listen. Next thing I knew, he shoved that poor boy as hard as he could into a table and came after me. Mr. Howard pulled him off. Then we smelled smoke and saw that a kerosene lamp had been knocked over, and fire was crawling up a tablecloth. It spread fast."

Isaac started coughing bad. Nathan come in to listen to his chest. He shook his head. "You need to come back later. Isaac needs to rest."

Elijah said, "Can I ask him just one more question?"

"Go ahead."

"Did you know the man causing the trouble?"

"He wasn't from around here," Isaac whispered. "Never seen him before."

Nathan followed us out of Isaac's room. He put his hand on Elijah's shoulder and told him how sorry he was about Albert. Elijah got that look on his face I saw only a few times, when he was mad and gone to what he called his dark place.

"Don't go do nothing foolish, Elijah," Nathan said. "This was a terrible accident. It's nobody's fault."

"The hell it was!" Elijah turned and stormed away.

Nathan stopped me from following him. "I'm worried about him," he said.

I nodded 'cause I felt the same way. "Albert meant the world to him. I don't know how he's gonna get over this."

"We need to calm things down. I'm gonna send for my brother-in-law. Maybe Herbert can help folks focus on rebuilding instead of revenge."

Chapter 38

"From Sorrow to Hope"

The man Isaac saved lived to tell his story. Seems he and another fella drank too much whiskey early in the afternoon and staggered up to their rooms to sleep it off. Just when Isaac and George thought they got everybody out safe, someone shouted that two men was still upstairs. The fire was raging through the hotel, but Isaac and George couldn't leave those fellas to burn to death in their beds.

They got ahold of one man and put him on the floor. George started dragging him by the feet, while Isaac scooped up the other man in his arms and ran for the stairs. He thought George was close by, but just as he got to the front door, the roof and walls fell in behind him. He knew then that neither George nor the man they called Smithy made it out alive.

The stories about Isaac and George traveled all around Hardin County. Both men were heroes in the eyes of everyone who lived near Uptonville. For the rest of his days, Isaac carried a sadness with him that he survived the fire but George did not.

Elijah and Lela decided to hold one service for both Albert and George a few days after the fire. Thataway, folks only had to come once to pay their respects. Edward gave them a fittin' send-off, and we buried them in the cemetery behind the church. Most everyone from around these parts come to the funeral.

Herbert Smith attended, and my brother James come from West Point. Doc was there, along with Pa, my brothers and their wives. Miss June sat with our young'uns so she could mind them. Sally Ann come with Henry, who was suffering the loss of Albert near as much as Elijah was, since his daddy had worked for him all those years.

After the burials, we all gathered in the meeting hall for dinner. We had quite a spread that day, sure enough. One thing about country folks never changes. It doesn't matter a lick whether it's a wedding or a funeral; people cook up all the food they got to share.

Edward offered up a prayer to bless the bounty of the food. He asked people to stay awhile after dinner so Herbert Smith could have a word with them.

Herbert was the most successful man I ever met. By this time, he was running the railroad with his Uncle Milton. Yet he was still as plain and polite as he was the day he told Sally Ann how good her cooking was. I could tell by the flush of his cheeks that he felt uneasy speaking before a crowd. But he cleared his throat, cleaned his spectacles and got right to it.

"I know you've suffered a terrible tragedy," he began. "Not only the deaths of Albert Fry and George Howard, but also the loss of your beloved town. Before the service, I had a meeting with Garrison Upton, Doc Middleton and James Van Meter to discuss the town's future. Here's what I want you to know. You folks are important to all of us at the L&N Railroad. We've counted on your business for many years. Now you can count on us to help you rebuild, if that's what you elect to do."

Folks were so filled with sadness that nobody had given much thought to how they'd build back the town. Where was they gonna get the money to do that? A man in the crowd shouted out, "Just how does the railroad plan to help?"

Herbert said, "We plan to donate a substantial sum of money to get you started. Miss Lela, we'd like to work with you to rebuild the hotel because it's real important that we have a place for people to stay when they have business in these parts."

My brother James spoke up. "I'd like to give back to the town where I was born. Elijah, I'd be proud to help you get Albert's store up and running again if you want."

Elijah's forehead wrinkled up. Finally, he said, "James, I'd be pleased to see my pa's store rebuilt, but I don't know who would run it. I stay plenty busy with our farm and I can't do both."

Much to my surprise, Daniel had something to say. "Pa, I always liked Pappy's store. Maybe you'd consider letting me run it."

I could feel the mood in the room changing from sorrow to hope.

People started asking all kinds of questions about what it would take to rebuild the town. James had some fine thoughts. He said, "We done this very thing in West Point. We gotta begin by deciding what people want."

Everyone started talking, and Herbert had to try to get ahold of things. But it was all right 'cause folks were excited and not carrying on about nonsense.

The barber said he and his wife would like to build back their place. Another man talked about starting a creamery. The blacksmith, Mr. Henley, said he'd start over if we could raise the money.

Herbert said, "Garrison Upton told me that he wants to reopen the bank."

Then James asked for people's attention. "If you're gonna start over," he said, "then let's do it right. Why, you could have telephones, electricity and paved brick streets. You're gonna need a mayor and maybe even a sheriff."

"And some kind of firefighting contraption!" a woman called out. "I don't never want to depend on no fire brigade again!"

Everyone agreed with that! Herbert and James said they'd be glad to get things rolling, finding investors and seeing what other towns our size had going good for them. Folks decided to meet again in a couple of weeks.

I saw a smile on Lela's face for the first time since her daddy died. And not too long after that, we come back to the little church so Isaac and Lela could speak their vows in front of God and Edward and begin their new life.

As time went on, it become clear that the young folks, like Isaac, Lela and Daniel, would rebuild the town to suit their needs. It took a few years, but sure enough, the day come when Daniel ran the general store and Lela had a fine hotel with electricity, indoor toilets and a telephone.

But I'm getting ahead of myself. Before the rebuilding, one more thing had to happen, and it was Henry who made that possible. I'd always had a tender spot in my heart for Henry Jackson, but never more than when he told me what he done that same day.

Chapter 39

"Hateful Men"

Henry had many fine qualities, but two things stood out. First, he was a good judge of character, and second, he was a wise man. After the meeting ended, he asked Doc if he, Elijah, Herbert and James could meet with him at Doc's house. That afternoon, Sally Ann settled the men in the library and fetched their tea. Then Henry come in. He was nervous at first, but Doc put him at ease. He sat down in a chair beside Elijah, facing the other men.

Henry said, "I like what you had to say about rebuilding our town, Mr. Smith, and you too, James. And there's nobody I respect more than Doc and Elijah. So I'm hoping you can help my friends before something bad happens to them."

Herbert set his cup down, and James did, too. "How can we help?" Herbert asked.

Henry turned to Elijah. "I knew how bad you was hurting after you found Albert dead, so I went looking for the two colored fellas who worked at the hotel to find out what happened. When I come upon them, they was scared for their lives."

"Why were they scared?" Elijah asked.

"Jerome knew exactly what happened 'cause it was on account of him the trouble started."

"What do you mean?"

Henry looked at each of the men in turn. "I'd like you to hear it straight from him, if that would be all right."

Everyone said that would be fine. So Henry went and fetched Jerome and his daddy, who everyone called Cook. Doc told the men to get chairs from over by the gaming table and to sit down next to Henry and Elijah.

Cook and Jerome acted real skittish, but Herbert had a way of calming them down so they could tell what happened.

Jerome said, "Well, sir, I was helping out in the dining room just like always. When Mr. Howard hired my daddy as the cook, he told me I could be a waiter as long as I dressed in a white jacket with black pants and learned to serve people proper. I done a good job of that for near on a year before this happened."

"What happened on Saturday?" Doc asked.

"Well, the hotel was full up for a big meeting. We heard it was about white folks not liking coloreds. That made Daddy and me real nervous."

Cook was staring at his gnarly old hands.

"I figured my daddy would be all right in the kitchen 'cause them men wouldn't see him. But I asked Mr. Howard if'n he didn't want to find a white boy to serve up their supper."

"What did he say?" Herbert asked.

"He told me I was the best waiter he ever done seen, and nobody was gonna keep me from doing my job. I was proud he thought highly of me, but I was still scared."

A heavy silence hung in the room for a minute or two. Then Doc said, "Tell us what happened next."

"I went about my business serving up their suppers. They been drinking liquor most of the afternoon and was getting ugly in their talk. I hoped things would settle down once they got food in their bellies. I was wrong. The talk about coloreds kept getting louder. My hands started shaking, and I spilt some water on the man leading the meeting."

Jerome stopped talking 'til Elijah asked, "Then what?"

"That man spit in my face and called me a stupid nigger. Then he got ahold of me by the collar and yelled that I was a low-life nigger who didn't know my place. That got them men riled up good. One fella yelled for the others to hush up 'cause they was going too far. And that's when the fighting started."

Jerome had to stop to catch his breath. "That's when I saw Mr. Howard and Isaac come running. The man still had me by the collar, and I couldn't breathe. Mr. Howard told him to let go of me. The man shoved me into the table ... and one of them lanterns fell over and set the white cloth on fire. Them drunk men kept fighting and knocking over more lanterns. Pretty soon the dining room was all lit up!"

He started shaking all over. "Then what happened?" Doc prodded gently.

"I don't know for sure, sir. I ran to get Daddy and we come out the back door. The last thing I seen was Isaac and Mr. Howard trying to get everyone out of the dining room."

Jerome couldn't stop shaking. Cook put an arm around him.

Herbert said, "Jerome, you're not thinking the fire was your fault, are you?"

Tears started streaming down Jerome's face. "Well, sir, that's what them men yelled at me when they found us back behind the hotel just before it fell in."

"What men?" Doc asked.

"The one who shoved me into the table. He was with three other white men. He said the fire was my fault and that if'n I told anybody what happened, he'd see that me and my daddy hung from a tree."

Finally, Doc asked the question everyone had on their minds.

"Do you know who that man was?"

Jerome started to answer, but Henry interrupted. "I got something to say first." He looked Elijah in the eye. "You got to promise you won't do nothing about it."

"What are you talking about, Henry?"

"I seen you go crazy before."

Henry knew about that dark place Elijah went to when he got mad. He didn't go there very often now, but when he did, it scared folks. Doc spoke up right away.

"Elijah, we need to know what happened. You got to promise you won't do anything foolish. Do I have your word?"

Elijah stayed quiet.

Doc spoke a little louder. "Give me your word!"

Henry told me that Elijah's jaw set hard, and his eyes got real shiny. But in the end, he give Doc his word.

Herbert said, "Tell us the name of the man."

Jerome said, "I heard him called Carlton Helmstead."

Herbert looked surprised. "Carlton Helmstead from Elizabethtown?"

"That's him," Cook said. "You know him?"

"He's running for the United States Senate."

"That no good bastard!" Doc said.

Then Herbert said, "You did the right thing by telling us what happened, Jerome. And you have my word that no one is gonna blame you for the fire or hurt you in any way."

"Thank you, sir, for your kind words," Cook responded. "But these men ain't like you. I don't want to find my boy hanging dead from no tree."

James hadn't said nothing yet, but he started nodding when he heard that. "These men are pure evil. Cook and Jerome will never be safe here."

Everyone in the room understood that what James said was true.

"I'd like to take the two of you back home with me," James said. "We have a fine hotel in West Point where you can work, and I can provide you a place to live. We don't have trouble like this in West Point. I'll guarantee your safety myself."

Cook and Jerome spoke quiet to each other for a minute. Then Cook said, "Thank you, sir. We'd be pleased to come with you to West Point."

"We'll leave first thing in the morning," James said.

Doc said, "Henry, you're a fine man, and I'm proud of you for bringing this to us. You go on now with Cook and Jerome. We'll figure out what needs to be done." Henry stood, briefly put a hand on Elijah's shoulder, then left the room.

After the door closed, Doc, James, Elijah and Herbert sat for a few minutes lost in their own thoughts. Finally, Herbert broke the dark mood.

He clasped his hands together and smiled. "Gentlemen, I have a plan."

Chapter 40

"Herbert's Terms"

Early the following week, Herbert arrived at Helmstead's home in Elizabethtown. It was a dark, rainy afternoon—quite fittin', Herbert would recall later, for a meeting with such a man. He rang the bell of the big brick house, set right in the middle of town. He was surprised when an old, white-haired colored man answered the door.

The man led Herbert to the parlor, where Helmstead was waiting. He invited Herbert to sit in a stuffed chair across from him. A little table between them held liquor bottles and glasses.

"May I offer you a brandy, sir, or perhaps a whiskey? I pride myself on only serving Kentucky's finest bourbon."

It was not quite three in the afternoon, so Herbert asked for a glass of water instead. Helmstead obliged, and then poured himself two fingers of bourbon.

Herbert studied Helmstead while he fixed their drinks. They were opposites, to be sure. He himself wore a plain black suit. His shoes were scuffed, and his spectacles dusty from his travels. Helmstead, on the other hand, wore a lacy white shirt and high polished boots. He was a hefty fella, who looked about to burst the buttons of his fancy shirt. Herbert recalled Doc's telling him how Helmstead dressed like a dandy when courting Mary. Seems like he hadn't changed much except for his fat belly—and his crushed cheekbone and crooked nose, courtesy of Elijah Fry.

Helmstead tried to engage in small talk, but Herbert cut him short. "We're both busy men," Herbert said, "so let me get right to the point. I'm here to discuss two important matters."

"What are they?"

"Coal cars and your Senate campaign."

Helmstead sat back and sipped his bourbon with a look that Herbert described as a cat about to eat a tasty mouse.

"Well, sir," he said, "those are two of my favorite topics of conversation, so please go right on ahead."

I guess I better take a minute to tell you what was happening in Kentucky at this time. In the early 1900s, coal was in great demand for heating houses and the like. But the mines was turning out coal faster than the railroad could haul it away 'cause their trains was too small. The L&N decided to build a factory to make more railroad cars. They'd settled on two possible sites, Cincinnati and Elizabethtown. Herbert was the man who would make the final decision. So the truth was that Herbert was the one toying with the mouse.

Herbert said, "You played an important part in getting the L&N to consider building the factory here in Elizabethtown."

"Yes, that's a fact," Helmstead said with a smile. "We've been working hard to show you folks what a fine city we have here, with workers who will do the job right."

Herbert merely nodded. "I presume that winning this factory for Elizabethtown would be important for your Senate race, since the revenues would benefit Kentucky instead of Ohio."

Helmstead lowered his head like he was feeling humble. "While it's true that I want the fine people of Kentucky to prosper, I hadn't thought about it much in terms of my campaign."

Herbert set his glass on the table. "Well, I certainly have."

Helmstead smiled. "Can I count on your support, Mr. Smith? That would mean a great deal to me."

Herbert leaned back in his chair and folded his hands in his lap. He waited a spell before saying, "Here is exactly what you can count on, Mr. Helmstead. I know damn well that it was you who led the hate-filled meeting at the Uptonville Hotel that resulted in the fire that killed two people and burned down the town's main street."

Helmstead's cheeks got red, Herbert later said, and he started to sputter. "It was that dumb nigger who started the fire!"

Herbert put his hand up to silence him. "Do not utter the word *nigger* in my presence!"

Helmstead said, "You can't prove a damn thing about that fire. I have witnesses. It's my word against the nig ... colored boy."

"You are right about that, Mr. Helmstead. You will never be found guilty in a court of law."

Helmstead smoothed his lace shirt and settled back in his chair.

"However," Herbert said, "I have a great deal of influence in the court of public opinion, where I guarantee you will be found liable. I believe we have some important matters to discuss. Do I have your attention, sir?"

The red disappeared from Helmstead's cheeks. Now he turned rather pale. Herbert repeated his question. "Do I have your attention?"

Helmstead nodded.

"I have not made a final decision regarding the factory site, and I would not want to penalize the citizens of Elizabethtown because of the actions of one despicable man. However, the L&N Railroad will not be associated with hate. Therefore, we need to come to a resolution about these matters before I make my choice."

"And what would that be?"

"The good folks of Uptonville want to rebuild their town, but they need money to do so. I would like to give you the opportunity to help. I would deliver your check myself."

Helmstead asked, "Are you attempting to blackmail me, sir?"

"Not at all, Mr. Helmstead. I am merely giving you a chance to do the right thing." Herbert paused, then smiled. "However, I will tell you this. The feature article scheduled tomorrow in the Louisville *Courier-Journal* is about the coal-car factory and some ethical concerns I have with one Carlton Helmstead of Elizabethtown."

"What?"

"The article will be vague about the details. However, the reader will be left with no doubt that if Cincinnati is chosen over Elizabethtown, it will be because of you. I have no doubt that would effectively end your Senate campaign."

The flush returned to Helmstead's cheeks, but he kept his temper in check. "What else do you require, Mr. Smith?"

"To begin, you are never again to set foot anywhere near the town of Uptonville, and no harm shall come to any of its citizens, colored or white, as a result of your hateful actions."

Helmstead knew better than to speak; he could see there was more to come.

Herbert said, "Your bigotry disgusts me, and I have the power to ruin you. If you want any chance of a political career, or a coal-car factory in your city, you will cease all further attempts to pit one race of people against another. Do I have your agreement?"

It took Carlton Helmstead another shot of bourbon before he agreed to Herbert's terms.

The following Sunday, Herbert presented the townspeople of Uptonville with two matching checks. One was for $25,000 from the L&N Railroad. The other $25,000 was from Carlton Helmstead.

It took us a few years to rebuild, but in the end, we had us a fine town with a brick street, a mayor and a lawman. And Herbert even brung us a firefighting wagon from Louisville.

Nothing could make up for the loss of Albert and George, but we made something good out of what was bad. We changed the town's name from Uptonville to Upton, 'cause that made us think about what was new instead of what we lost.

Elizabethtown got the coal-car factory, and Carlton Helmstead was elected to the Senate. He never showed his face anywhere near Upton again, and no harm come to any of us citizens 'cause of him.

The sad thing was, there was no way for Herbert to stop the hatred that Carlton Helmstead passed on, not only for coloreds, but also for white folks who treated them as equals. Years down the road, we come to know that first hand.

Chapter 41

"Sisterhood"

I never thought I could love a woman like a real sister. I come to be fond of my brothers' wives, but I didn't spend much time with them once I got married. Miss June and Sally Ann were the ones that give me the gift of true sisterhood, but it come wrapped in a package of sorrow.

Albert had been in the ground just eight weeks when the time come to harvest our tobacco. It was hot in the morning when the menfolk started hanging our crop in the barn to cure. Elijah and Henry got the sticks going while Thomas, Daniel and Benjamin climbed the beams to hang them, just like my brothers had done for Pa. I come out to help, but I was feeling poorly. I reckoned it was the heat. I decided to go back to the house and sit for a spell. I got about halfway there when my insides started cramping bad, and I fell out from the pain.

I must've screamed 'cause Miss June come out on the porch with Viola, Clifford and Irene. She wasn't walking good by then, so it took her a spell to get to me. My babies got there first and began crying and hollering up a storm. Elijah and Henry come running from the barn.

Miss June saw the blood on my skirt and told Elijah to carry me into the house straightaway. Henry rushed off to fetch Doc.

I felt the blood coming out of me, and I was scared to the bone. I had an idea what was happening, but Doc confirmed it when he got to me awhile later.

He said, "Molly, I'm afraid you're losing a baby. Did you know you were with child?"

"I thought I might be." Elijah, who was holding my hand, looked surprised and sad. Doc told Elijah to get on back to the barn 'cause there wasn't nothing he could do for me. Elijah fussed 'til Doc promised to come fetch him if needed.

It took hours of pain before the baby come out.

"The baby looks to be about seventeen weeks along. It's a boy."

I started to cry. He patted my hand and then kissed it soft. "Molly, I think the stress of the fire and losing Albert caused you to miscarry the baby. I can't see any other reason for this happening because it was perfectly formed."

My heart felt heavy, but I knew what would happen if Doc told Elijah why I lost the baby. Since Albert's passing, he'd had a rage boiling inside of him. He'd made a promise to Doc that he intended to keep. But he'd break that promise for sure if he knew he'd lost both his pa and a son on account of Carlton Helmstead.

"Doc," I said, "you got to tell Elijah that the baby wasn't right and had to come out before something bad happened to me. He'll believe you. I know how he grieved for Mary, and he doesn't want nothing like that to happen to me."

Doc done what I asked, but he got worried. I'd lost a lot of blood, and though the baby come out, Doc couldn't be sure I wouldn't start bleeding again. If that happened, there wouldn't be nothing he could do to save me. "Molly, you got to stay in bed for a few weeks to heal up."

I tried to argue, but Doc had a way of putting things in the proper light. "Molly, I'm not sure you can have babies after this. But if you want a chance, you got to rest and get strong. That's the only way you'll ever suckle another young'un. Do you want to have another baby?"

I was twenty-seven years old and past my prime, but I still wanted more babies with Elijah. So I agreed. I was worried about how all the chores would get done, but Miss June and Sally Ann figured all that out. Miss June took care of the young'uns and chores. Sally Ann come to tend to me and do the cooking. Doc said he would look in regular, leaving Elijah and Henry to tend to the farm.

I spent a miserable few weeks of doing nothing. But in another way, it was a blessing. I come to know Sally Ann as a sister.

Most afternoons, we whiled away together once the menfolk finished their dinner and she'd done up the dishes. Sally Ann would sit in my rocker while I rested in bed. We talked about all kinds of things. One day, I finally got up the gumption to ask her something I'd wondered for a long time.

"What was it like being a slave?"

"I don't know nothing different, Molly."

I was surprised when she said that 'cause she'd been a free woman since long before I was born.

She said, "Me and Isaiah grew up together on Doc's daddy's plantation. We couldn't get wed like white folks do. We had to ask the master if'n we could live together. He said that would be fine 'cause we was good breeding stock. We jumped the broom when I was sixteen."

"What's that mean?" I asked.

"Jumpin' over a broom holding hands is what coloreds did when they wanted to act like they was husband and wife. It showed people they was gonna sweep out their cabin together from then on."

Sally Ann said Doc come to the plantation that same Christmas with Miss Madeline to say they was getting married. "His daddy thought it would be fittin' to give them Isaiah and me as a wedding present."

That shocked me good.

"They had me do the cooking, and Isaiah looked after the farm. They built us our own little place out away from the big house, so it worked out fine."

"What happened when they done away with slavery?"

"Doc told us we was free to leave, if'n we wanted 'cause we wasn't his property no more. We was scared 'cause we didn't know where we would go. Doc said he hoped we'd stay where we was, since he and the missus was fond of us. He promised to pay us from then on, so that's what we done. Not long after that, our Henry was born a free boy."

"How come you only had one young'un?"

"I couldn't have no more babies after Henry. But I is content with the one I have."

I told her that Henry was a fine man, and we was thankful to have him to help us. I thought about her story well into the night. The next day when she come to sit with me, I had to ask her one more thing.

"Why did you stay here all these years, Sally Ann? Didn't you want to get away from the folks who bought and sold you like you was mules?"

Sally Ann got a strange look on her face.

"Molly, once you is a slave, you can't never be free."

"What do you mean?"

"The Middletons was good to us. And we heard stories about coloreds who left their masters and wished they hadn't."

"Why?"

"At least they had food to eat and a place to sleep. They didn't have to worry they'd get hung just 'cause they was colored."

After a moment she said sadly, "It don't matter that we're free, Molly. White men make the rules we got to obey. I'm gonna tell you something I ain't never told another living soul, not even my sweet Isaiah."

"What's that?" I asked real soft.

"Henry ain't no free boy."

"Why you say that, Sally Ann?"

"If'n white men decide we should be slaves again, there ain't nothing Henry could do about it."

I started to say that would never happen, but then I thought about the man who stirred up white folks against coloreds. I held my lips shut together.

Sally Ann must've been thinking the same thing. She said, "I never seen a man look at me with so much hate just 'cause my skin ain't the same color as his."

Tears started falling from that poor woman's eyes.

"Me and Henry gonna live out our days right here 'cause we know you folks ain't like that."

I asked her to lean in to me close so I could tell her something. I took her hand and held it tight.

"We don't never want you to leave us, Sally Ann, 'cause we love you and Henry."

For a long time that afternoon, we stayed like that, just holding hands and being quiet. I liked the look of my white hand tangled up in her black one. We both knew what I said was true, and that's what made us sisters.

Chapter 42

"MiJu"

In no time, I got back to my ornery ol' self, but I was worried about Miss June. She couldn't see to mend clothes like she used to. One day, she went to grab a glass of water, and it fell right out of her hand.

I paid Doc a visit to ask him about her. He told it to me straight out. "I'm not going to lie to you, Molly. Miss June won't last out the year. I think she's worn out from the MS and is getting ready to die."

I felt my heart break. Miss June was more than a mother to me. She was the only grandmother our babies knew. They adored her. I didn't know how they would get along without their MiJu.

"Use the time you got left to let her know how much you love her," Doc said. "That way, you won't have any regrets when she dies."

Well, that's exactly what I done. We sat outside on the porch near on every day when it was warm. Once in a while, Miss June could talk clear, and I listened to her hard. Most times, we just enjoyed being quiet together, listening to my rocker as it creaked back and forth.

One evening when supper was over, Miss June found she couldn't get up from the table no matter how hard she tried. Elijah carried her to bed. I got her all settled under the covers. I kissed her forehead and started to leave. She grabbed my hand, and even though she couldn't speak, I knew she was afeared to be alone. I told Elijah to bring my rocker, so I could sit close to her bed.

Miss June's eyes weren't focusing, and her breathing sounded like someone trying to blow on a whistle. I wouldn't leave her for nothing. But when I couldn't keep my eyes open another minute, I kissed her cheek and said, "I love you, my sweet mama." Miss June squeezed my hand tight, and I knew she heard me. Just as the sun was coming through the window, I woke up. Miss June wasn't breathing no more.

Doc come and pronounced her dead. He sent Thomas to tell Edward to let folks know we'd be burying her the next day. Sally Ann and I washed Miss June and put oils on her body so she wouldn't start smelling bad. Then we dressed her proper and wrapped her in my best quilt. Elijah and Henry built a fine box to carry her to the grave.

Miss June told me she didn't want folks gawking at her after she passed. She wanted to be remembered like she'd been. So Elijah and Henry lifted her out of the bed and set her down in the box. Then we got the young'uns to stand around her. Elijah said a prayer, and Henry nailed the box shut.

The next morning, we loaded her in the back of our buckboard. The older boys rode with Elijah. Henry drove Sally Ann and the rest of us in another buckboard he'd borrowed from Doc.

Edward decided Miss June should be buried beside the schoolhouse instead of in the cemetery 'cause she belonged in the place she'd love the best. The burial was scheduled for ten o'clock, but a crowd gathered an hour early. It pleased me to see how many people come to give her a proper send-off.

After Edward got done praying, he asked folks if they had something they wanted to say. One after another spoke about how much Miss June meant to them. Men and women alike was weeping as they told stories about her. Miss June taught them to read and write, to be sure. But more important, she'd made them believe in theirselves and dare to try things they'd never thought possible.

That was the last lesson Miss June had to teach me. You don't have to be famous to make a difference. The young'uns she taught never forgot her.

As the men throwed dirt on her grave, Sally Ann put her arm around me. "Come spring, let's you and me come back and plant flowers on her grave," she said. We decided on tulips 'cause they was Miss June's favorites. She said they was colorful and regal.

It was hard to get over the loss of Miss June. A few days, later Sally Ann come to me and said, "Molly, there's one thing I know for sure. The good Lord don't intend for you to stay sad. Whenever He takes someone from you, He gives you something special in return."

The following year, I come to understand what she meant. I grew as big as a barn with child. I felt scared at first that I might lose another baby, but Elijah made sure I ate good and rested a lot.

When my time come, which was a mite earlier than we expected, labor went quick. Nathan was on hand as I give a final push and out popped a fine boy. I thought I was done, but another big pain come on. I pushed more, and Nathan caught a baby girl. Lord have mercy, no wonder I got so big. I done had two babies inside of me! The good Lord took my sweet Miss June to heaven, but He gave me two babies in return. That was a powerful fine thing He done, for sure.

Chapter 43

"Black Ice"

The next few years flew by fast. We stayed busy and happy with our farm and our young'uns. Then in late November 1912, we faced another loss.

The tobacco was curing in the barn, and we planned to haul it to market in a few days. That night it started raining ice, and we was afeared the crop would freeze and be ruined. None of us slept much that night. Henry got up before sunrise to go to the barn, to see after his crop and ours. He told Sally Ann he wouldn't need no breakfast 'til he got back. She got some biscuits for him to eat on the way, but Henry left before she could give him the pail.

Sally Ann ran after him, not knowing the porch steps was covered in black ice. She slipped and fell hard on the ground below. Henry heard her screaming and come running. He carried her inside and laid her down on the bed. Then he fetched Doc, Elijah and me.

When we got to the house, Sally Ann was screaming in pain. Her hair was wet with sweat, and she wasn't making sense when she tried to talk. Her eyes looked glazed. I think she knew we was there, but her mind wasn't tracking good. I got a rag with water to wipe her face. Doc checked her over, then he put his hand on Henry's shoulder. "Your ma's hurt real bad. I think she broke her back and maybe her hip, too."

Henry said, "But you can fix her, can't you, Doc?"

"There's nothing I can do for her but try to ease the pain some. Older folks don't recover good from broken backs and hips. Most times, they die in their bed from a stroke or pneumonia 'cause they can't get up and around."

Tears started rolling down Henry's face. Doc give Sally Ann a shot of morphine and tucked her in good. He promised to come back the next day. We got the older boys to watch the young'uns so we could stay with Henry. In the middle of the night, the morphine wore off, and Sally Ann started baying and thrashing about like a deer caught in a fence.

When Doc come back the next morning, Henry took ahold of his arm before he went into her room and said, "You got to do something, Doc. I can't stand to see Mama suffering like she is." Doc hung his head low and didn't say nothing.

Henry said again, "Do something, Doc!"

"Like I told you, Henry, there's nothing I can do but ease her pain for a while. I got to be careful with the morphine I give her. Too much can be lethal."

Henry stayed quiet for a spell. Then he looked Doc square in the eye and said, "Put her out of her misery, Doc. Make her go to sleep with the morphine and not wake up."

"I can't do that, Henry."

"You put your dog down when he broke his leg so he wouldn't suffer no more. Why won't you do that for my mama?"

Doc didn't say nothing. He just rubbed his crippled-up hands together.

Henry kept after him. "I know Mama wouldn't want to live no more if she couldn't be useful. She'd tell you that herself if she could."

"It just wouldn't be right," Doc said.

I could tell Henry was getting mad by the look in his eyes. He spoke a mite slower. "Are you saying the misery of my mama ain't worth that of your dog?"

Doc looked like he'd been stabbed in the heart. "You know I'm not saying that, Henry."

"Then do something! I'm begging you!"

I'm not sure whether it was the tears rolling down Henry's face or the sound of Sally Ann wailing, but Doc finally give in.

"I'll do what you ask, but we can't let nobody find out." Doc shifted his gaze to Elijah and me. "I got to have your word that this will remain between us. I could go to jail if someone found out." We promised Doc to keep the secret.

Doc told Henry to go in and say his final goodbyes while he got all the morphine he had out of his bag. In them days, a doctor could get morphine easy. After Henry come out, Doc went into the room and shut the door behind him. He returned a few minutes later.

"She's gone. We got to get her in the ground today. We'll bury her up on the hill near Mary."

Doc sent Henry and Elijah to dig her grave. I asked him if they could build her a box after they got done with that.

"No, Molly. We don't have time to build a box. I reckon it will take most of the day to dig a hole 'cause the ground is hard. We got to get Sally Ann buried before dark so nobody finds out what I done. I'll go back to the house and get some sheets to wrap her in."

There was one thing I had to do, and I didn't care how much time it took. I was gonna wash and oil Sally Ann just like we did for Miss June.

I took off her nightdress and covered up her private parts while I worked on the rest of her. I started with her hair, which was pure white now. Then I moved down to her face. Her lips was turned up a little like she was gonna smile.

I got ready to wash her arms next. I put my arm against hers, and they was different as could be. I rubbed my fingers on her skin to get a good feel of it. Her black skin was thick like leather, while mine was pale and thin.

I wondered why God made us different like that. I remembered what she told me about growing up a slave and being scared after she got free. I reckoned she needed thick skin to protect her from white people's hate.

I rubbed oils on her, kissed her and wrapped her in the sheets Doc brung. We buried her up on the hill just before dark. Now both of the women I loved most in the world was gone, and the hurt in my heart took a long time to heal.

Chapter 44

"Treasured Times"

Doc was never the same after that. His joints hurt bad, and he couldn't get around much. He got mean-spirited from being in pain all the time. One summer day in 1914, he told Elijah he wanted to have a meeting with him, Thomas, Daniel and Benjamin 'cause he had important matters to discuss. He knew his time on earth was short and he wanted his affairs in order.

When he got home from the meeting, Elijah didn't say much, and I knew better than to push him. What he did say was that Doc was leaving everything he had to Mary's sons, since Martha and Miriam were married to wealthy men. He deeded his land to Benjamin 'cause Thomas was now a doctor, and Daniel had the store to run. His money would be divided among the three of them.

He told Thomas and Daniel to use their money wisely and help folks as best they could. He was more direct with Benjamin.

"Buy up all the good land you can with the money I'm giving you. A man can steal your money, but nobody can take your land away from you. Will you do that for me, son?"

Benjamin promised his granddaddy that he would do just that.

Doc died the week after they had their meeting. We buried him up on the hill with Sally Ann and Mary.

Now here's what I couldn't understand at the time. Thomas, Daniel and Benjamin was gonna have plenty of money to live a good life. But Elijah come home from that meeting in his dark place. He stared at me with sad eyes for a time after that. I wouldn't understand his sadness for some years to come.

Pastor Brown used to preach about the evils of money. He quoted a Scripture about how hard it was for a rich man to get into heaven … something about poking your eye with a needle. I never knew what that meant, but it didn't sound like something a body would want to do. We didn't have much money, so we didn't have to worry none about its evils. But the money Doc left Elijah's sons changed them.

Thomas used his inheritance to set up a medical practice in Louisville for poor people. He was a fine man, and money weren't no evil for him. Benjamin done good, too. He loved the land and took care of it. He hired men to help him farm his acres and looked after his people real good. I was proud of him for that.

It was Daniel who changed for the worse once he had money. He wasn't content to run the general store no more and hired a man to run it for him. He wanted to taste what he called the good life. He decided to leave Kentucky and settle in New York City. He started putting his money in what they called the stock market. He told us he had a knack for picking winners and was getting rich fast. That's when he started buying fancy duds and acting like he was better than everybody else.

In 1915, I got the surprise of my life. When I was thirty-six and Elijah forty-nine, we had another baby. That baby girl was the prettiest little thing I ever done seen, with dark curly hair and fat rosy cheeks. I asked Elijah if we might name her after the two women we'd loved most in life. We called her Tula, which is the Dutch word for tulip, Miss June's favorite flower. We give her Mary as a second name 'cause Elijah still carried his first wife soft in his heart.

The next few years was the happiest of my life. Elijah's sons had been on their own for a while now, so we could concentrate all our love on the family we had together. Viola turned fifteen the year Tula Mary was born, and she was a big help with the young'uns. Clifford was fourteen and spent every minute he could helping his daddy and Henry with the farm. At twelve, Irene liked going to school and learning new things more than anything else. Many a night, I had to get after her to put her book down, blow out the lantern and go to bed. Our twins, Eva and Earl, grew into fine young'uns who thought baby Tula was about the greatest thing to happen to our family.

Some of my favorite times was having supper together of an evening. I remembered when me and Ma had to wait 'til the menfolk finished their meal before we got ours. We ate our cold food in silence 'cause we was wore out after doing all the house chores. With my own family, all the children pitched in to help with chores, so none of us was too tired to laugh and carry on when we ate supper together.

One conversation we had brought back some bad memories. Most evenings Henry ate supper with us, but he wasn't there one day 'cause he felt poorly. When we asked the children that night what they was learning in school, Clifford said they was studying about slavery and the Civil War.

Even though Isaac was their uncle, they had to call him Mr. Van Meter at school. Irene said she was bothered by something and asked him, "Do white people like coloreds now, Mr. Van Meter?"

Isaac said, "Some do, Irene, but a lot of folks still hate coloreds just 'cause their skin isn't white."

Irene was upset when she told us that. She loved Henry just like the rest of us. "Do people around here feel thataway about Henry?" she asked.

We hadn't had no trouble in Upton since Herbert Smith made the pact with Carlton Helmstead. But we heard about a group called the Ku Klux Klan that stirred white folks up against coloreds, just like Helmstead done the night our town burnt down. One thing I knew for sure. We'd raised our children to treat everyone as equals. We taught them that the color of a man's skin meant nothing. His character was all that mattered.

"People around here like and respect Henry for the good man he is," Elijah told her. "So don't you worry none about Henry. He's part of our family and always will be."

During this time, lots of changes was going on in the world. Folks was paying near on $300 to buy one of them newfangled automobiles instead of buckboards. A lot of places had electric lights, so people could see good after dark. Folks in town got telephones and could talk to each other whenever they wanted. But they had to go through an operator on a party line to call somebody. I heard tell that they could listen in on each other's conversations, and that just didn't seem right.

We stayed simple folks, living on our farm with no electricity or telephone. We got dressed before the sun come up and went to bed after it set. We didn't need no electric lights after dark 'cause we had lanterns, and we didn't have no use for a telephone. Who was we gonna call? Most everybody we loved was right here. Even Henry.

One by one, our young'uns left home to make their own way in life. I was grateful that each of them finished the eighth grade. Unlike Benjamin, none of our young'uns wanted to stay here and farm. Isaac taught them about all kinds of exciting places outside of Hardin County, and that made them want an adventure.

Viola married a boy from town and moved to St. Louis, Missouri. Clifford got a job working on the railroad in Tennessee. Irene become a schoolteacher and married a preacher's boy in Lexington. I had a feeling Miss June arranged that from above so she would have a righteous life 'cause Irene had always been her favorite.

When it came their time, Eva and Earl traveled together to Louisville and stayed with Thomas and his family for a while. Eva went to work in a ladies' dress shop, and Earl got a job laying bricks. I thought about our children every day and couldn't wait to get their letters. I liked hearing all about their adventures, but I fretted about them being on their own far away from home—except for Eva and Earl, who had each other and Thomas.

The house was much quieter with only Elijah, Tula Mary and me, but she brightened our spirits every day with her laugh and smile. She loved school and made friends easy. Isaac said she was about the sweetest child he'd ever had in class. She was smart, too, and loved to read. I know a mama isn't supposed to have favorites, but Tula Mary was mine. She was my surprise baby, and I knew I wouldn't have no more. I cherished every moment we spent together.

My childhood ended when Ma died. Spending happy hours with Tula Mary made up for all the time I lost. Sometimes when we played outside, I felt like a young'un again. Growing up, I was mad I'd been born a girl, so I acted like a boy. But now, with Tula, I finally got to like the little girl part of me, even though I was an old woman in my forties. Why, Tula even brung her schoolwork home, so I could learn new things right along with her. Oh my, those were happy times.

Chapter 45

"The Lie"

In the summer of 1925, Elijah began feeling poorly. His back ached, he couldn't keep his supper down, and he felt hot to the touch. At first, I thought he'd get better with rest and mineral salts. But when it come time to bring in the tobacco, Elijah just couldn't do his share of the work. That's when I knew something was really wrong.

When his face got puffy and he stopped going to the outhouse, I made him go with me to see Nathan. We sat for a spell while Nathan looked in his medical book. When his head started nodding, I reckoned he found what he was searching for.

"Elijah, I think you may have Bright's disease. It affects your kidneys."

"Is that why he don't go to the outhouse no more?"

"Yes, Molly. And you hurt in your manly parts. You've had that going on, haven't you, Elijah?"

Elijah told him that was so.

"I'm gonna give you something to make you go to the outhouse. I want you back here in a week. You hear?"

Elijah started going to the outhouse again, but he stayed puffy in the face, and his back hurt him bad. Nathan put some kind of contraption on his arm, then pumped it up and let it out. He said it measured blood pressure. Too much blood pressure wasn't good for you. Elijah must have had too much 'cause Nathan had to do more treatments.

Elijah began to see Nathan regular for warm baths and bloodletting to make the blood pressure go down. It helped some, but Elijah never did feel right again once he got the Bright's disease. Nathan said he hoped the disease was acute, which meant it would go away. If not, it was called chronic Bright's disease. If Elijah had that, there wasn't much he could do. I prayed it was that acute one. But after things went on the same way for a few years, I knew it was the bad kind. In June 1928, Elijah went to see Nathan right after he bought us a Ford pickup for the farm. He'd been going to his dark place more 'cause he was tired of feeling bad. But that day after he come back, he seemed better. I asked if maybe Nathan gave him a new medicine.

But Elijah said that wasn't it at all. He bought something in town that he wanted me to put away in a safe place. "I was having dinner at the hotel after I saw Nathan. A fella came over and introduced hisself. He asked if he could show me something he was selling. He seemed nice enough, so I told him to have a seat."

I hadn't seen Elijah smile in months the way he did when he said, "I bought a life insurance policy."

"What's that?"

"It gives you money, Molly, if something happens to me." I'd never heard the like. "What did it cost?"

"Just a few dollars. It'll pay you much more than that when the time comes."

I didn't understand why you would pay someone money one day just to get money later. Why not just keep the money you got? But I was grateful for whatever it was that helped Elijah come back to his old self. That good feeling lasted 'til November.

Elijah got up that morning of November 17, 1928, hurting bad. There wasn't nothing more Nathan could do to relieve his suffering.

Henry done most of the hard work bringing in the tobacco crop, and that made Elijah feel worse.

It was raining cold that day like when Sally Ann died. We worried it might start to ice up come nightfall. Henry and Elijah had been out in the barn making sure the tobacco was dry. Near on suppertime, Henry come into the house alone.

I was busy and didn't pay him no mind at first. Then I saw him standing there holding Elijah's pocket watch.

"Oh, my Lord, Henry! Is Elijah all right?"

"He's fine, Molly."

"But you got his watch!"

"He give it to me."

My voice got louder. "What did he say to you?"

"He wanted me to have it 'cause we is brothers."

"What else?"

"That's all, Molly. What's the matter with you? I didn't take the watch. Elijah done give it to me."

"What was you talking about before he give it?"

"The roof was leaking, and Elijah wanted to climb up to fix the holes. I made him promise he would let me do it in the morning. He give me his word."

I took off running for the barn, with Henry and Tula right behind me. I called out for Elijah, but he didn't answer. I ran back behind the barn and saw the ladder up against it and the hammer and nails on the ground. Then I saw Elijah. He was lying with his neck cocked to one side. Blood was coming out his mouth, and his eyes were open. My head started spinning, and everything went dark.

We buried Elijah up on the hill next to Mary. I took some comfort knowing they was together again. But I was lost, even with all of Elijah's children, except Daniel, there to grieve with me. Thomas said he got word to Daniel, but he was too far away to come for the burial.

Edward had us pray and said kind words about Elijah before we threw the first dirt. By this time, Pa had been gone for several years, but my brothers and their wives come to pay their respects. After everyone left, Benjamin asked if he could have a word with me.

"Molly, do you remember when Elijah went to see Doc before you got married?"

"Yes. He told me they come to some kind of an agreement, but he didn't say what it was."

"Granddaddy told him that he'd give his blessing on one condition."

"What was that?"

"Doc gave Elijah forty acres of his land when he married my ma, Mary. He said he'd approve your marriage if Elijah deeded the land back to him. They drew up a contract that said he could farm the land, but he'd be the caretaker and not the owner. Elijah could keep the house he built, and Henry could stay in his."

"Why did he do that?

Benjamin's voice got low. "He wanted to keep the land in the Middleton family and not let it go to you, or the children you had with Elijah."

"Why are you telling me this now?"

Benjamin looked troubled. "Doc left all his land to me, including your farm and Henry's ten acres. He made me promise to use the money we got from your tobacco to buy more land."

Benjamin wasn't looking me in the eye. "That means you and Henry won't be growing the crop no more. I'll see to it. You can stay here in the house as long as you live, and Henry can stay in his, but you won't have no more money coming in from the sale of the tobacco."

I felt my cheeks start to burn. "Well, how am I gonna see to Tula Mary then?" I asked. "She's only thirteen. She's not ready to make her own way yet."

Benjamin took my hand and patted it. "I'll look after you, Molly. I promise you that. I'll see to it that you have money for whatever you need, and Henry, too."

That made me think of that insurance policy. I got the box where I kept the papers and showed Benjamin.

He studied them. "This here is an accidental death policy."

"What's that mean?"

"The insurance company has to pay you five hundred dollars, since Elijah had an accident and didn't die from natural causes."

Benjamin told me he'd send the paperwork to the company for me. After the money come, I should put it in the bank where it'd be safe. Then he hugged me tight and told me not to worry.

I sat in the rocker for a long time after he left. My mind was spinning 'cause things made sense now. What I feared deep in my heart was true. Elijah done planned his accident.

That evening, Henry come around. He made sure the fire in the fireplace was going good and then asked if he could sit with me for a spell. He took out the watch and stared at it. I could tell his heart was hurting as bad as mine.

"Elijah told me he wanted me to have his watch 'cause I'd been a brother to him since we met fifty years ago. He give me his word he wouldn't try to fix the roof, since the rain had stopped and the crop was dry. He told me to go up to the house and wash up for supper. He wanted to puff on his pipe for a few minutes."

Henry looked up from the watch to me. "How did you know something bad had happened, Molly?"

"It was on account of the watch, Henry. Didn't Elijah ever tell you the story about it?"

"All he said was that Albert give it to him when he turned sixteen."

"Albert told Elijah that the watch was to remind him to be true to his word. But if there come a time he had to tell a lie for a good enough reason, then he was to give this here watch away, like Albert done give it to him."

Henry looked like he'd been kicked in the gut. "I should never have left him alone in the barn. Why did he try to fix the roof hisself when I promised I'd do it in the morning?"

I let out a big breath and said, "There's nothing you could've done to stop him, Henry. His mind was made up."

I had to wipe my tears with the sleeve of my dress before I could go on. "Elijah wasn't out to fix the roof. He climbed on top of the barn so he could jump off. He killed hisself, Henry, but made it look like an accident."

"Why would he go and do that, Molly?"

"I reckon Elijah didn't want to live no more 'cause he was in pain all the time. But he knew when he died, our land would go to Benjamin. He bought a life insurance policy to take care of us, Henry, when we didn't have no more money coming from the tobacco crop."

Henry just sat there, his shoulders shaking with sobs.

I felt closer to Henry that night than ever before. Neither of us owned our land, and Elijah was lost to us forever. I reached out and patted him. "Looks like we is all we got, Henry, so we better look after each other good."

MOLLY and HENRY

Chapter 46

"The Grand Life"

I don't know how we got through the first few weeks after Elijah died. Most days, I didn't want to get dressed, and more nights than not, I lay awake 'til dawn just 'cause the bed was too empty to sleep in. For a long time after her daddy died, Tula Mary lost the sparkle in her eyes. It broke my heart to hear her crying into her pillow at night.

Henry hauled our tobacco to market and sold it for a good price. We needed every penny 'cause this was the last time we'd have a crop to sell.

Folks dropped by from time to time to see how we was getting along. Edward come and prayed with us. Benjamin saw to it that we had plenty of food and wood. Isaac brung us supplies from the store, and my children wrote me letters regular.

Then one day in April, I got two visitors I wasn't expecting. I was sitting in my rocker mending clothes while Tula Mary was at school. I noticed a strange sound that just kept getting louder, like something was about to blow up.

I went out on the porch to get a look. And Lord, to my surprise, here come Daniel driving one of them fancy new automobiles I'd seen in a magazine. It was called a Model T Ford with a rumble seat. Daniel got out and nodded to me. He wore a fancy suit with a white silk shirt.

Daniel walked around to the other side of the automobile and opened the door. A woman got out with a cigarette hanging out of her mouth. She dropped it on the ground and crushed it with her shoe. She had brown hair cut short with waves rolling through it. The wind was blowing, but her hair didn't move none. Her dress was so tight, I thought she might bust a seam, and it didn't even cover her knees.

As they come up on the porch, Daniel said, "Molly, this is my wife, Catherine DuPont. We wanted to come by for a few minutes to pay our respects." Then he leaned in to give me a kiss, but his lips didn't touch my cheek.

I could barely find my voice, much less my manners. I was too busy looking at the blue powder above this woman's eyes. Her cheeks were much too rosy to be natural, and her mouth was all painted a bright shade of red!

Finally, I asked them to come in and sit a spell. When Daniel come in the door, he looked around, then frowned. "The place is much smaller than I remember."

Daniel and Catherine sat down in the wood chairs near my rocker.

"It's good to see you, Molly."

"You've been gone a long time, Daniel. We was sad you couldn't make it to your pa's funeral. He's buried up on the hill next to your ma."

"Yes, Benjamin told me that. We've just come from the big house. I wanted Catherine to see where my mother was raised."

"I've never seen a tobacco farm before," Catherine said. "I'm a city girl. We live in houses that sit side by side. I can't imagine owning this much land!"

I had a hard time understanding what she was saying 'cause she didn't sound nothing like the folks around here. I guess people up north talk fast, all up in their nose.

Looking at Catherine, Daniel said, "My mother's family had money and did well." Then he turned his face to me. "My daddy and Molly came from much more *humble* origins."

Squeezing his hand, Catherine said, "Well, rising above that is what made you the man you are, Daniel."

Looking pleased, he said, "Catherine's daddy helped me invest money in the stock market. Remember, I told you all about the stock market, Molly, last time we talked."

I nodded my head but didn't smile. Giving money to somebody to make more money without doing a hard day's work didn't make no sense to me then, and I figured it wouldn't now, so I didn't ask nothing more about it.

Daniel said, "You should let me invest your money, Molly. I heard that you got a settlement from the insurance company after Daddy died. What did you do with it?"

I didn't think that was any of his concern. I just said, "Benjamin told me to put it in the bank."

"That's good. I'm glad you got it with the Bank of Upton. They're a smart operation. I had them take some of their surplus money and invest it in utility stocks. That's the hot ticket now. So I guess in the long run, you invested that money in the stock market, Molly, and I'm happy for you."

I didn't understand a word he said, so I changed the subject.

"When did you get married?"

"We got married a couple months ago. We went to Boston for our wedding trip. Then Catherine decided she wanted to see where I was raised. I explained there wasn't much to the town of Upton, but she wanted to come anyway."

"Well, Catherine, what do you think of Upton? Must be a shock coming from a place like New York City."

I guess I was staring at her legs 'cause Catherine tried to pull her dress down, but no matter how hard she tugged, it stayed up above her knees.

She said, "Oh, Molly—may I call you Molly or should it be Mrs. Fry?"

"Molly will do," I said.

"I think Upton is quaint."

"Quaint?" I repeated.

Daniel must've known I didn't know what the word *quaint* meant. "What Catherine means is that she thinks Upton is a nice little town."

"Oh, yes," Catherine said. "It's a sweet place."

"Do you think you might like living in Upton one day?"

Catherine's red mouth dropped open. She looked at me and then at Daniel.

"We don't plan to live here in Upton, Molly," Daniel said. "We'll head on back to New York in a few days."

"But what about the store?"

"I'm going to sell the store when it suits me. In the meantime, my hired man will keep it going."

Catherine said, "Daniel's working for my daddy now. He's a broker on Wall Street and plans to make Daniel a very rich man."

"Well, don't that beat all," was all I could say.

I asked if they'd like a glass of lemonade.

"We can't stay, Molly," Daniel said, getting up from his chair. "We're having dinner at the hotel with Isaac and Lela, but thank you just the same."

Catherine said, "It's very nice to meet you, Molly. Perhaps one day, you'll come visit us in New York."

Daniel took Catherine by the elbow and hurried her out the door. I heard him say, "Molly wouldn't do well to visit us. She only went to school for a couple of years. That's why she's better suited to a *simpler* way of life."

I watched him light a cigarette for her and one for hisself. Then they drove away in their Model T Ford with the rumble seat. When I couldn't see them no more, I went back inside and sat down in my rocker. It was plain to see that Daniel was living a grand life, but he'd lost his heart. My tears started flowing. For the first time since Elijah died, I was glad he wasn't around to see what had become of his son. I had a good cry for the both of us.

Chapter 47

"Falling Dominoes"

Me and Henry had some dollars saved back. We bought seeds to plant a big garden. With no more money coming in, we had to grow our own food. When the weather got warm, we tilled a nice big plot out back of the house and planted beans, potatoes, beets, carrots and squash. We had the time now to tend a garden proper. We planned to can as much as we could for the winter. Come July, we'd pick the blackberries that grew wild all over the place so we could make jam to have all year long. We had some nice apple trees, too, so we didn't have to worry none about growing more fruit.

Working with me and Henry in the garden brung the sparkle back to Tula Mary. She loved being outside, digging in the dirt, enjoying the warm sun and fresh air. After months of a pale face and sad eyes, her cheeks took on a pink color now. And when she saw the first seedling she'd planted burst through the earth, she shouted out with joy. Then she took my hand and Henry's and had us dance around in a circle, laughing and carrying on like we used to. That's when I knew we was gonna be all right 'cause we felt part of the new life springing up around us.

We bought two cows and some chickens so we'd have milk to drink and eggs to fry. Joost and Jansen helped Henry build a little barn out back near the garden for the milk cows, with a chicken coop beside it for the hens and rooster. We kept everything away from the tobacco fields and barn 'cause that wasn't ours no more. Besides, I didn't want to go anywhere near the barn. Every time I seen it, I pictured Elijah jumping off the roof, and I wondered what went through his mind before he hit the ground.

I taught Tula how to milk a cow proper, but I never showed her how to wring a chicken's neck. Her heart was too tender to kill a critter like Ma made me do. Besides, we had to keep our hens alive to lay eggs. We couldn't afford to kill animals for their meat. And I was glad of it.

I asked my brothers to help Henry dig out a cellar up close to the house where we could store our canned goods. I also wanted a place to hide if the weather turned bad. They fixed it up good with steps I could climb down and shelves to store things up off the ground. I took my special box down there when they got done.

It was a darn good thing we did all that 'cause later that year, something happened that caused a panic. They come to call it the Great Depression.

It began on Tuesday, October 29, 1929, but I didn't learn about it 'til later when Benjamin took me to town. I could tell he was troubled. He told me Isaac and Lela wanted to meet with us to discuss some important business.

As we drove, he tried to explain what was happening, but I didn't understand none of it. He told me the stock market had crashed on Black Tuesday. I asked if he was talking about a building falling down. He said it was a whole lot worse than that.

"Folks are jumping out of windows 'cause they done lost everything they owned. People are breaking down the doors to banks to get their money out before it's too late."

I asked him what any of this had to do with me.

"It has everything to do with you, Molly," he said.

I hadn't been to town but a time or two since Elijah died, and I wasn't prepared for what I seen. What few folks was out on the street was gathered in front of the bank. I saw women weeping and holding their children tight, while men were slumped over, just staring at the ground. It reminded me of the morning after our town burnt down, except this time the buildings was still standing and there was no smoke in the air.

We met Lela and Isaac in the hotel dining room. I knew whatever they wanted to talk about wasn't a good thing. I was surprised to see Nathan and Martha there, too, sitting at a big round table with places for the rest of us. Lela had sandwiches and tea brought to our table so we could eat while we was talking.

Isaac said, "I've been listening to the radio ever since Black Tuesday, and things are getting worse, not better. Seems like banks are failing all over the country, just like the Bank of Upton."

I was surprised to hear that. I asked Isaac to explain it to me.

"Molly, do you remember when Pa and I used to play a game of dominoes? When one domino falls, they all fall down. Well, it's kind of like that. Seems like a lot of people took their savings and invested in the stock market. Now that it's crashed, they've lost everything. Other folks kept their money in the bank to be safe. But what they didn't realize was that the bank took their money and bought stocks with it, trying to make more money. All that's gone, as well."

"So are you saying folks who had their money in the Bank of Upton can't get it no more?"

Benjamin said, "That's exactly what I'm saying, Molly. I'm so sorry, but that means you lost the money you got from the insurance company."

"Did you lose your money, too?" I asked.

"I lost some of what I'd saved. But most of my money is in my land."

"What about you, Isaac? Have you and Lela lost your money?"

They looked at each other and nodded. "We've lost our savings, but we still got the hotel 'cause it was paid for."

"And you, Nathan? You and Martha all right?"

Nathan gave me a look I'd grown to know so well. He had a kind smile, even when he was feeling sad. "Well, Martha and I are all right, but my family's business is in trouble. We're going to Cincinnati to see if we can save it."

"How long you gonna be gone?" I asked,"

"We may be staying there," Nathan answered.

Nobody said nothing for a few minutes. I could tell by their faces that there was still more bad news. I asked them to tell me straight out.

Benjamin finally said, "It's Daniel, Molly. We don't know what's become of him. Phone lines were jammed after the crash, but he finally got through to Isaac at the hotel. Tell Molly what he said, Isaac."

"He was sobbing so bad, I had a hard time understanding him. He said that he'd lost everything, including the store. He'd margined it, which means he used the store to borrow money to put in the stock market. And the investors were gonna take ownership of the store in place of their money."

Well, that scared me for sure.

"How are folks around here gonna get their supplies?" No one had an answer.

"Daniel said Catherine's daddy killed himself," Isaac told me, "just like the rest of the fools who jumped out of building windows. Daniel didn't know what would become of him. I told him to come home, but he was too ashamed."

"Why is that?" I asked.

"He's the reason folks around here invested in the stock market. The bank, too. They trusted him and thought he knew what he was talking about. He feels responsible for everybody losing their savings."

I didn't much like the man Daniel had become, but he was still Elijah's son, and I'd raised him as my own. "We have to find him," I said, "and bring him home."

Benjamin said, "I agree, Molly. But nobody knows where he's

at. I've hired a man to go find him. I'm gonna sell off some of my land so I can try to get the store back."

I turned to Isaac and Lela. "Are you gonna be able to keep the hotel open?"

"It's too soon to know," Lela said. "But never mind that. What are you gonna do without the money Elijah left you?"

"Don't you worry about me none. Me and Henry planted a big garden. We got milk cows and chickens, so we got food to eat and a warm place to stay. We'll be just fine. You look after yourselves."

I kissed Nathan and Martha goodbye and told them how much I'd miss them. I couldn't stop my eyes from shedding tears over that.

Me and Benjamin didn't talk much on the ride home. I kept thinking about what I said at the end of our meeting. *We'll be just fine.* I prayed to God that what I said to them was true. After Benjamin left, I went down to the cellar and opened my box. The money from the insurance company was all there, and that gave me a measure of comfort.

Elijah must've been watching over me good. He never put money in the bank. We didn't know from one year to the next if we'd have a good tobacco crop. Most years, we made enough to get by with a few dollars left over. But there was times we had to count on every coin. Elijah always wanted to know exactly where his money was, and how much he had on any given day. I figured if that was good enough for him, I might as well do the same, in spite of what Benjamin thought.

I kept the truth about the money to myself. I felt betrayed that Benjamin took our land. Maybe that's what Doc wanted, but it just didn't seem right. Benjamin had more land than he could manage, and he was well-off like his brothers, while my children all had to leave home to fend for themselves. I wasn't sure how long five hundred dollars would last us. But it was a heap more money than a lot of folks had now, and I was grateful.

Chapter 48

"Presents From the Heart"

Christmas come upon us fast that year. Nobody was in a mood to celebrate much. I was determined not to let other people's dark moods creep in on Tula Mary and me, or Henry neither. Like I said, we didn't have nothing to do with folks losing all their money, so I made up my mind we wasn't gonna suffer on account of their mistakes. But we didn't have no money to spend on Christmas presents or a fine dinner.

I'd always liked Christmas 'cause of the birth of Jesus and all. Ma used to make it special for us young'uns. We'd get a handmade toy and sweets in our socks, and she'd always make me a new dress to wear to church. But after she died, Pa didn't want to celebrate no more, so we didn't.

Elijah didn't make a fuss over Christmas either after Mary died. But all that changed when we got married and Miss June come to live with us. She loved Christmas and set us straight about celebrating it proper as a family. She made us hot chocolate and read us Christmas stories every night around the holiday.

We never did take to the notion of Santa Claus like folks do nowadays. That's on account of there being no way a fat man could come down a wood-stove pipe from the roof. Why, he wouldn't have been able to get his arm down the chimney, let alone his belly! No, sir, that story didn't make no sense to us.

But we did like the notion of giving gifts. Me and Elijah saw to it that our young'uns had four presents each on Christmas. They got one thing they needed, like socks or shoes. Then we made each of them something special. I made rag dolls for the girls, and Elijah carved out wooden toys for the boys. The third present was a sweet in their socks. Hard candy was their favorite. And, finally, our young'uns got to choose something special they wanted to have with their Christmas dinner. That made for a fine meal with lots of side dishes.

Now with Elijah dead and all the young'uns but Tula Mary gone, I didn't know how to make Christmas special. But Tula Mary come up with a fine idea of something to give Henry, and he told us not to worry none about presents 'cause he had something for each of us.

I'd been frettin' about what to cook for Christmas dinner. We didn't dare slaughter a cow for beef or a hen for roasting. We needed milk and eggs through the year much more than beef or chicken for Christmas dinner. But I didn't want to fix no plain meal of beans and cornbread.

A few days before Christmas, Henry come over grinning and told me not to worry about Christmas dinner. There was a surprise coming. Then on Christmas Eve, Isaac drove up in his Hudson automobile and delivered our whole supper. The hotel had a fine cook making Christmas dinner for the folks staying there or coming just to eat. Isaac had him make up our supper, too. He brung a whole roasted turkey with brown gravy and chestnut stuffing, sweet potatoes cooked up in butter, sugar and cinnamon, green beans, cranberry salad, rolls, and a pecan pie for dessert. I don't know when I'd ever seen a finer Christmas dinner.

I asked Isaac if he could stay and eat with us, but he said it was gonna snow soon, and he had to get back to help Lela. Before he left, he handed Henry a box wrapped up real pretty. I told Henry to go ahead and open it, but he just smiled and said it was for later.

We decided to eat our supper straightaway while it was fresh and warm. We barely spoke while we was eating. I don't think we'd tasted food this good since Sally Ann died.

We ate 'til we was about to explode and still had plenty of food left over. Me and Tula Mary done up the dishes, while Henry put the rest of the turkey and fixin's down in the cellar for Christmas Day.

It was getting dark, and we felt sleepy after that fine meal. Tula lit the lanterns, and Henry brung in more wood for the fireplace. Our house was warm and cozy. I sat down in the rocker near the fire, with Henry and Tula in chairs beside me. I was missing Elijah something awful, but I didn't want either of them to feel my sadness. I kept looking into the fire and rocking in my chair.

Finally, Tula said, "Mama, can we give Henry his present?"

I told her to go on and do that. We wrapped it up the best we could in some pages from the Sears and Roebuck catalogue. Henry looked plum surprised when he undid the paper.

"We thought it would be fittin' for you to have Pa's pipe," Tula told him. "And we found a tin of tobacco he hadn't opened yet."

Henry got thick in the voice when he said, "I can't take this, Tula. Why, it was special to your pa."

Tula gave him one of her beautiful smiles. "Well, I'm not gonna smoke it, so you might as well have it." She excused herself to go to the outhouse.

Henry said, "Molly, I can't take this pipe. It belonged to Elijah. Why, I saw him smoke it all the time when he was thinking hard about something."

I leaned in to him and spoke from my heart. "I wish you would take it, Henry. Elijah would be pleased for you to have it. Besides, I don't want to keep it no more."

"Why's that?" he asked.

"It was still warm when I found it in the barn after Elijah died. I know he smoked it before he jumped off the roof. He must've been thinking about what he was gonna do."

Henry nodded and put it away in his shirt pocket. When Tula come back inside, he said, "I'm pleased you give me your pa's pipe, Tula. I thank you."

He reached into the pocket of his pants and took out a little box tied up with red ribbon. "Now I got something for you, Tula Mary, and I hope you like it. It belonged to my mama."

Tula carefully undid the ribbon and lifted the lid. Inside was the prettiest hair comb I ever done seen. I don't mean the kind you pull through your hair. It was one of them fancy things that rich ladies wear after they fix up their curls. The yellow comb had five pearls on it and two small peacock feathers.

"Oh, Henry," Tula said. "This is so beautiful." She turned to me, and there was big ol' tears in her eyes. "Mama, put this in for me, please."

Well, I just looked at her 'cause I didn't know how to put a fancy comb in her hair.

Henry grinned. "Give it here," he said. "I seen my mama do this a hundred times."

He told Tula to lean in to him. He took some of her hair and rolled it up. Then he carefully placed the comb right where it would keep it in place. Tula Mary looked all grown up with that comb in her brown hair. And Henry looked real pleased with hisself.

"My daddy, Isaiah, worked for your granddaddy Albert. You never knew Albert or Isaiah, but they was both fine men. My daddy saved back as much money as he could from his wages and asked Albert to help him buy something nice for my mama. Albert found this here comb, and that's what my daddy give her for Christmas that year. Mama was so surprised, she cried for days whenever she looked at it. Poor Daddy thought, at first, he'd done something wrong, but he got it straight in time how much she loved it. I know she'd be real happy knowing you was wearing it."

I don't think I'd ever seen my Tula Mary so tickled with a present. She jumped up and hugged Henry around his neck.

"I love it, Henry. Thank you."

"Well, you look real pretty, Tula, and that's a fact."

We sat there just smiling for a while. Then Henry reached down by his chair and put the present Isaac done give him on his lap. Both me and Tula Mary thought it was for him, so we waited for him to open it. But Henry cleared his throat and handed it over to me.

"I asked Isaac awhile back if'n he could think of something special I could give you, Molly, to say thank you for cooking for me and making me feel so at home. Isaac give it some thought and then brung me this. He said there wasn't nothing you'd rather have."

I took my time undoing the fancy wrapping paper, and then my breath caught in my throat. I looked at my present and I looked at Henry. Then I just started bawling. Poor Tula thought something was wrong.

"What is it, Mama? What's the matter?"

I looked again to make sure I done read the title of the book right. I was fifty years old and hadn't laid eyes on this here book since I was eight. That's when Miss June read it to us at school. It was my favorite story ever 'cause Jo was a tomboy like me.

The book was worn, and a few of the pages was torn in the corner, but that didn't matter. Inside the front cover, plain as day, was Miss June's name. She'd kept the book all these years to read to her young'uns in school. That must've been where Isaac found it. But I thought none of them other young'uns could've loved this book as much as me. Now it was mine.

I opened the first page, hoping I could still read good. I asked Tula and Henry to come in close. I slowly began saying out loud the first words of *Little Women*, by Louisa May Alcott.

"Christmas won't be Christmas without any presents," grumbled Jo, lying on the rug. "It's so dreadful to be poor!" sighed Meg, looking down at her old dress.

I looked up from my book, first at Henry and then at Tula Mary. He was puffing on Elijah's pipe, even though it didn't have no tobacco in it, and she was touching the comb in her hair. I had my favorite story in my lap after forty-two years without it.

That night, it didn't matter a lick what we'd lost or that we was poor like them March girls. Henry, Tula and me had the best Christmas presents a body could have 'cause each of them touched our hearts.

Chapter 49

"Seen Together"

In 1930, Tula Mary turned fifteen and got ready to make her own way in the world. Her sister Eva found her a job in Louisville working for a family that owned a grocery store. They wanted Tula Mary to mind their two young'uns and help tend the store. In return, she'd live above their garage and be paid a small wage.

Times was hard during the Great Depression. Those who had jobs was fortunate. I had to let my last baby go, but I took some comfort knowing that Eva and Earl would look out for her.

The morning she left, Tula wore her best dress and coat 'cause she wanted to look nice when she met the family. She had the comb from Henry tucked in her hair. Henry drove us to the train station in Elijah's Ford truck. It was chilly that morning, but the sun was shining. We waited inside the depot 'til we heard the train coming, then we walked Tula out onto the platform.

I felt the tears coming, but I held them back. I looked at my baby girl one last time, trying to paint a picture of her in my mind. She'd been a joy in my life, and I treasured the years we'd had together. As the train come to a halt, I reached into my purse and gave Tula fifty dollars.

"I can't take this, Mama," she said.

"I want you to have it, Tula. Put it somewhere safe in case of an emergency."

"But I'm gonna be earning a wage, Mama."

"I'll sleep better at night knowing you got it."

Then the train conductor yelled, "All aboard!" Our time together come to an end. I held her close and kissed her. "I love you, Tula Mary."

"I love you, too, Mama. I promise to write you letters every week."

Henry hugged her and said, "We'll miss you, Tula Mary."

"I love you, Henry," she said.

She picked up her suitcase and started for the train. The conductor helped her up onto the step. Then she turned and waved at us one last time. Me and Henry stood on the platform with tears falling down our cheeks as we watched the train roll away.

Three years later, at planting time in early April, we drove to town to buy our seeds. My children sent us money from time to time so we could buy supplies. We held off as long as we could to make our money last. A lot of changes had taken place in Upton. People was still suffering from the Great Depression. A group of men took over the Bank of Upton after it failed. They ran it different than the Uptons had 'cause they didn't know folks in Hardin County personally. When a farmer didn't bring in a good crop one year, the Uptons used to let him wait to pay his mortgage 'til times was better. The new owners just took over a man's farm when he couldn't pay what he owed. Then they sold the land off cheap. That's how come there was strangers now living around Upton.

Benjamin bought the general store back from the investors after Daniel lost it. He hired a man and his wife from Elizabethtown to come and run it. I'd only met them once when Benjamin took me to town. That day when me and Henry walked in together, everybody stopped what they was doing to stare at us. We didn't recognize the other folks in the store, and nobody said hello. The way them folks was looking at us made me nervous. Henry, too. We picked out our seeds and paid for them. The shopkeepers weren't nearly as friendly as the day I'd been there with Benjamin.

As we started to walk outside, a man said, "Damn nigger with a white woman!" I turned around and saw him spit on the floor. I started to say something, but Henry hurried me along. People on the street stared at us as we got in the truck and drove away. I'd lived over fifty years around these parts, and Henry longer than that. Folks always treated us kindly and with respect. But on that April day in 1933, both of us knew that Upton was no longer the place we remembered.

A few days later, Benjamin paid me a visit. I hadn't seen him in a while. I invited him in to sit a spell, and I got him a glass of lemonade. He asked after Tula Mary and told me he hadn't found Daniel yet. Then he set his glass down and said, "I need to talk to you about something, Molly."

"What's that?"

"I heard what happened at the store the other day."

I told him how bad Henry and me felt about how we was treated.

"Things have changed around these parts, Molly. It's not like it was when I was growing up."

"How do you mean?"

"My granddaddy saw to it that Sally Ann, Isaiah and Henry were treated well. My daddy and Henry were best friends as boys, and nobody thought nothing about it."

"That's right," I said. "Henry's always been a part of our family."

"Well, that was all right with folks as long as Daddy was alive. But he's been gone now awhile, and folks don't like seeing you alone with Henry."

I started to say something, but Benjamin shushed me. "Let me finish, Molly. I think it would be best if you go to Louisville to live. We could find you a little place near Tula Mary. I'd pay for everything."

"But my home is here."

"Then we'll have to send Henry away."

My cheeks got hot. "You'll do no such thing! This is Henry's home, too!"

"That's where you're wrong, Molly. This is my land, not yours!"

I felt a cold chill come over me when he said that. "You got the papers Elijah and Doc signed when your daddy and I got married?"

"I got them," Benjamin said.

"They legal?" I asked.

"They are."

"Then you better read them again. They say I can stay in this house as long as I live, and Henry can stay in his. And that is exactly what we're gonna do."

Benjamin started to argue, but this time I shushed him. "Me and your daddy raised you better than this, Benjamin Fry. He'd be ashamed of you if he was here now. You can leave my home now."

Benjamin got up and walked to the door. Before leaving, he said, "You stay then, Molly. And Henry, too. But don't be seen in town together. It's not safe."

Chapter 50

"Mighty Fine People To Love"

We thought there'd come a day when folks got over their hatred of coloreds and the white people who loved them. But they never did, so me and Henry kept to ourselves, except when my children come to visit. I was tickled when Tula Mary got married and had young'uns of her own. I got to rock each of my grandbabies in this here rocker, and I loved every moment I spent with them. But all too soon they left, and the house grew quiet again.

In time, Benjamin and me softened toward each other, but a wedge remained between us. He come to see me one day to bring news about Daniel. "We found him in St. Louis, living in a Hooverville," he told me.

"What's a Hooverville?" I asked.

"It's a shantytown for folks who can't find work. They call them Hoovervilles 'cause they blame President Hoover for not doing more to help people during the Depression."

"Is Catherine there with him?"

"No, Molly. She's long gone. Daniel doesn't know what became of her."

"Are you gonna bring him back to Upton?"

"No," Benjamin said. "Thomas went to fetch him. Daniel's sickly from not eating good and living in a shantytown. But Thomas thinks he'll get well with proper care."

Benjamin asked if I needed anything from town.

"No," I said. "Isaac's been good to bring us supplies."

"Well, let me know if you need anything or want me to take you to town."

I told him I would, but I never did.

~ ~ ~

Henry and me grew old together. We enjoyed a simple life. Every spring we planted our garden, and every winter we sat by the fire. We took our noon dinner together, and Henry come by most evenings for supper. We never got tired of each other's company. We was the best of old friends.

We shared a lot of memories of Elijah, Sally Ann, Miss June and the children. We talked for hours about all kinds of things, like growing up with Pa and my brothers or how life was for Sally Ann and Isaiah as slaves. Sometimes we just sat on the porch watching the sunset together, not having to say much of nothing.

One talk we had that stuck in my mind. One day, when we come out on the porch after dinner, we could see the tobacco crop growing good in what used to be our field. I didn't know how much land Benjamin owned now, but I reckoned it was several hundred acres, most all of it planted in tobacco. When Henry lit up his pipe, I wondered about something.

"Henry, you and me spent nearly all our lives growing tobacco. It provided us money, but I never had any other use for it. It isn't a crop you eat. Most of my kin don't smoke, and you wasn't fond of it 'til we give you Elijah's pipe."

"That's right, Molly. My daddy never smoked. Albert chewed tobacco some, but I never saw Doc use it."

"Yet look what happened to us on account of it," I said. "First Doc and then Benjamin got greedy and wanted more land to grow it. And now, here we sit after all our hard work, not owning much of nothing. I wonder if it was worth it."

Henry puffed on his pipe. When he let out a breath, he watched the smoke rise up in the air. "Know what I think about?"

"What's that?"

"Three hundred years ago, my people was first brung here in chains to make white folks rich from tobacco. Might never been slavery if'n for tobacco. Yet I'm a free man who grew the same crop that made us slaves."

I pondered that for a spell. Then I had a thought that made me smile. I reached over and patted him. "We're finally free, Henry."

"What you mean, Molly?"

"In a way, we was both slaves and tobacco was our master. We depended on it for everything. Now it don't matter a lick if the tobacco grows good or not. All we got to do is tend to our garden and spend time together. Can't say the same for Benjamin or the men who work for him. Seems like they're the ones in chains now."

The last day we shared was a nice day in June when I was near on seventy years old, and Henry was almost eighty. That afternoon, I asked Henry if we could walk up the hill to visit the graves. We took our time 'cause we didn't get around so good anymore. A warm breeze was blowing, and the sun felt good on my face.

We paid our respects to Elijah and Sally Ann. I thought about Elijah every day, even though he'd been gone for some twenty years. I remembered the day we buried Sally Ann after I washed and oiled her skin. Henry held my hand while we offered up a little prayer.

I turned to go back down the hill, but Henry said he needed to rest a minute before we got started. The sun was shining through his thin white hair, and I noticed his face was sagging more than it had. I didn't want to think about how much time we had left together. I reached up and patted his cheek. I closed my eyes when I felt his lips touch mine.

I had something I been wanting to tell Henry. I took his sweet old face in my hands and spoke the truth Miss June taught me. "You don't get to choose who you love, Henry. God does that. You only choose if you'll love that person or not."

Tears come to my eyes. "I love you, Henry Jackson. You're the best friend I ever done had." We kissed for the first and last time that day.

While I was back at the house starting supper, a dizzy spell come over me. I went outside and sat in my rocker. I closed my eyes and waited for it to pass.

When I opened my eyes again, I saw Tula Mary sitting in my rocker. I found myself in a strange bed and didn't know where I was.

"You've had a little stroke, Mama, but the doctor thinks you'll be just fine."

"Where am I?"

"You're in Louisville with me."

"What happened?"

"You must've been cooking something on the stove when you had your stroke. It started burning and set the house on fire. Henry got to you just in time. Saved you and the rocker, but everything else is gone."

"Where's Henry?"

Tula Mary held my hand. I asked her why she was crying.

"Henry carried you away from the fire, but then his heart gave out. Benjamin found you and Henry lying together in the yard."

I've thought about my life a lot since then, and that's why I been telling you my story. I lived a lot of years on this earth, with good times and bad times, joys and sorrows, all mixed in together. I never got the book learning I wanted, but I come to understand something important. It doesn't matter a lick whether you're pretty or homely, got money or not, whether your skin is white or it's got color. It's the heart you got beating inside of you and the character of your soul that mean the most.

God chose some mighty fine people for me to love. And I'm powerful glad I didn't let nothing or nobody stop me from loving them ... or them from loving me.

Epilogue

"Our Greatest Joy"

It was after midnight when we finished listening to Molly's recording. We were so touched by her story that we didn't say much. What we felt couldn't be put into words. While Larry put the reels away, I sat down in Molly's rocker. I put my hands on its worn old arms and started rocking slowly back and forth, listening to it creak, just like it had in the recording. I thought about all the furnishings gracing our house, his ... mine ... and ours. Blended families, stuff and things.

I realized then that this beat-up old rocker was our greatest possession.

And the love we shared was our greatest joy.

Final Thoughts

"Molly's Enduring Message"

We hope you have found *Molly's Rocker* a thoughtful and inspiring experience. Sadly, the racial, religious and gender biases that Molly and her family confronted in the 1800s are still intensely relevant today. Enabling a deeper, empathic understanding through honest exploration can truly make a difference. We are committed to fostering heartfelt, multigenerational dialogues and ongoing lessons to examine and discuss these vital issues.

To connect with us and join the unfolding conversation, we invite you to visit us through our growing communications outreach:

For those seeking educational resources to assist with deepening Molly's message, we have developed the evolving *Molly's Schoolhouse* program, a blossoming, interactive guide to the lessons Molly offers, including video vignettes and exercises. You will also discover a way to access and purchase the audio version of *Molly's Rocker* here. Visit mollyschoolhouse.com to explore!

We invite you to visit our websites oflovecreations.com and thewayoftheone.org for information about *Molly's Rocker* and other books by Susan M. Hoskins.

Our expanding social media and email outreach related specifically to *Molly's Rocker* and *Molly's Schoolhouse* will continue to be updated and communicated on the mollyschoolhouse.com site. You can also follow Susan M. Hoskins and The Way of the One on Twitter, Facebook and Instagram.